JOEL AUSTIN

NOMAD

vinci

BOOKS

By Joel Austin

Frank Sherman Thrillers

To the remarkable, often unseen people who make life worth stepping into every day.

Vinci Books

vinci-books.com

Published by Vinci Books Ltd in 2025

1

Paperback ISBN: 9781036705350

Chapter One

Time was against the three men. A faded day's warmth still smothered the desert sands, and their shirts clung like wet rags. They worked with a quiet concentration that enveloped them deeper than the surrounding darkness. Soft red lights barely illuminated the bed of a dilapidated truck. It held three long wooden crates about the size of children's coffins, which took up the entire area. Large block letters emblazoned the sides, announcing their provenance.

Using crowbars, two of the men pried apart the nails securing the wooden lids, while the third watched the horizon. They worked efficiently, fueled by an abiding sense of urgency. Outside of the packaging, the contents were incriminating. Inside the crates, they would lead down a straightforward path to the death penalty.

"Start laying them out," whispered the tallest of the three men.

The second man solemnly unwrapped the contents. He took them out one at a time and laid them out on the tailgate and truck bed. Thirty new M4A1 carbines glistened in the pale light. The guns smelled of oil and industry.

"Boot, help me with the crates."

The third man swiveled and started tossing the crates into a shallow trench in the sandy ground. Deep enough for a body, the ditch spread out and away from the truck. All three crates went to the bottom before he started shoveling small mounds on top. The sand plopped and spread like a scoop of melting ice cream.

Over the southern horizon, two dots of light appeared, accompanied by the low growl of a domestic engine.

"Contact," barked the tallest man. "Are we clear?"

"Clear," repeated the other men.

"Good. Boot will take the left flank. Hadz will stay with me. Questions?"

"No, sir," they echoed.

A wide country smile stretched across the tallest man's face and his eyes glistened in the oncoming light. "Ain't no sirs out here. Now, let's make some money, boys."

"Yut," they exclaimed in unison.

The headlights swayed like tired dogs across the undulating terrain. From mere pinpricks, they grew in intensity with each passing minute. Audible above the engine noise, a car stereo rumbled across the flatland.

"Deet, who the fuck is this guy?" Hadz asked.

"A local," replied the tallest man.

"And he checked out?"

Deet might have seethed at the comment were the stakes lower, but he gave the question some leeway. "Nothing in the databases and Jones vouched for him."

"Jones is a drunken hack."

"He's a repeat customer."

"I'm just saying, it's a lot of hardware for a first-timer."

"I know."

"And this guy is driving like the Dukes of Hazzard."

Deet's upper lip quivered with anger at the arrival's reckless behavior. "I know."

An ear-splitting heavy metal song poured out of the oncoming truck with enough bass to thump their chests with the pressure change. The driver did nothing to conceal their presence and parked in front of the men with no pretense of discretion. Anyone watching could have seen the odd meeting and the guns lying in the back of the truck. As the vehicle stopped, the giant plume of dust it created swept over them and cast a ghostly ochre pall.

The driver hopped out as the lights flicked off and the screeching sounds faded into the night. Deet eyed him up like a bully on the first day of school. He was average all around. Neither tall nor short, but thin and wiry. He wore working man boots with deep scuffs, and stains of grease covered his Carhartt pants. Shabby, unkempt brown hair fell to his neck and two days' worth of scruff clung to his chin. Compared to the three men standing quietly in the darkness, he was gruff.

Deet stepped forward, frothing with anger. "What the fuck was that entrance?"

"That's no way to greet a customer," replied the driver.

"Are you Steve?" asked Deet, challenging the man to confirm something he already knew.

The driver gave a lopsided grin. "No, I ain't, but I imagine you ain't expecting no Steve."

Deet didn't reply.

"I'm Elmore. What should I call you?"

"D."

"D? Well, that's vague, unless your mama wanted to be mysterious."

"You ain't paying for my family history," Deet said.

"Fine. Don't get your buzz cut in a ruckus. And your friend?"

"H."

The newcomer laughed like a kid with milk squirting out his nose. "Do I get to meet A?"

"No," replied Deet with unequivocal stiffness.

"Live a little," Elmore added with a gesture up towards the starry night sky twinkling above.

"You got the cash?" asked Deet.

Elmore pointed behind them. "If that's the stuff."

Deet nodded towards the tailgate of the much older truck. The one Hadz bought from a salvage place for eight hundred in cash the week before. It was twenty years older than Elmore's ride, but Deet guessed the local's pink slips were legit.

Hadz pulled back the tarp covering the rifles, and Elmore let out a low whistle of joy.

"Hot damn, boys. These look fresh off the assembly line."

"Newer than mother's milk," replied Hadz.

Elmore picked up a rifle and inspected the action with the eye of someone familiar with the design.

"Have you ever shot one of these?" asked Deet with a kernel of suspicion bouncing around his gut.

"And here I thought we weren't sharing our family history."

Deet was in no mood for small talk and moved on with business. "They're three grand a piece, not including ammo."

A frown scrunched up Elmore's face. "Jones said he got them for two Gs each."

"Jones is a repeat customer."

"Maybe I'll just take one as a trial."

"Minimum order is ten," said Deet flatly. "However, we'll throw in the magazines for free."

"But not the ammo?"

"Next time."

"Can I try one out?" asked Elmore.

"Sure, after you buy them and go on your merry way."

Elmore continued inspecting the rifles. "How do I know they're genuine? Fakes are popping up everywhere these days."

"Ask Jones," replied Hadz with a chilly edge in his voice.

"Oh, I did, but one can never be too careful."

"Don't fuck about," growled Deet. "Are you buying or not?"

"I'll take a crate."

Deet and Hadz exchanged a quick glance. They buried the only crates around under the sand, and they wondered how the stranger came to such a descriptive term.

"I've got six Gs on me now," Elmore continued. "I'll get you the rest later."

"This ain't Rent-A-Center," countered Hadz. "You pay upfront and in full."

Elmore looked at the men standing straighter than a pair of two-by-fours. "The economy ain't great now. Things are tight. I can take three off you now for two thousand apiece. I'll come back for the other seven next week."

"Jones said you were good for thirty."

"I am," assured Elmore with a wave of his hand. "But not tonight."

The two men exchanged another look. A litany of felonies passed between them without a word.

"Alright," agreed Deet. "But only because Jones vouched for you."

Elmore smiled and carried three of the rifles back to his truck. Reaching under the seat, he pulled out a roll of twenty-dollar bills held together by rubber bands and tossed it over to Hadz.

"Good doing business with you," he added while climbing into the truck.

"Don't forget the magazines," reminded Deet in a soft voice.

Elmore flashed a self-conscious smile and walked back towards the two men. "Right, I don't want to forget those."

As he reached out to grab them from Deet's outstretched hand, the taller man twisted at the waist and landed a brutal strike to Elmore's solar plexus. The devastating blow doubled Elmore over, and he vomited on his shoes. Before he could draw air back into his lungs, Hadz came from behind and slipped a thick plastic bag over his head.

Panic exploded across Elmore's face. He flailed his legs about, searching for something solid to push against. All he found was sand. It was not enough to budge the man standing behind him. Hadz held firm like an anchor sunk in the seabed.

Unable to move, Elmore scratched at the plastic, hoping to puncture its surface or anything to get a puff of air. Deet stepped forward and locked down the local's wrists with a grip capable of juicing whole oranges. That face with its aquiline nose and heavy black eyebrows was the last thing Elmore saw before the night sky lost all its twinkle.

Hadz gripped the bag for another two minutes until he was sure Elmore was dead and long after the fight disappeared.

"Boot!" shouted Deet.

The man appeared from the gloom with his rifle in hand.

"Grab the E-tool and make some space by the crates."

Boot nodded and started frantically spreading sand with the small shovel. Knowing that Elmore would never wake up, Hadz pulled the body towards the widening gap in the ground. The two worked with purpose. Within minutes, they had a shallow grave into which they rolled Elmore's body.

Deet retrieved the rifles from the dead man's truck and wrapped everything up with canvas tarps. They said nothing until the work was complete and met between the two vehicles. Dawn still waited over the horizon some five hours out.

"We need to get rid of his truck," Deet began. He did not hurry his words, but they came across as urgent.

"I could drive it over the mountain and leave it in the valley somewhere," offered Hadz.

"Do it, but stay off the highways. We don't want any cameras to see you. Boot and I will unload the gear at the shed and then he can pick you up. Remember, don't be late."

The men nodded. They needed no further orders, motivation, or prodding. The risks were abundantly clear.

Chapter Two

Shimmering walls of morning heat hovered above the pavement. The distortion twisted the horizon into silvery puddles of nothingness. Captain Frank Sherman shrugged off the temperature as no different from Iraq or Syria or parts of Afghanistan. Each country had its own version of the furnace called summer. The difference that day was one of location and severity. He was only ninety miles from the Mojave Desert and a digital thermometer on the bank sign across the street read 107°F. A heat wave for most of California, but for Buford, it was another Thursday in July.

He did not hurry. No one hurried in that kind of heat. Everything slowed to a crawl as the body coped. The other pedestrians he passed carried a similar look of resignation on their faces. Burdened by their passage, but not unduly.

Twenty minutes earlier, he'd found a decent cup of coffee, but despite the heat, he couldn't bring himself to order it iced. It was a principle of the beverage to be served hot. The cafe also made a decent corned beef hash.

It was more praise than he could say for his motel room,

which had a bed and not much else. The air conditioner ran intermittently with a tepid breeze, but it was clean and cheap. A relic of the fifties, the building clung to the ground like it might be bulldozed for something newer at any moment. Most importantly, it was the closest thing to his mother's nursing home.

The Desert Rose Retirement Village was a star-shaped building with all the dour architectural grace of the seventies. It sat at the end of the street brooding over a dried-out wash optimistically called a river. Back when the paint was fresh, it would have been a pleasant place. Such glory had faded over the decades until only the memory remained.

Sherman waved at the jovial attendant behind the front desk as he walked inside. He could not understand how someone in such a dreary place could stay so positive, but he appreciated the effort.

"Good morning, Stan."

"Hey, Frank, good to see you again. How are things?"

"Still alive."

A sympathetic but morbid smile crossed Stan's face. "Glad to hear it. She just finished breakfast. Go on back."

"Thanks," replied Sherman as he ambled down the dim hall.

His mother glanced up as he entered the room. The year since his last visit had not been kind. Sophia looked like one of those tablets people throw in a glass of water for hangovers, slowly dissolving away at the edges. The fiery Greek mother of his childhood was still there, but dulled and diluted.

Piles of mail and sticky notes stitching together her life covered a small side table next to the bed. A half-eaten plate of gloopy food perched precariously on top. Seeing her like that left Sherman with a profound sense of sadness. He grieved for the years lost and for those lying ahead, already bereft of joy and possibility.

"Franky," she chirped. "There's my boy."

"Hey, Mom. How are you doing?"

She was remarkably lucid and attentive. "Everything hurts and they keep feeding me this goddamn mush, but *c'est la vie.*"

Sherman smiled and took a seat in the threadbare chair next to her bed. The chair belonged to her mother, and she never parted with it even after the fabric disintegrated from years of use.

"It looks hot out there," said Sophia as she took his hand in hers.

"Triple digits," he admitted.

She shook her head in disbelief. "The young man on the news. You know the one I like to watch. He was saying something about how the earth is getting warmer. As if this place can get any hotter."

Sherman smiled. Her relationship with the present tense was fragile.

"Did your father say what time he's off duty?"

There it was. The complete break with reality. Sherman took a deep breath and steeled himself for the conversation.

"Dad's dead, Mom. He has been for years."

Her face flooded with terror, confusion, and a hint of embarrassment as if she should have known such a profound fact. Those beautiful green-orange eyes of hers, the ones passed down to her son, flashed around the room searching for something familiar. Resignation sank into the corners of her mouth in a way that only those suffering from memory loss could truly understand.

"Oh," she began. "I'm sorry. I forget a lot these days."

"It's okay, Mom," he replied and squeezed her bony hand with its knuckles gnarled by arthritis.

A knock sounded on the door and a gentle voice piped through the opening. "Mrs. Sherman, it's time for your vitamins."

The door opened and the nurse slipped into the room. She was slender and short, with tawny skin and big brown eyes that Sherman felt could see genuine joy in the world. Her name was Vanessa, and she had been his mother's nurse for over five years.

"Frank," she said with a wide smile that curved steeply upward in the corners. "I didn't know you were in town."

"I got in late last night."

She handed Sophia a little paper cup filled with a finely woven tapestry of opiates, stool softeners, blood thinners, and cholinesterase inhibitors.

"Well, how have you been? Or better question... where have you been?"

Sherman chuckled, and his mother looked over with genuine interest and clarity. "Not much has changed since I saw you last."

"Frank, that's not much of an answer," scolded Sophia.

"Classified?" asked Vanessa.

"Most of it."

She shrugged, having heard the same answer for the last five years, but the mystery made it interesting, and she hadn't stopped asking.

"Sophia, my dear, how are you doing this morning?"

Sherman's mother threw up her arms as high as they could travel, which was not much further than her shoulders. "I hate peaches."

Vanessa looked over at the uneaten pile of canned

peaches. "Oh, dear. We got a new cook. I'll tell Jorge you don't like them."

She motioned towards the door, and Sherman stood to follow.

"I'll be right back, Mom."

Sophia smiled and turned on the morning news.

Beyond earshot, they stopped in the hallway with its color-coded paint and blistered wallpaper.

"Jorge has been here longer than you," said Sherman.

"I ran out of excuses."

Sherman leaned against the opposite wall. "Is she that bad?"

Vanessa moved closer as if unsatisfied with the distance, and Sherman felt a fleeting rush of youth. "Honestly, she's gone downhill over the last six months."

"Has she seen the doctor?"

"The diagnosis hasn't changed."

"What about her meds?"

"He upped the opiates," Vanessa admitted.

"Why?"

Her shoulders dipped. "Quality of life."

"So, it is that bad."

"I'm sorry, Frank. Getting old isn't pretty."

Sherman ran his hands through his beard. It didn't conceal his fingers, and the length left him feeling suddenly exposed. He had cut it hours before hopping on a flight out of Al Udeid in Qatar. The trim was on a whim, but the fear of his mother not recognizing him weighed heavily on his decision.

"Thanks for being good to her."

Vanessa gave him a playful shove. "She's still a firecracker, but some days are better than others."

He nodded and headed back towards Sophia's room.

"Frank," Vanessa called out. "I'm off at 6:00. Do you want to grab a drink afterwards?"

Sherman didn't hesitate. "My treat."

"Great. Let me get cleaned up first. Can you meet me at my place at 6:30? I'm just a few blocks over."

He would have met her in Nevada if she'd asked. "Sure, that works."

Vanessa smiled and returned to her rounds.

As soon as Sherman sat back down, Sophia gave him a nudge. "It's about time you two went on a date."

"You heard that?" he asked incredulously.

"I'm old, not deaf."

"It's just a drink."

"That's how my marriage to your father began."

"Mom," he began but left the thought unsaid.

Their marriage baffled him. His father was the epitome of a good Marine—straight, hard, and no-nonsense. His mother was wild, wicked, and funny to her core. Not a match made in heaven. Thinking back, it surprised him they lasted so long. Until cancer killed off the old man. That was another surprise. The tough bastard had beaten everything and everyone that crossed his path, only to be undone by his own body. Although, Sherman knew it was the desk job that got him in the end. Take the rifle away from a man like that and death doesn't look so bad.

"Take her somewhere nice," his mother suggested.

Sherman looked out the window at the dusty town at the edge of nothing. "Like where?"

Sophia looked around like she was grasping for some memory from when Cal worked at the nearby Marine Annex, but the past was slippery and she gave up. "What do I know? All I get is goddamn peaches."

Sherman patted her hand and helped himself to the syrupy fruit.

Chapter Three

The sedan reeked of sweat, stale coffee, and the consequences of excessive fast food. Crumpled wrappers littered the passenger side floor, and it resembled a cheeseburger graveyard. Sour air wafted out of the vents and the engine of the old Crown Victoria sputtered. The temperature gauge needle stood at the top, swathed in red.

Special Agent Megan Landers rolled down the windows and turned off the ignition. Her partner, Javier Martinez, shot her a look of disgust.

"You should have requisitioned a new car from the depot," he complained.

Landers rolled up her sleeves and settled herself into what she saw as a miserable day. "You should man up. This isn't half as bad as Kandahar."

"Don't start with your army days."

"I'm just saying, Javi, you lived a simple life in Florida."

"Miami ain't an easy beat. We had fifty-one homicides the year before I moved out here."

"We call that Friday in Afghanistan."

Javier shook his bald head and beads of sweat rolled down his temples. His white button-down shirt stuck to his skin, and he made a big display of shaking his shirt for Landers.

She said something but he cut her off. "And don't tell me it's a dry heat like that is better. I don't buy that shit for a second. Look at me, I'm still sweating either way."

"You sweat in winter."

Javier scowled at the comment and the truth behind it. "How long are we going to watch the sister?"

"As I recall, you didn't have any better ideas."

"The guy disappeared in the middle of the night. I'm guessing he is sleeping one off or he's dead in the desert."

"Your callous disregard for human life astounds me," Landers added in a mocking tone.

"He doesn't have much of a life from what I've seen. Not exactly upstanding citizen material."

"Need I remind you, he was our only lead."

"You don't. And I know that is up in smoke. But sitting on the sister's house gets us what? Heat stroke?"

"You ask too many questions."

"I'm a detective. It's my job."

"You're an FBI agent," Landers corrected.

"Still a detective at heart."

"Then detect what happened to our missing confidential informant."

"Trouble like him usually finds a hole in the ground to hide. He'll either crawl out in a couple of days or we'll send in the cadaver dogs."

Landers felt impatient for her partner to make the next logical leap. "Which means?"

"He's likely a dead idiot."

"Sure, but idiots around here have a long shelf-life. So, our suspect pool must be small."

"We'll find another source. Everybody around here is looking to make a buck."

Agent Landers silently disagreed with her partner. Their C.I. was not reliable nor particularly capable, but he had something most of them lacked—a conscience. Combined with his connections, the man was the perfect bait for catching a much larger fish.

The cold shower in her hotel room beckoned unseen over the horizon. Four hours remained until dark. The day was not looking up, and she thought wistfully back to her year in Afghanistan. She had slow days and scary days, but not prosaic ones. The war buried any such boredom.

Chapter Four

Sherman left the nursing home fifteen minutes before Vanessa ended her shift. When he arrived, the hotel room was not much cooler. Walking inside felt like opening a fridge that lost power the night before. Everything smelled musty and the air was lukewarm. Sherman stripped and headed straight for the shower. He knew it was a futile effort, and when he reached Vanessa's, he would look no different from when he left the nursing home. Still, it was worth the effort because she was worth the effort.

Drying off proved useless. The towels had the same absorbency as cardboard and the texture of sandpaper. Sherman slipped on his newest shirt, the same pair of jeans, and flip-flops. His army boots sat in the corner—a reminder of his limited time back home. Seven days of leave and he had already burned through one.

Sherman glanced at a cheap Casio watch around his wrist. He added a couple of minutes of travel time and thought it better to be early than late. Then he stepped out into the oven called Buford.

Everything in and around the door expanded from the heat and the thing barely shut. He pulled hard enough to grunt and just managed to engage the lock.

Over the years, his body had accepted the desert as its home climate and adjusted accordingly. He sweated but not profusely, and not without significant exertion. A blessing and a curse. It helped him to not look like a cold can of beer left next to the barbeque, but it left him open to heat stroke.

Off the main street, there were no sidewalks, and Sherman meandered in the dirt strip between the asphalt and the fences demarcating private property. Most were simple chain-link affairs—some had strips of fake wood woven between the metal to give some approximation of class.

Vanessa's house was almost the same color as the ubiquitous sandy dirt stretching for miles in every direction, and it created an optical illusion of not knowing where the house began and the yard ended. She stepped outside as Sherman walked through the front gate.

"You didn't have to get all dressed up for me," she teased.

Sherman looked down at himself. "These are the nicest things I own."

Vanessa wore a pale blue tank top with thin straps and gray shorts. For Sherman, it was a revelation. He had never seen her in anything but scrubs, and it painted her in a whole new light.

"What a strange life you lead," she added.

"Where to?" he asked.

"I'm guessing a black-tie affair is out of the picture."

"I have a black t-shirt back at the motel."

"There is a bar a few blocks over. Nothing fancy but not a complete dive."

Sherman shrugged and followed her out the gate. "I like dives."

"Frank, why does that not surprise me?"

Out of the corner of his eye, and not even consciously, Sherman caught sight of a silver sedan parked in the dirt two blocks over. It was easy to see because there weren't that many houses. Each block resembled Swiss cheese, with a smattering of homes and lots of empty space in between. His brain registered the fact but kept on moving.

"You okay?" asked Vanessa.

"Good enough," he answered with a genuine smile.

"Can I ask you a question?"

"Personal or professional?"

"Maybe both," she said.

"Go ahead."

"How do you turn it off?"

"With the power button," he deflected. Sherman knew where the question led and the answer often frightened people.

"I know how much it hurts to see her like that, not knowing left from right on some days. That must mess with your system, it does with mine after a long day. How do you turn it off when you leave?" Vanessa asked.

Sherman paused for a moment and considered. "You have it backward. The question shouldn't be how I turn off my humanity when I leave here."

"I wasn't insinuating—" she began but he cut her off.

"Don't worry, I'm not taking it personally. I was saying the better question is how I turn it back on when I come home."

She angled her head to one side and waited for more.

He continued, "Once you let go, it's hard to find it again."

"It?"

"Humanity, sanity, a moral compass—take your pick."

"And do you?"

Sherman locked her face in his gaze and peered at her with the same eyes as his mother. Sophia's gaze was so full of mirth, wild and humorous, but his contained something animal. A look long ago lost in the world of superficial desires and the niceties of culture.

"So far," he answered.

Vanessa bit her lip and Sherman wondered if she was about to get all professional and ask about PTSD or encourage him to seek treatment, but they had reached the bar and it didn't seem like an appropriate conversation to have over a pint. Besides, it was only their first date.

Sherman held the door open in a modest gesture of good manners that also gave him a moment to look inside. The bar was just that and nothing more. No tables or dining options that he could see. Two pool tables sat in the far corner while an L-shaped bar consumed the space. They grabbed a couple of stools on the side so he could see the front door.

One beer turned into two. The conversation veered across their checkered pasts, but it crossed no lines. A respectful first date from two people well past their twenties and the surges of youthful lust. Sherman enjoyed her company and had nowhere to be the next day.

"Another round?" he asked.

"I wish, but I have an early shift tomorrow."

"Can I walk you home?"

"How quaint."

"Call me old-fashioned."

"Sophia would approve."

Sherman ran his hand roughly through his hair. "Let's leave my mother out of it."

Vanessa laughed. "Sure."

The sun had made excellent progress on its descent towards the horizon, but the heat stubbornly persisted. They walked unhurriedly on the dirt shoulder between pavement and private property.

Arriving at her gate, Vanessa leaned in and gave Sherman a quick kiss on the cheek. Then she turned and hurried inside like she was running away from a future bad decision.

Sherman stood there for a moment, disappointed in himself for not taking a chance and kissing her back. With nowhere to be, he turned towards the main street, hoping to find another bar.

Two blocks later, his conscience failed to produce a decent argument for staying the course. Regret was not something he took lightly. He turned back and retraced his steps.

The gate was open and Sherman's mind whirred to life from the incongruence. He had watched Vanessa shut it not five minutes earlier. Somewhere deep in the bottom of his brain, where the basic instincts of humanity lived, warning bells rang. He reached the front door in six long strides and knocked hard.

No one answered.

Not someone to knock twice, Sherman tried the door handle and, finding it unlocked, barged inside. The knock had given away any pretense of subtlety or surprise.

Vanessa was sitting on the couch. A thin rivulet of blood oozed down her chin from a split lip—the result of a quick jab to the face. Nothing hard, but a punch that got the recipient's attention. She looked frightened but oddly defiant.

Two guys towered over her. One in front and the other behind. They were wiry and wore shirts with geometric designs. Both were covered with dull tattoos and three large numbers adorned the inside of their forearms: 909. An area code, Sherman assumed.

His arrival caught them by surprise. Either they thought the door was locked or that no one was dumb enough to interrupt them. Vanessa shook her head from side to side as if imploring him not to get involved, but it was too late.

"Hey, fellas," said Sherman.

"What the fuck!" shouted the man with a shiny gold spiral on his shirt.

Sherman shut the door and closed the gap. He couldn't tell if the men were armed, but his gut said they were. People like that lacked the confidence for weaponless violence.

The man with the spiral shirt took two steps towards Sherman, unable to temper his aggression. He went to shove Sherman in the chest but might have well announced the end of a movie.

Sherman twisted out of the way and caught the aggressor's face with one hand as he passed, tilting his gaze up towards the ceiling. Off balance and unable to react, he could do nothing as Sherman threw him to the ground head-first. There was a dry crack as the skull met hardwood.

After watching his accomplice get knocked unconscious in a heartbeat, the second guy pulled up his shirt to show the pistol handle sticking out from his waist as if the act alone would solve his problem.

Such a sight didn't stop Sherman. He picked up speed

and closed the gap before the goon could get the gun unstuck from his overly tightened belt. The guy looked up in time to see a heavy glass candle holder Sherman found on a side table flying at his face. It hit him on the chin like an out-of-control high school fastball.

Staggered by the impact, he could not prevent Sherman from landing a scything right hook to the temple. As his fist connected with flesh, Sherman knew the fight was over. The man's eyes rolled backward in the sockets and he crumpled to the ground in a contorted heap of limbs. For a second, Sherman thought it might have been fatal, but he spotted faint signs of breathing.

He grabbed the gun and went to check the first guy who had nothing but a phone. Sherman took the cash out of their wallets as compensation for acts of irredeemable stupidity. The total came to less than fifty dollars. The pistol was equally cheap and bore more scratches than a lineman's helmet. Coming in at under a hundred bucks, it only worked up close and he didn't even know if that was true.

"You okay?" he asked Vanessa, who had not moved from the couch.

"No, Frank. I am not okay."

"Good. Tell me about it on the drive."

"What?" she stammered.

"Round up a few clothes. We're leaving."

"My car is in the garage," she suggested.

"We're going out the back door. Do you know of a car we can borrow? Or steal?"

"My mom's, I guess, assuming she's not out playing the slots."

"Grab your stuff."

Vanessa could not stop staring at the result of Sherman's outburst. "You shouldn't have done that."

"I'm old-fashioned."

"They won't see it that way."

"They'll be lucky to remember the night," he added.

"Or live through it," she countered.

"More reasons to leave now."

"Are there others?" asked Vanessa.

"There is a car parked two blocks over. It's been sitting there occupied since we went to the bar. I'm guessing they're not the neighborhood watch."

"I'll get my bag," she announced.

Chapter Five

The FBI agents arrived minutes later and knocked on the door. Something about the sister's date's entrance caught their attention, but formality and law prevented them from barging into a house without a warrant or just cause.

Nothing happened.

Agent Javier Martinez waited a beat and knocked again. Loud thuds echoed on the other side.

Still nothing.

Agent Landers edged against the wall and peeked through a window. Between tiny cracks in the metal curtains, she could see a pair of boots. The toes pointed straight up towards the ceiling and they weren't moving.

"I see a body," she announced.

Javier crossed to the right side of the door, while Landers waited on the left. She nodded and he tried the doorknob. It turned and opened a sliver. *Moment of truth*, Landers thought, and she nodded for Javier to enter.

The anticlimax on the other side of the door was a welcome relief. There was no shooting or immediate danger. Two guys lay on the floor, breathing but not moving. Landers checked their pulses, which were weak but consistent. Both men were non-responsive but stable. *Out cold,* she thought.

Javier cleared the modest two-bedroom home. He circled back moments later. "All clear."

"Except for these two," she added.

"Yeah, well, no sign of the sister or the other guy."

"Call the locals and an ambulance," instructed Landers. "These guys are prime candidates for some sort of traumatic brain injury."

Javier went off to make the call while Landers emptied the pockets of the unconscious men. She took out two driver's licenses and the random clutter often lingering in wallets.

"Inland Empire addresses," she said as Javier finished his call.

"Some Hemet boys this far out?"

"Let's check with Hemet P.D., I imagine they are in the system. Maybe they will have some known associates."

Javier scribbled down the action in a small notebook.

Agent Landers concentrated her memory on the man who showed up on the doorstep twice. A nominally average male. Six feet tall and muscular without being bulky. He had short but unkempt hair and a trimmed beard.

"Did you get a good look at her friend?" she asked.

"Run of the mill, minus the flip-flops," answered Javier.

"He held the door open for her at the bar."

"So, he has manners."

"Maybe it was a date. It looked like she gave him a kiss before he left."

Javier shrugged. "Friend or friendlier. Who knows these days?"

"She opened the door for these two like she was expecting someone."

"Someone like him," Javier added.

Landers nodded. "And then he shows up a few minutes later."

"Maybe they were all friends."

"Does this look like a friendly conversation?" she asked.

Javier chuckled at the men's misfortune. "Okay, so assuming these two shitheads aren't on a first-name basis with the sister, then why are they here?"

"You're the detective," she joked.

Javier squatted next to Landers and asked, "Do you think they are the sellers?"

She lifted an arm sticking out of the spiral shirt and haphazardly dropped it back to the ground. "They don't look the part."

"Could be middlemen or other buyers. Maybe our C.I. shorted them on the deal. It wouldn't surprise me."

"Me neither."

Javier tapped his fingers against the floor. "We never found out where Elmore got the money. Aside from his truck, the guy lives worse off than my oldest boy and he's working his way through college."

Landers stood. "It's a good angle. I bet Elmore skipped town with the goods and these two are looking for leverage."

"Family is the best kind."

She poked her head in the garage. "Car is still here. They must have left out the back. See if you can find her next of kin. They could be down the street."

Javier grabbed his phone and made another call.

The sound of sirens trumpeted in the distance and Landers stepped outside to meet the incoming police and paramedics. She held out her badge as they arrived. It was the easiest way to end any pissing contests or latent sexism. As soon as they saw those big block letters, everyone fell in line. She might get a few barbed comments behind her back, but experience built Landers of tougher stuff and she did not wince at such trivial words.

Javier stepped outside to meet her while the paramedics worked to stabilize the two men. "They'll be lucky to eat solid food again."

Landers nodded absentmindedly. The heat had transported her across the world to Kabul, when she wore a uniform and soldiers saluted as she passed.

"Next of kin?" she asked.

"Yeah. Her mom is just a couple of blocks away."

"Let's go."

They headed south as the setting sun clung to the vestiges of day. Landers walked fast with an easy loping stride while Javier sweated through his shirt again.

"What if she runs?" he asked.

"She's already running."

Their two-person parade came to a stop in front of a sagging beige house standing resolute against the heat. Not a single blade of green existed in the rocky front yard. Landers undid her ponytail, let her hair drape around her shoulders, and cracked an easy-going smile she had practiced for years. The feminine touch. Then she rang the doorbell.

A thin woman in her late fifties, with wispy streaks of gray hair and a leopard print blouse, answered the front door but declined to open the metal security door. "Can I help you?"

"Hello, ma'am, I'm Special Agent Megan Landers with

the FBI. We're investigating a ring of car thieves operating in the area. Did you recently report a missing car?"

The woman frowned in confusion. "No, I didn't."

"You didn't report a missing Toyota Tundra?"

"I drive a Civic."

"And it's here?"

"My daughter borrowed it. She was having some… uh, boy troubles, but I reported nothing."

"My mistake, ma'am. Have a good day."

The two agents retreated with a practiced ignorance and walked back towards their sedan as Javier made yet another call. The conversation was brief.

"I put out the BOLO on the mother's Honda."

"Did you hear what she said?" asked Landers.

"Boy troubles."

"What does that mean to you?"

Javier shrugged. "Not my department."

Chapter Six

A rusted bell hanging over the door clanged as Sherman walked into the motel office. The years had not been kind to the interior, and it came across somewhat cleaner than a strip club after closing. A timeworn man emerged from a small room hidden behind the dirt-smudged front desk. He slid on the glasses hanging around his neck and nodded.

"What can I do for you, Mr. Sherman?"

"Good evening, Harold. I need to upgrade my room."

"Oh," replied the owner, looking down the length of his nose.

"Something with two beds and an AC that works."

Harold narrowed his eyes at the insinuation of disrepair, but he didn't insult a paying customer. His eyes scanned the keys hanging neatly from pegs against the wall. "I have a double queen room, but it's twenty dollars more per night."

Sherman smiled and handed over a hundred-dollar bill. It covered the upsell for the rest of his stay.

"Did you get your stuff out already?" asked Harold.

"I did."

"Alright then," replied Harold and they exchanged keys.

Vanessa was standing in the shadow of a vending machine outside the office, trying to stay out of sight. She caught Sherman's eye as he exited and handed over his backpack.

"Is that all you brought?"

Sherman nodded and considered the bag well stocked. There was enough clean underwear to last him the entire week.

He pointed towards the exposed stairway leading up from the parking lot. "We're on the second floor."

"I've never been here before," she said as they walked up.

"Why would you? You live here and this place is a dump."

Vanessa glanced across the brittle horizon visible from the second floor. "Did you ever live here when your dad was stationed at the annex?"

"No, I was long gone by then."

"You joined the army after 9/11?"

"Yeah," he answered, although the memory seemed faint and otherworldly.

"That doesn't surprise me."

"I was trying my hand at college."

"But that is surprising. What was your major?"

"Undeclared."

Vanessa laughed. "I can't see you as a gangly, pimple-faced freshman wandering through the dorms."

"Not your experience?" he asked.

"No. I got my nursing degree the cheap way. Took most of my classes at a community college before transferring to a university for the last year. So, I guess I missed the whole keg stand, party scene."

"No shame in being responsible."

"No fun either."

They stopped in front of off-kilter gold numbers. With a grand gesture, Sherman opened the door. "Here we go."

The room was marginally larger than his old one. It checked all the boxes he'd requested. There were two queen beds, and the AC spat out cool, if not cold air. Otherwise, it was a cheap room in a rundown motel at the edge of nowhere.

Vanessa glanced at both beds, paused for a moment as if to consider the options, and took the one furthest away from the door. She dropped her bag on the floor, stripped off the worn aquamarine comforter, and lay down on the bare sheets.

"Thanks again, Frank."

"Of course."

"I mean, thanks for everything."

Sherman gave a sympathetic smile, but the truth of it was, he enjoyed smashing on the two guys. In situations like that, his lines were black and white. Compared to the war and its many shades of gray, such clarity was a welcome relief.

"Dare I ask what is going on?"

She rolled onto her side, facing his direction. Even in the feeble lamplight and her best efforts to counter it, he could see the swelling in her lip and bruising on her chin. She had taken a decent punch to the face.

"In all seriousness, I'm not really sure," she answered.

"Start with the basics," he said. "Who were those guys?"

"Sleaze-ball friends of my brother."

"I didn't know you had a brother."

"Half-brother, from my dad's troll of a second wife."

It struck Sherman how little he knew about Vanessa or

her life. Family barely tipped out into the open during their date, if they bothered to call two drinks such a thing.

"Some friends. What did they want?"

"Besides being pricks and slapping me around, they wanted to know where Elmore is hiding."

"You don't go punching your friend's sister in the face over a missed night on the town. Is he in trouble?"

"They said he owed them money, which is nothing new. Elmore owes everyone money. He bought that fancy fucking truck off the backs of his family. Begging and borrowing one day and then driving up with that overpriced manhood compensator the next."

There was a quality about Vanessa that Sherman enjoyed but couldn't put his finger on. *Spunky*, he thought, yet with a darker edge.

"Your brother… is he usually on the wrong side of the tracks?"

"This town is on the wrong side of the tracks. You know there ain't much choice for boys like him. Most of them leave, and the ones that stay drift about like tumbleweeds."

"Which way did he go?"

"He started out straight enough, working some minimum wage night shift at the dollar store. I even got him a part-time gig at the nursing home. But Elmore had a notion that this world owed him more. He had a side hustle with some boys from across the pass. I'm not sure what happened after that, but we stopped talking on the regular. He was too busy, and I was just that working stiff sister with no dreams."

Such a transformation did not surprise Sherman. From Syria to Iraq, the disenfranchised and unemployed youth gravitated towards the fringes. Over fifteen years of war, he'd buried more than his fair share.

"Only one thing to do then," he began.

"What?" she asked.

"Find your brother."

"I'm not sure he deserves help," Vanessa lamented.

"Better to have him take the next beating than you."

"You make a convincing argument, Mr. Sherman."

"We'll start in the morning, after coffee."

"I guess I'm calling in sick after all."

Sherman thought to ask what she meant, but Vanessa was halfway unconscious, eyes shut against recent events. She hadn't even bothered to undress and he tried not to think about a different outcome. One where she wasn't bruised and bleeding. One where he needn't have changed rooms. But sleep was a rare commodity in Sherman's world, and it didn't take him long to follow suit.

He left the loaded pistol on the nightstand.

Across town, in a modernly furnished room with orange triangles painted on the walls, Agent Landers flipped through her case files. A small glass of whiskey sat cooling around a single cube of ice. Javier lay on his bed, shoes still on but half-asleep.

Of the dozen crime scene photos in the manila folder, all contained a similar theme. From bank robberies, shootouts, murders, and gangland executions, the perpetrators all used military weapons. Not civilian copies, but the real deal. Most of the serial numbers were missing, but some remained. Those that did were traced back to weapons lost during decades of war. Weapons shipped to or from conflict zones in the Middle East.

Logistical leakage was the official term, but Landers

knew better. Someone was selling off the surplus and she'd seen the damage American hardware wrought. M4A1 rifles had a cyclic rate of 950 rounds per minute, while the M240 could decimate a human body from over eight hundred yards, and it came standard with fifty rounds. Combined with extended-capacity magazines and military body armor, the criminals were outclassing even the most well-equipped police departments.

"I don't like the timing," she said.

Javier groaned and lifted his head. "You're right. It's late. Go to sleep."

"You know what I mean."

"Elmore is in it for himself and whatever dollars he can beg, borrow, or steal. Skipping town with the guns or cash ain't exactly surprising."

"Something feels off. He said the meeting was all set up and good to go. I don't think he'd run, not after getting this far."

"You can't predict idiocy," Javier said offhandedly.

"That's unusually pessimistic, even for you."

"It's late. I'm beat. And our one lead on this case is missing."

"You're wallowing."

"I'm being realistic."

Landers sipped her whiskey and brooded over the setback. "We need a contingency plan."

"Like I said earlier, there are plenty of people around here willing to make a buck. We just need to lay out the cash."

"Let's stay on the sister for now. I get the feeling she is somehow connected."

Javier raised his hands in surrender. "Fine. Can you turn off that damn light?"

Chapter Seven

Hours later, Sherman awoke to the metallic rumble of the air conditioner and a stirring sun. Thin strands of light snuck through the worn vinyl blinds. Vanessa was curled into a much smaller form and still asleep. Sherman guessed it was early. His watch confirmed it.

He padded across the shabby blue carpet with its interlocking diamond design and peeked through the blinds. The window overlooked the street behind the motel where they parked the Honda. Across from that was the cafe he found the previous day—the one with a decent cup of coffee and edible breakfast.

Sherman grabbed some clean clothes and slipped into the bathroom for a shower. He let the cool water run through his hair and down his neck. It helped him think, but the outcomes all looked bleak and his gut said Elmore was in serious trouble.

"I need some caffeine and an aspirin," Vanessa groaned as he left the bathroom.

He pulled a small bottle of Bayer from his bag and

placed it on the nightstand. "I'm gonna grab us some grub."

Vanessa waved him off and Sherman shambled through the motel parking lot and across the street into the cafe. He ordered coffees and breakfast burritos and got a refill on his to-go cup before the food was ready.

Not wanting to give Vanessa a scare, he knocked on his way back in. She was still lying on the bed but showered and dressed. Her shorts were the same, but the shirt was new and snug. Sherman tried not to stare for too long.

"Breakfast," he announced before handing over a Styrofoam cup and foil-wrapped burrito.

"You're a hero twice over," she replied with a cheerful smile that seemed more forced than genuine. The swelling had subsided some, but her bruises were the color of an ink stain.

"Don't give me too much credit."

She sipped her coffee slowly and with purpose. "I'm thinking Cullen might know where Elmore is hiding."

"Who is Cullen?"

"His best friend since kindergarten."

The longest tenure of friendship Sherman ever had was ten years, and Tillerman was dead. "I'm ready if you don't mind eating in the car."

"Let me put some makeup on. I don't want everyone thinking you're just another boyfriend."

Sherman said nothing, but the remark filled in the sketch of her life with rather harsh lines.

They made their way down the street to her mother's Honda Civic. Vanessa headed for the passenger side door, but Sherman beat her to it.

"Don't you want to drive?" she asked. "Men around

here assume the wheel like it is some privilege of their sex handed down through evolution or providence."

Sherman laughed at her directness and the kernels of truth embedded in it. "Cars and I have a checkered past."

"Would you tell me if I asked?"

"Depends on how long of a drive we take."

Vanessa pulled out into traffic and headed west along the dusty main road that crossed Buford. "I can take the long way."

"Like Utah?"

She laughed, and it felt like a lost friend coming back to visit. "I'm afraid it's only ten minutes."

"That might get you one question."

She didn't blink before asking, like the question was loaded and ready. "How did you know I was in trouble?"

"The gate was open."

"And that was enough for you to barge in?"

"I said one question," he replied.

"And I'm still driving."

Sherman laughed and held up his hands in mock protest. "Yes, that was enough."

"And if it was just me?"

"I'd have some serious apologizing to do."

"And if it was three or four guys?"

"You'd be putting some makeup on me."

She drummed her fingers against the steering wheel and Sherman thought his false modesty might have fallen on deaf ears.

"Cullen works at the garage up ahead."

In the distance, past a lone house with plywood signs advertising tax and notary services, was a series of low-slung yellow buildings. Clumped together, they looked like a set of cubes cut in half and buried in the dirt. Vanessa pulled in and parked between faded white lines, fighting against neglect and the sun.

A thick-shouldered man stepped out as they approached. Cullen was about Sherman's height but forty pounds heavier, with the forearms of someone accustomed to ratcheting. He wiped off streaks of grease and smiled at Vanessa.

"Hey, V. What are you doing here?"

"I'm looking for Elmore."

Cullen eyed Sherman warily like a dog twice bitten.

"We haven't been hanging out much lately," he admitted.

"Any idea where he might be?"

The mechanic shrugged and looked at Sherman. "He in trouble?"

"Sorry, Cullen, this is Frank. Frank, meet Cullen."

"You look like trouble," replied the younger man.

"He's just a friend."

"The kind that gave you that shiner?"

Vanessa self-consciously touched her chin. "No. I'm done with those kinds of friends."

Sherman said nothing but already liked Cullen. He didn't look the type to take shit from anyone.

"Look, I need to find Elmore. He owes money to some guys and they came to visit me."

Cullen's eyes narrowed in concentrated anger. "Fuckers! I told Elmore to stay away from those assholes but he wouldn't listen. He was always looking for a shortcut, never willing to work for it."

"Where can I find them?" asked Sherman, speaking up for the first time.

"You don't want nothing to do with them. Believe me."

"I'll be fine."

"You got some balls, dude. How do you know?"

"The same way I know you've got a flathead screwdriver in your back pocket in case this went sideways."

Cullen reached back and patted the overbuilt tool. "Alright, alright. No disrespect. Elmore used to meet them over at Trotters."

"Thanks, Cullen."

"Be careful, V. You know they ain't a wholesome bunch."

She waved and Cullen watched as they got back into the Honda and pulled back onto the asphalt. The air conditioner blew at full tilt, trying to keep up with the outside temperature.

"Trotters?" asked Sherman.

"It's a bar on the edge of town. Should we swing by and look?" she asked.

"Not that I mind, but isn't it a little early for a bar to open up?"

She looked at the dashboard clock. It read 8:00 a.m. "At this hour, it might just be closing."

Chapter Eight

The **BOLO** worked. Not immediately, but Javier received a call from a local officer during breakfast. They talked briefly as the man barely concealed his distaste for running federal errands. Agent Landers dropped her fork and grabbed the last strip of bacon but didn't finish her plate of eggs. Minutes later, they were back in the foul-smelling Ford, driving across the desolate city.

"This place is strange," Javier observed as they passed by an empty block. "It's like one of my kids' coloring books where they forgot to fill in half the shapes."

Landers nodded in agreement. The disjointed nature of the area also struck her as odd. She was used to overcrowding, where people took up every available inch. Buford felt splotchy, as if they had cast a small town across a much larger footprint.

"Reminds me of California City, only with more people."

"What's the population here? Ten thousand?" he asked.

"You've spent too long in Miami to have a concept of size. Last census said fifty thousand."

Javier whistled and let the warming air wash over his hand as he stuck it out the window. "What a shithole."

"It's got running water."

"Okay, Christ, no more war stories. I take it back. This place is the epitome of pleasantness."

"Pull over," instructed Landers. "I see the car up ahead."

Javier eased the sedan into the desolate parking lot of a pool supply company. Faded blue paint hung on the walls, and the sign was missing an O. He pulled out a camera with a telephoto lens and took a quick picture.

"They're talking to someone."

Agent Landers glanced over at the LCD screen. "Isn't that Elmore's friend?"

"Yeah, Cullen. But why are they talking to him?"

"Looks cordial," she added.

"You mean he's still standing."

"I mean, this looks like a normal conversation with three people engaged in a civil back and forth."

"I'd say they're looking for Elmore too."

Landers nodded at the first decent conclusion to come from Javier all morning. "Agreed. The question is, why?"

"Ain't but two things worth asking about in this arid pan of shit—money and drugs."

"She's family," countered Landers, although her intuition followed a similar logic.

"All the more reason to find Elmore. Business and family don't mix. If you had siblings, you'd understand."

"My parents aren't Catholic."

"Nothing wrong with a wholesome, loving family,"

Javier countered. "Minus the layers of unending guilt and incessant nagging about grandchildren."

"My point exactly," she said, although Landers never experienced the blinding warmth of a large family. Her parents had been professors at a small private school in the Midwest. One of those recognizable names that no one could find on a map.

"You should stay for Thanksgiving one of these years. The whole mob would be there—Benny and his three boys, plus Juanita and her mess. I think she just had her sixth kid."

"I'll keep to my container of takeout."

Javier shook his head. "Don't you go home? If you have a home."

Landers gestured around the sedan. "This is my life."

"Work isn't everything."

"Who said this is work?" she joked, although neither of them believed it. Landers was a lifer. Once bitten but never cured of the itch for another case. She jumped from one gruesome slice of humanity to the next.

The Honda turned north onto a wide boulevard with a median covered in dirt and dead grass. The patchwork of buildings continued thinning until the spotty development of Buford faded away, leaving a land bereft of any semblance of humanity except for the road. And what a road.

Heading dead north were two extra wide lanes built for the land-ship-sized sedans of the sixties. Two more lanes headed south on the other side of the median. Both were lined with sidewalks and tall curbs and plenty of room for street parking. A perfectly planned development, save for one inconvenient fact—no one ever built a thing. Only the faded asphalt and concrete carcass remained to tell the story. Even that had cracked and buckled under the blazing sun and cold winters.

Javier slowed down and let the Honda race out ahead of them. There was no other traffic on the road and nowhere to hide.

"I've seen nothing like this. It's like the Twilight Zone out here," he observed. "A graveyard of dreams."

"I don't think dreams had anything to do with it," countered Landers. "This is hubris, plain old fucking American hubris."

"So is Vegas."

"Or Miami," she retorted. "You're only feet away from rising ocean levels."

Javier waved the notion away. "It ain't my house sinking."

"No, but it's your grandkids who will be left holding the bill."

A pale shimmer rose in the distance, and both agents squinted at the distant monolith.

He shrugged. "Where does this go?"

Landers looked at her phone for a few seconds, squeezing together her two fingers, hoping to answer the question. "Nothing but some abandoned buildings and an old dog racing track."

"What twisted bastard made dogs run in this heat?"

Landers didn't have an answer that would satisfy her partner's ire about the mistreatment of canines. His soft spot for the species was unmatched.

"It is just beyond the city limits," she added.

"Only way to make gambling out here legal, I imagine."

A quarter-mile short, Landers gestured towards the right and they turned onto a street that led nowhere with asphalt that petered out, turning into large black chunks that would have looked at home on the side of a volcano. The digital thermometer in the car read one hundred and three.

"You want to wait here, don't you?" asked Javier, glancing uneasily at the dashboard temperature gauge.

Landers pulled out the camera. "I don't see anything closer."

Javier undid his collar and rolled up his sleeves.

"That won't help," she added.

It didn't, and the air licked their faces like an open oven door.

"What do you see?" he asked.

"Looks like a party. Twenty or thirty vehicles. Mix of trucks and cars. Most look like racing versions. Either muscle cars or imports. The place is packed."

"It's not open for business, is it?" asked Javier. A tinge of concern hung in his voice for the fate of any animal left outside.

"Not for dog racing," answered Landers. "But it looks like the bar never closed. I can see neon signs in the windows."

"A little early for the bar scene."

"I think it is just closing," she replied. "Everyone is heading back to their cars."

Chapter Nine

The roof of the racetrack rippled like waves in a stormy sea. Each tip cascaded down and then back up, giving the building a viscous appearance. Its very shape fought against the encroaching desert, thumbing a nose at the parched expanse. Once-mighty windows had shards dangling down like stalactite like the broken teeth of a shattered past.

Nothing existed around the structure except for buckled pavement and tumbleweeds. Cars were parked close to the entrance in haphazard rows. No one cared much for straight lines or efficiency.

Trotters existed on the ground floor of the defunct track. Once-stylish circular windows had been covered over with plywood and the ends of discarded industrial-sized cable spools. Twenty or so people in varying stages of inebriation had gathered in front. Sherman stepped out of the Honda and eyed up the crowd.

"Welcome to Trotters. The sleaziest bar in the state," announced Vanessa with hints of shame and pride on her face.

"How are they even open?"

"Technically, we're outside of the city limits, so the cops can't do anything and the sheriff is stretched so thin, he doesn't want to risk a raid."

Looking at the clientele, Sherman understood why rolling up with sirens blaring might produce an unanticipated result. Most were drunk, some were high, and quite a few covered both categories in some strange Venn diagram of vice. Worst of all, they were armed.

"Am I going to get my ass kicked if I go in there without you?"

Vanessa nodded. "How many drunk idiots can you handle?"

"Not that many."

"Then we should go in together."

He motioned ahead. "After you."

No one seemed to take much interest in Sherman. The same could not be said for Vanessa. Some of the guys out front whistled while the women gave her long, hard looks that drilled down to some ritual core. Fashion in the crowd trended towards shiny shirts and belt buckles. Sherman knew it to be a look, but beyond that, he was lost.

"Are we asking everyone about Elmore?"

"Just the bartender," replied Vanessa as they approached the door."

She opened the heavy steel entryway and a wave of stale beer and piss accosted their senses. The standard dive bar smells, but worse. Magnified or multiplied by the heat and a complete disregard for sanitation. It reminded Sherman of a claustrophobic place in the bowels of Mumbai.

Years ago, he was training some Indian officers as part of a goodwill anti-terrorism tour sanctioned by Uncle Sam, and they invited him out for drinks one night. Some drinks turned into many. They wandered the bustling streets filled with the cacophony of everyday life and the buzz of neon. The last place they stumbled into had the same smell as Trotters—beer going in or coming out.

Vanessa waved to a man standing behind the bar. "That's Benton," she whispered.

The bartender was tall and thick with enough ink on his arms to fill a book. From a single look, Sherman knew the guy could handle himself. Given the work environment, he reckoned it was suicide any other way.

Benton turned towards them with a discerning eye. "V, what the hell are you doing here?"

"I'm looking for Elmore. Have you seen him recently?"

Benton raised an arm and scratched his shaved head. "Sorry, not for the last few days. He's usually passed out in his truck right about now."

"It's not outside."

"Sorry, V. If he ain't out there and he ain't in here, then I don't know. Maybe ask Cullen."

"We did. They had a bit of a falling out. Is there someone out there he's been running with lately?"

Benton cast a sideways glance towards Sherman and some semblance of a mutual respect passed between them. "It might be best if you waited for him to turn up. He's probably sleeping one off somewhere."

"Oh, how sweet. You're looking out for my safety," Vanessa mocked.

"I don't think you'll have an issue with your friend around."

Sherman said nothing.

"Fine, it's your funeral," added Benton. "Ash is outside."

Vanessa deflated at the name. "Shit."

"I've seen Elmore dipping into that pool a few times. I must stress, he ain't pleasant to converse with right now, but you know that, V."

She touched a scar just above her belly button and her eyes went wide. "Thanks, Benton."

"My advice, not that you'll take it, is to leave this well enough alone. Elmore ain't the sharpest chisel, but he's hard enough. Don't join him in the shitstorm."

Sherman could see by her reaction they were headed right into the heart of it.

"Let's go," she motioned towards the door.

As soon as they left the damp, stale interior, murmurs of recognition from the crowd grew and Sherman knew they were not going to the crowd. The crowd was coming to them—four confidently muscular guys with a few girlfriends trailing behind for a view of the action.

"This is gonna suck," whispered Vanessa.

"Didn't expect to see you back here," yelled a man with gnarled knuckles and a twice-broken nose.

"I wasn't planning on it, Ash."

"Because I distinctly recall you saying that you'd never be caught dead with the likes of us again. I did hear that, right?"

"Right," chirped one of the women, swaying with intoxication.

"With words like that, I am left wondering why you're standing here looking no different than a two-bit hooker."

Vanessa swallowed like she was choking down her pride and touched her swelling lip. Sherman watched her body language change but said nothing.

"And who's the bearded sugar daddy?" asked Ash with unhidden conceit.

"A friend."

Ash laughed and the others joined in until the jeers overlapped into a single roar. "You ain't picked a decent friend since second grade. Is she giving you a little taste on the side just to string you along?"

Again, Sherman said nothing. He still saw a few ways the conversation ended with everyone standing.

"Does he talk?"

"He doesn't need to. I just want to know where Elmore is."

"Funny you mention that, V. I had the very same question. That dipshit brother of yours owes me some money."

"Half-brother."

"Half or full, it doesn't matter. You're both tainted by that drunken father you share. The trash doesn't fall far from the tree."

Vanessa clenched her fists so tightly, the knuckles turned white. "Did you send those 909 boys to my house?"

Ash bent forward and looked down the length of his nose. "Those fuckers ain't welcome here no more and I don't need any inland bitches to get my money back. I'll take it from Elmore the next time I see him. Piece by bloody piece, if needed."

Few differences existed between the Trotters regulars and the two men who dropped in on Vanessa. Sherman could differentiate between a Haqqani and Yaqoob fighter in the mountains of Afghanistan, but everyone in Buford looked the same. All of them were wiry and caked with dust, showing complexions singed by the heat.

"Let's go," Vanessa whispered to Sherman.

They skirted around the throng, who hurled insults and the occasional cigarette butt in their direction. Vanessa walked fast without running while Sherman lingered a pace behind her. The sound of boots crunching over the crumbling pavement caught his attention. One of the men from the crowd jogged past and yanked Vanessa's wrist, unwilling to let her go without a final word.

Sherman didn't hesitate to whip the edge of his hand into the guy's throat. It happened so quickly that the others didn't notice until their friend fell to a knee struggling to breathe. By then, Vanessa had the car started.

"Go," ordered Sherman, jumping into the car. He wanted to be gone before Ash pieced together why his friend was drooling on the dusty asphalt with bloodshot eyes.

The Honda launched out of the parking lot onto the road with a screech of metal. Several men ran behind in its wake with shiny pistols sparkling in the early morning sun.

"Well, that was interesting," said Sherman.

Vanessa checked the mirror like she expected to see someone, and Sherman knew his actions came with consequences, but only dust swirled behind them. A gift of timing and inebriation.

"You shouldn't have hit him," she said. "You're like a firework launched from the tube and waiting to explode."

Again, Sherman found himself smiling at her unique way of painting him with words. "He shouldn't have grabbed you."

"He was drunk and stupid, nothing more."

"Sometimes it helps to lay the ground rules with guys like that," explained Sherman. "Now he knows the game entails risk."

"Colt, the guy you hit, I watched him kick in the teeth of a Burger King manager for not giving him enough ketchup."

"Knowing that, I should have broken his jaw."

She glanced in his direction several times like she wasn't really sure who was in the car.

"Where do we find the other guys?" he asked.

"What do you mean?"

"If Ash didn't send those idiots to your house looking for Elmore, then who did?"

"Yeah, I know someone to ask."

Chapter Ten

Four long wooden crates perched precariously on the front of the forklift. Deet lowered the mast and drove down a long corridor lined with green boxes and metal containers. Piled up by the dozens, the crates towered over the cab like a canyon of government excess.

"Sergeant," shouted a voice over the sounds of heavy machinery.

Deet stopped and saw the Battalion Commander, Colonel Brandon Wakefield, marching in his direction. A ramrod straight pole of shit and polished brass.

"Colonel, sir. What can I do for you?"

"Did you finish the latest shipment?"

"Not yet, sir. The crates were a mess."

"I don't give a shit if they were in pieces. We have a schedule, and the next batch is arriving this afternoon. You better not be skating, Sergeant. I don't appreciate a bunch of fucking slackers ruining my quotas."

"No, sir. We'll get it done."

"Goddamn right you will."

The colonel stomped off like the stick went all the way up his ass, and Deet snarled until he was out of view. He dropped the load of crates on top of an identical stack and looked down at his watch. Lunchtime.

"Chow time," shouted Hadz from across the aisle. His fatigues were caked with dust from moving gear outside, but there was a smile on his face.

Deet parked the forklift and followed the corporal out of the warehouse and towards a Roach Coach parked next to the golf course. Some local named Raul owned the food truck, and it was the next best thing to home cooking, which said very little in Deet's book, but it was better than the commissary.

"What did Old Man Spit-and-Polish want?" asked Hadz.

"Quotas," sighed Deet.

They sat on a faded concrete table shaded by thread-bare umbrellas that Raul had bought secondhand from a closed-down burger joint. Behind a thin ribbon of chain-link fence, the golf course flags waved in the searing wind. The fairway grass had burned up in the desert sun decades earlier, back when the paint on the base was still fresh. Some genius had replaced the greens with astroturf, which made the place look like it had a strange viridescent rash. Dots of green on what was one giant sand trap.

"Did he say anything else?" asked Hadz.

Deet detected the concern in his friend's voice. "Nah, he'd never get those boots dirty enough to check."

"And the other thing?"

"They've probably stripped the truck by now."

Hadz nodded. "Nothing but a bunch of cracked-out thieves. But it leaves us short a buyer."

"I'm working on it."

"I don't want to speak out of turn here, Sarge, but we might have to dream a little bigger. The fire sticks are one thing, but we might have to up our game."

Deet didn't need to consider the request. He had already given it much thought over the preceding weeks. Selling rifles was easy, but the margins were low and the risk high. Making a hundred guns disappear out of inventory wasn't hard. Selling them was another story.

"I'll reach out to Jones."

"Are you gonna tell him what happened?"

"Hell no. That prick is just a middleman."

Hadz shoved a bite of carnitas into his mouth and chewed through his concerns. "You think Elmore was a…?"

Deet shrugged. "He was a liability."

"And Boot?"

"He's fine. Family counts for something with us."

"Alright. Hey, are you coming to the movie?"

"What are they showing?"

"The Expendables."

Deet almost spat out his taco from laughter. "Ain't that about right. Expendable sums up this whole goddamn place."

"Exactly why they won't miss a few crates here and there."

The men finished their tacos without another word, but not in silence. The whine of the food truck's generator and the whoosh of the freeway were reminders they were stuck in the armpit of America.

Deet finished his shift a few hours before dark. They'd managed to siphon off one more crate of lightly used M4 carbines and another of careworn M240B machine guns. Even in their current state, the heavy weapons were worth fifty grand.

Getting full value, however, was proving difficult. He had a supply. Plenty of people had the demand. Bridging that divide kept Deet up late at night. He found himself visiting internet cafes in Arizona and payphones on the streets of L.A.—anything to keep his internet history a secret.

A fellow NCO shouted something about the movie but Deet waved him off. He fished out the keys to his trailer and mounted the three metal steps. There was a housing shortage on the base and everyone under the rank of lieutenant got relegated to temporary housing.

The door to the trailer creaked open on twenty-year-old hinges. It didn't fit in the jamb anymore, but complaints never made it out of the box. What once was temporary now existed in another state of being. Not temporary, but not permanent. An interim constant.

Deet cracked a beer and sank into the grimy brown couch he found on a corner in Las Vegas with a cardboard sign reading FREE attached by packing tape. It almost supported his weight, which was high praise in comparison to the trailer.

Two weeks prior, a PFC hung himself with his belt from the monkey bars on the playground. Nothing in his "temporary" trailer could hold his weight. Deet found him the next morning, twisting in the wind for some poor kid to find.

One bottle turned to three. The Bud Light clock on his wall reminded Deet he only had six hours until the night shift. Afghanistan lingered like a pleasant dream in his mind. At least his life had meaning back then.

He spotted the cheap flip phone under some junk mail and opened it up. The number he dialed came from memory.

A male voice answered.

"How did it go?"

"More bang than bust," replied Deet.

"Oh, I thought for sure he was good for it."

"He came up short and took off running."

"Sorry to say, it doesn't surprise me, but I thought he'd changed. I'll keep my ear out for something else."

"Do that," replied Deet before hanging up. He would have blamed the man but had not found success on his own either.

Chapter Eleven

Cold air from the car vents had done nothing to cool Vanessa's nerves. She fidgeted nervously in her seat, checking the mirror every other second. The expansive road to nowhere passed by in one brownish-orange smudge as she tapped her fingers on the steering wheel.

"You really shouldn't have hit him. I know you have some code or whatever soldiers call it, but this place isn't yours. You don't recognize the subtleties or know the culture."

Sherman sighed and leaned into the leather headrest. "You're right, I don't know this place or your history. And you've no obligation to share it. God knows I've got enough secrets to choke a giant. And maybe Colt wouldn't have left any scars back at Trotters, but I know those two guys in your house were not there to chat."

Vanessa was silent for a moment. She stared straight ahead while Sherman watched her face slacken in the corners. Just beyond her cheekbones, a flash of silver shrouded by tumbleweeds caught his attention—a lone sedan parked on the side of the road.

"I'm sorry," she began, regaining Sherman's attention. "I'm not one for accepting help of late. Hell, I've never accepted much help in my life. Years ago, I made some mistakes. You've heard these types of stories before. I hung out with the wrong kids, drank too much, did drugs, slept around… the whole shebang."

Sherman nodded but said nothing.

"When I hit the bottom, and I fell for quite some time, it fucked me up." Her lips quivered at the memory. "It took a lot of searching and a lot of reflection to find my way out. But I did. I pulled my sorry ass off the ground and went back to school and made something of myself."

"You're not like them," assured Sherman.

"I used to be and I'm afraid of being pulled back into their world. Into Elmore's world."

Sherman scratched his beard and sniffed the air. "You're much too wise to fall for that shit again. Youth has a way of polishing the ugliness in the world, while age gives everything a good scuffing. It's hard to ignore all those imperfections when you see them with older eyes."

"And what do your old man's eyes see these days?"

"Lots of dirt, not a lot of shine."

"Would you have done it differently? Hindsight and everything. Would you have enlisted?"

Despite his reticence of late, Sherman had never truly considered the question. Not once had he inspected it with the attentiveness that jewelers give a diamond.

Vanessa answered his look with another question. "You don't know, do you?"

"In all honesty, I'm not sure. The past doesn't change. I can't undo any of it."

"But would you? God knows I would revisit a few of my worst nights if I could."

"Sure. I have regrets. I've lost friends. Too many to count. But I can't change their deaths any more than I can change my high school hairstyle."

Vanessa gave him an inquisitive smile.

"I had a surfer phase. Anyways, I try not to dwell on what I cannot change and focus only on what can be done. The past is for learning from, not for hiding under."

"Don't take this the wrong way, but you sound a lot like your mother. *C'est la vie*."

"I suppose I had to get it from somewhere."

"Not your father?"

"I don't think he ever considered anything but windage, elevation, and temperature."

Vanessa looked back lost, missing the connection.

"He was a sniper."

"Oh," was all she thought to reply.

"Tell me about this guy you know," added Sherman, steering the conversation away from his own past. He'd already shared enough of that.

"Jones."

"Is that a first name or a last?"

"I don't know. Everyone calls him Jones, nothing more."

"What side of the tracks does he sit on?"

"Depends on the week... hell, maybe even the hour. He calls himself an entrepreneur, but Jones likes fancy words and fancy booze."

"If he had a business card, what would it say?"

"They all use LinkedIn these days."

Sherman said nothing.

"Right, uh, he does a little bit of everything. He sells drugs and women and real estate and insurance."

"A real renaissance man."

"Growing up poor will do that to you," she countered.

"Well, what face will we see?"

Vanessa shrugged. "We're headed to his office, but who knows."

The checkerboard patchwork of buildings returned and then turned left, heading east back towards the truncated downtown stretch. It was still morning but the temperature hovered at the precipice of triple digits. Sherman glanced down at his flip-flops and considered his exposed feet like long-lost friends who only appear on holidays.

"That's his place, up there."

Vanessa was pointing to a narrow building with white siding and red trim around the roof. It reminded Sherman of some cheap approximation of a Christmas shop or some other North Pole-related structure.

A wide field of empty plots surrounded the office, and beyond it lay a neatly laid grid of sidewalks. One lone house stood in the background—a solitary reminder of a lost dream. Faded signs with giant arrows pointing inwards advertised a great development opportunity: *Homes from the high 100s.* Judging from the outcome, Sherman assumed the price point was not a great opportunity.

"More failed dreams?" he asked.

"This town is full of them."

As Vanessa pulled in, there were two cars in the small dirt lot behind the building. A late nineties BMW coupe and a large Ford truck, built decades ago. Both were covered with a thin film of brown dirt.

Through the window and blinds, Sherman could see a figure standing from behind his desk and waving his hand. A moment later, the front door opened, framing a thickset man with red cheeks and curly hair that stood gazing in their direction.

"V!" he shouted. "What the hell brings you here? You're not selling, are you?"

"Hey, Jones. No, nothing like that," she replied.

"If you need someone, let me know," he said, then looked at Sherman. "Oh, shit, where are my manners? Come on in."

The interior of the office was practically arctic—at least forty degrees cooler than the parking lot. Sherman guessed Jones spent a fortune each month on air conditioning, but maybe that was the point. The temperature served as some strange sign of success or means. Or maybe the guy liked it cold.

Jones sat down behind his desk and the chair squeaked under his weight. "If you're not selling or buying, what brings you to my side of town?"

"Elmore," announced Vanessa.

"Elmore? As in your brother?"

"Half-brother."

"Right. What about your half-brother?"

"Have you seen him recently?"

"Sorry, V. We don't run in the same circles."

"You'd be surprised," she quipped.

"Oh?"

"Do you still work with the Hemet crew?"

Jones drummed his hands subconsciously against his desk. A nervous twitch of sorts. He looked at Sherman and then back at Vanessa. "I'm a broker. Real estate and insurance."

"Sorry," she replied, realizing her mistake. "This is Frank. He's an old friend of the family."

"Friend or not, I'm afraid I can't help you. I haven't

done any business on that side of the pass for quite some time."

"They came to my house and gave me this souvenir." She pointed towards her bruised lip.

Jones blinked rapidly as if he could not decide on his next salvo of words.

"I didn't know," he stammered. "Like I said, I've been flying the straight and narrow these days. But," he paused.

"But what?"

He took a deep breath. "I ran into Elmore a few weeks back. We got to drinking Jack and it loosened his tongue. He mentioned some side projects."

"With who?" demanded Vanessa.

"Didn't say, but he had a grand scheme."

Vanessa knew her brother—half or otherwise. "Where was the money coming from?"

Jones tapped the desk again. "He asked Ash. I don't think it went well. He might have asked over the pass too."

"Where do I find them?"

"They come into town every few days. Usually, they stop at Oil Valley and drink until they piss themselves."

Vanessa nodded at the name. "Thanks, Jones. I'll give you a ring if I ever sell my place."

He smiled uneasily and looked at Sherman with some sparkle of recognition. Sherman said nothing as they left.

"Who else was in there?" he asked once they were back inside the Honda.

"I'm not sure, but I don't recognize the truck."

Chapter Twelve

The Crown Victoria was overheating and Landers rolled down all the windows before switching off the ignition. Another day of sweat and stench, sitting and watching. They had followed the Honda from the garage to the abandoned racetrack and back to town with a stop at a realtor's office. Nothing made much sense, but she could feel some underlying pattern. The sudden stop and a dingy motel fit into a bigger puzzle, but it had her confused like a sky jigsaw piece with no distinctive pattern.

Javier was watching the motel intently. "What do you think they're doing inside?" he asked. "Banging it out?"

"One track mind," replied Landers.

"You can't blame a single guy for curiosity."

"You're separated, not single."

"And you're splitting hairs."

"Did you get a good look at what happened back there?"

"Not really," Landers admitted.

"We could arrest him for assault. That ought to stir the juices of conversation."

"You think the other guy will press charges?"

"Once the shame rubs off."

Landers adjusted her ponytail and slid lower in her seat. "What about the realtor? Any news?"

Javier glanced down at his phone, but the gesture was moot. Nothing had changed in the five minutes since he last checked the device. "The L.A. office is checking on him and I left a message with a local detective, but they don't seem in a hurry to do any favors for us federals."

"Do you think the guys at the racetrack and the sister's house are the same crew? Maybe she was confronting them."

"I don't think so. Wrong uniform. The boys at the bar had collared shirts on."

Agent Landers agreed, but it helped to hash it out to be certain. "It feels as if the sister knows the system or at least the players. The parking lot looked like high school after a homecoming dance."

"Maybe she is dipping a toe back in or maybe she and Elmore were working together."

"And the new guy is what... muscle?"

Javier nodded. "He's been effective so far."

"Too effective. It's like I've seen it before."

"Street gang?"

"No," answered Landers as her memory floated off into the past. "Afghanistan."

Images of Kabul's crowded streets and the mountains rising taller than a tsunami on the horizon came rushing back. Her mind unspooled the good with the bad—the cases she solved as an MP and the everyday violence that tore through the fabric of society.

A misplaced shadow brought Landers back to the present and she glanced up at the rearview mirror. In that briefest of glimpses, it all came together.

"Javier, don't move."

"What?" he replied before a bearded face bent down next to his open window.

"A little hot for suits, don't you think?" asked Sherman.

Javier reached for his gun, but Sherman caught his bicep and squeezed hard.

"I don't think that's a good idea."

"Are you threatening a federal officer?" demanded Javier, bewildered and in pain.

"Are you threatening a commissioned officer in the United States Army?"

The dots in Landers' spotty pattern suddenly connected in a series of obvious lines. Of course, she recognized the move. Of course, it was from her tour. The guy was a soldier.

"I apologize for my partner," Landers began. "The heat makes him testy."

Sherman glanced across the interior and she could see his eyes drinking in all the details in giant gulps.

"You don't need the Glock," he replied, nodding towards Landers' hand.

She had been holding the pistol just out of view below the seat but tucked it under her leg in a show of goodwill.

"Alright, can we start with some ID?" asked Javier, his arm burning from the stranger's grip.

"You first," replied Sherman.

Landers slowly took out her badge and held it up for the soldier to see. It had big block letters and a shiny shield. FBI. His expression registered personal distaste that usually came from experience.

Sherman released his grip on Javier's arm and retrieved a Military ID from his pocket. He held it up but didn't hand it over.

Landers memorized the name and rank before repeating it out loud, "Captain Frank Sherman."

"Now that we're all friends, why are you following us?" he asked.

"Mutual interest," replied Landers.

"An active case?"

"I couldn't comment, Captain."

"That rank doesn't mean much out here."

"It still does to me," replied Landers.

Sherman watched her carefully like he already knew something about her.

"I suppose I should salute you," he added.

Landers didn't flinch, but the speed at which he'd arrived at the conclusion surprised her. *Once a soldier, always a soldier,* she thought. "Once upon a time."

Sherman lowered his head further down and gave a wide, conceited smile. "Since we're all on the same side, why don't you fill me in on this stakeout you're undertaking?"

"Need to know," growled Javier.

"Good. I'll let you know if I need you."

Landers held out her card and Sherman reluctantly took it before turning and walking across the street towards the motel, not the alley he used to sneak up on them.

"Captain," shouted Landers. "We need to chat. Please call my number."

Sherman waved his hand back in their direction without turning around. "You know where to find me."

"Who the fuck was that?" gasped Javier. He'd been

holding his breath without realizing it and the words whizzed out as if from an over-inflated balloon.

Landers placed her sidearm back in its holster and started the car. "The kind of guy who puts two assholes in a coma."

"Was that ID real?"

"Yeah… like the hundreds I've seen before."

"Why did he come back to the motel?"

Landers pointed at the feet of the retreating figure no longer wearing flip-flops. "He wanted his boots."

Chapter Thirteen

Concern spread in crinkled lines from the corners of Vanessa's eyes. Her nose twitched at the sight of Sherman crossing the street. He moved with the purpose of someone dodging an oncoming car. The sedan appeared old but reeked of law enforcement, as did the cheap suits.

No sooner were they out of sight did she ask, "Who are they?"

Sherman handed over the business card and thought of the woman in the car. Clean suit. Crisp and neatly folded. The ponytail was short. No longer than the bottom of a military collar. Regulation length. Everything else about the FBI agent appeared orderly. *Once an officer, always an officer,* he thought.

"FBI agents?" asked Vanessa like the card wasn't real.

Sherman nodded. "They're for real. One very competent woman and one inattentive guy."

"Why were they following us?"

"A mutual interest or so they said."

Sherman's nonchalance stoked Vanessa's panic.

"What the hell, Frank? I work in a nursing home. I don't run with that crowd anymore." She paused. "Except for today."

He motioned towards the Civic parked in the motel lot. "My guess, and mind you, it is pure conjecture, is that we share the same question."

Vanessa started the car with a worried look. "Where's Elmore?" she concluded.

"No other reason to follow us around."

"Shit, shit, shit." She banged on the steering wheel with the palm of her hand. "I figured he was sleeping off a bender or maybe a beating, but those two don't give a damn about drunken brawls or petty crime, do they?"

"Not in my experience."

"What is it, Frank? Did he rob a bank? Join Al Qaeda? Start a cult?" Vanessa's voice grew with each question until she came to the last and obvious one. "Is he dead?"

Sherman looked at the tears sprouting in the corners of her eyes but he couldn't bring himself to sugarcoat the answer. His brain wasn't wired for unbridled optimism.

"I don't know is not the answer you want to hear, but it's all I have to offer. I can say those two idiots at your house thought he was alive, so did Ash and his crew. I think the FBI is bowling down that lane as well."

"I feel like there's a but in all those words."

"I think your brother rattled the wrong cage."

"You're not wrong," she said.

"Let's hope I'm not right either," he added.

"Okay, you've got your boots. Now where do we go? Oil Valley isn't open until dark."

"You never said what that is?"

"Oh… uh, it's a motocross track outside of town, and like everything else around here, it has a bar."

71

Sherman nodded.

"Where to?"

"Your work," he answered.

"What?"

"I need to ask my mom a question."

"With the crazy already going on today, I'm not even gonna ask why."

Vanessa pulled into traffic and they drove in silence while a streak of silver trailed behind them. The bank thermometer read 114°F.

"Now they know where I work," she groaned as they parked in front of the nursing home and the FBI parked on the street.

"They already did."

"You're not helping."

From behind the front desk, Stan raised an eyebrow upon seeing them walk in together, but he knew better than to say anything.

The TV blared through Sophia's half-open door as they approached with the weather channel announcing dour news for the coming week. Another five days of extreme heat.

"Hey, Mom."

Sophia looked hazily at his face for a moment before the neurons found a well-worn path. "Hey, honey. How are you doing? It looks hot outside."

"Triple digits."

"Good morning, Mrs. Sherman," cooed Vanessa.

"You're not dressed for work, and stop with all that formality, Sophia is fine."

Vanessa laughed.

Some days were indeed better than others.

"Mom, where is Dad's stuff?"

"In storage."

"I gathered that, but where?"

She looked at him and the hope of an answer danced on her tongue, yet none materialized. Sherman knew the knowledge was there but it seemed stuck behind an impenetrable wall.

"I... I don't remember. I'm sorry, sweetheart."

"It's okay, I understand."

Sophia motioned towards the massive pile of bills towering over the small desk in the corner of her room. "You can check my Rolodex, if it helps."

Sherman sat down and started sorting through dozens of envelopes—some opened others not.

"Don't mess up my system."

"Do you have a system?"

"*P* means paid. Unopened means unpaid. *T* means trash. *J* means junk."

On the back of each envelope was a small red letter written in shaky ink.

Sherman turned one over. "What does *S* mean?"

"Shit."

Piles of each letter grew until Sherman found a cream-colored envelope with a hand-printed return address. The name read Bob's Ironclad Storage and **OVERDUE** was stamped in the middle above his mother's name.

"Bob's Ironclad Storage," he said.

"Yeah, that's the one. Didn't I say that?"

"No, Mom."

"Well, that's what I meant."

He looked at Vanessa and whispered. "Let's go."

"Say hi to your brother," added Sophia without taking her eyes off the TV.

"Mom, I don't have a brother."

"I know that," she said. "I was talking to her."

"Have you seen Elmore?" Vanessa's voice rose an octave with hope.

"He came around the other day or week." Sophia squinted in frustration. "Anyway, we had a good chat."

"About what?" Vanessa asked.

She looked up at the ceiling, concentrating on the moment. "The weather. You. Some lady friend of his that was playing hard to get. And some business venture he was cooking up."

"What business?"

"Something with big returns. He was excited. I gave him some extra cash and asked if I could get in on it."

"You gave him money?" Sherman grumbled.

"It's mine to do with what I like."

"How much?"

"Whatever I had laying around."

Sherman looked at Vanessa, who shrugged. "Mom…"

"A few hundred," she admitted.

"Did he say anything else about it?"

"I don't know, honey. You know me and business," Sophia continued, flustered by her imperfect recall. Then she smiled. "Something about street value greater than MSRP."

Sherman glanced down at the envelope and memorized the address before handing it over. "This one is overdue."

Sophia turned it over in her hands. "Damn it."

"I'll be back later, Mom."

She placed the bill on the nightstand and swatted them away with a flick of her wrist. "Don't forget your dad is home late tonight."

Sherman sighed, "Okay, Mom."

Chapter Fourteen

Bob's Ironclad Storage was nothing more than an overheated metal prison for excessive stuff. A purgatory of discarded items that never made it to the landfill or second-hand store. Rows of squat steel structures baked under red roofs and an unrelenting sun. Even the razor wire on top of the fence slumped from age.

The office building looked no different from the units it rented. Vanessa parked out front in a space stained by oil and they stepped inside. A middle-aged man with a cowboy hat tilted back off his forehead waved as they entered.

"What can I do for you?"

"Are you Bob?" asked Sherman.

"No, Bill."

"Was there ever a Bob?"

"Yeah, my dad."

"My condolences."

"Why? He's still kicking."

"Oh, well, mine isn't and I'm hoping to get inside the unit where my mom keeps his stuff."

"You don't need me to operate a key."

"That's the thing. She lost the key."

Bill cocked his head to one side and eyed them with borderline suspicion. "What unit?"

"Eighty-three."

"Hmmm, let me look." He walked over a spiral binder and flipped it open towards the end.

"The name on the lease?"

"Sophia Sherman."

"Well, it looks like your mother is a few months late on rent."

"She has dementia. Bills are not her strong suit anymore."

Bill scratched his chin and nodded, "Insidious, that one. I can let you in, but the bill is still an issue."

"How much does she owe?"

"A hundred and twenty. Looks like we haven't gotten anything for six months."

Vanessa stepped forward and handed over a credit card.

"You don't have to do that," Sherman began.

"Trust me, I owe you more than that."

Bill swiped the card and reached behind the desk for red bolt cutters. "You'll need a new lock after this."

He led them down a car-width-sized alley and stopped. A weather-beaten number hung askew above the garage-style door. Bill bent over and grunted over the effort of shearing off the padlock. The metal housing clanked to the ground and Bill regarded it like it was someone else's responsibility.

"Come and find me in the office when you're done. I can't stand being inside these things in summer."

"Thanks," replied Sherman.

They waited in silence until he was well down the row and out of earshot.

"Do you know what's in there?"

Sherman eyed the door pensively. "The past. It's either something or nothing."

"Feeling melancholic?"

"My father and I... we didn't have the best relationship."

"Did he leave your mom for some washed-up stripper with pink hair and a tattoo of Hulk Hogan on her ass?"

"Nothing like that," answered Sherman, laughing. "He couldn't even stomach Hooters. It was too much for his Baptist upbringing."

"So, what are you worried about? Besides spiders."

"I've come to realize just how much I'm like him. The good and the bad. And to be honest, I don't want to find out how close the apple fell from the tree."

"Open it. Even if it's something, it is still the past," she added.

"And I can always burn it all."

"That too."

The door slid open with a creak worse than fingernails on a chalkboard and a shiver ran up Sherman's neck. Dust wafted about in the afternoon light. Thousands of tiny specks danced around haphazard stacks of boxes. His mother never found much use in organization—a trait that drove his father mad. Not that he showed emotion, but Sherman knew it bubbled furiously behind those cold, calculating blue eyes. By God, how he feared those eyes. They could burn through a boy's confidence with one fleeting glance.

"This place is a mess." Vanessa swatted away particles

of dirt floating by her face. "Let me guess, Sophia packed it up."

"Her diagnosis has nothing to do with that mess on the table. She was born with it."

Vanessa nodded at the joke but didn't laugh. "What are we looking for?"

"Something big and metal."

Dozens of crumpled cardboard boxes leaned against the walls as if holding them up against outside forces. A dry-cleaning bag hung from a rusted nail in one corner while a cuckoo clock towered in another.

"My mom hated that clock," Sherman mused.

"It's, uh…"

"A noisy pillar of polished German crap?"

"I was going to say very brown, but yeah, I can see that."

"It used to scare the shit out of me as a kid. That stupid bird popping out and my dad yelling at me for leaving fingerprints on the glass."

Vanessa slipped through a narrow gap between the boxes and bent down to examine the timekeeper. She opened a small glass door—the one Sherman caught hell for touching as a kid. When she stood back up, there was a bottle of scotch in her hands and a look of triumph on her face. "Looks like Cal had some secrets."

"You have no idea."

Under a pile of newspaper clippings yellowed by age, Sherman found a metal trunk he remembered from his childhood.

"Is that it?" asked Vanessa, edging closer.

"Yeah."

"What's with the NY Times highlights?" She picked up a small article about the assignation of some Pakistani scientist twenty years prior. "This is some back page stuff."

One look at the crumpled body in the photo and Sherman knew why his father kept it. It was a trophy of his handiwork. A shot only the highest levels of government knew about but one that made it into the Times. There were dozens of articles spanning decades of carnage.

"Like I said, he had a lot of secrets."

It took a moment for Vanessa to catch the undertone of his comment before her face twisted in recognition.

The hinges creaked as Sherman opened the faded green trunk. He had never opened it himself, not even at the peak of his rebellious days when Cal deployed to some godforsaken place and only Sophia stood in his way. Not even with the threat of his father's belt thousands of miles away. Some rules Sherman respected in the face of all youthful urges.

"Don't those belong in a museum?" asked Vanessa, looking down at a glowing collection of polished wood and well-oiled steel.

"My dad was a collector."

"Do they work?"

"Probably, but the youngest one is still over a hundred years old." He pointed to a British Martini-Henry rifle. "My dad used to tell me this story all the time. How it saw action against the Zulu at the Battle of Isandlwana in South Africa. He said it killed a hundred men that day and would recount every detail. We even had to watch Zulu a half-dozen times. As if shooting a bunch of guys with spears was noble."

Vanessa took an unsteady step backward away from the morbid history contained within the container. "Is it ever noble?"

"No," he replied, slowly rubbing his chin. "When it

comes down to the piss and the blood, there's not much noble about it."

"Then why keep doing it?" she asked, but her words reeked of regret upon leaving her lips. "Never mind, you don't have to answer that."

Sherman stopped sifting through the trunk. She'd asked the very question that kept swirling around his mind, constantly being pulled into the whirlpool but never fully disappearing.

"Truth be told, I'm not sure. It is about the only thing I'm good at and I can't picture myself giving directions at Home Depot."

Vanessa gave a meek smile. "I didn't mean to pry."

"Do me a favor," Sherman said, changing the subject. "See if Bill will sell us a replacement lock." He handed over a wad of money.

"It's cheaper to go to the hardware store."

"I know."

She shrugged and headed back to the office.

Alone, Sherman pulled out the real reason for the visit. His father's Colt M1911. The man loved that gun more than any other possession. Given the choice between a house and the pistol, he would have picked the latter. He probably wanted to be buried with it.

He grabbed the gun, the magazines, and the leather holster. There were two boxes of .45 ACP ammunition. Sherman picked them up and looked at the lot number stamped on the side. For most people, the randomized grouping of letters and numbers meant nothing. Sherman was not the average shooter. The manufacturing date was around ten years prior. Given the conditions of the storage unit, he guessed it was still good.

"Got the lock," announced Vanessa.

"Great."

"Is that what you came for?" she asked, pointing to the gun and ammunition.

Sherman hastily slid everything into an old canvas bag. "Yeah."

"Are you hiding it?"

"Not anymore, I guess."

"And the rifles?"

"If we end up needing one of those, things have gone well and truly south."

"Can we go? I'm melting in here."

"Sure, I need some food."

"I know a place."

Chapter Fifteen

Only a few original parts of the Ford truck remained. Gone were the wheels, the seats, and the pieces of the media center. Even the engine, mirrors, and tailgate were missing. It resembled some early stage of the assembly process, but in reverse and in some darkened alley of Hemet.

"I'll give them an A for environmentalism," Javier began. "They stripped it down to the frame."

Landers surveyed the scene. It resembled the aftermath of an IED, but with straighter lines and no scraps of people to pick up.

"When did they find it?" she asked.

"A few hours ago."

"Do they know when it was dumped?"

"The officer couldn't say. More than a day, less than a week."

"Our last chat with Elmore was three days ago," she said matter-of-factly, but the days were melting together.

Javier flipped open his notebook and jostled the pages. "Monday afternoon."

Landers said nothing as her brain rearranged the possibilities between Monday and Thursday.

"We're lucky to have even got a call," Javier continued, inspecting the diminutive truck. "They took everything but the VIN."

"I'll give you a gold star for the BOLO later," she retorted, then paused. "Do you think he's dead?"

"A hundred percent. No way he leaves the truck here and disappears. Maybe the long-term lot at LAX, but who dumps their vehicle here and then runs?"

Scrunching up her face, Landers tried to grasp at a missing piece to their puzzle. "Fine. I'll concede he's dead, but the guys from his sister's house live here. If they killed Elmore and took his truck, why leave it here and why go back for the sister?"

The haphazard chop job was impossible to ignore, but Javier always filled in the silence. Landers assumed it had something to do with large families or maybe Catholic guilt.

"Maybe they didn't want the heat from a stolen truck but got greedy. Those parts might net seven or eight grand, but not much more."

"Elmore mentioned a thirty-grand buy-in."

"Exactly," Javier continued. "If he stiffed them on that kind of cash, well, I'd go knocking on some doors too."

Landers paced down the broken pavement of the alley and under a long strip of yellow police tape. Red and blue lights flashed against short stucco houses with security doors and barred windows.

"Would you say this is a nice neighborhood?" she asked.

"I would not."

"Did you see any other abandoned cars gutted for parts?"

"I did not," Javier concluded and jogged back to a

group of officers whiling away the night. They spoke briefly before he returned.

"The sergeant said most cars end up down the street at the very upstanding and legitimate auto repair shop."

"If there's a chop shop down the block, then why would those boys dump it here?"

Never one to sink with a bad idea, Javier pivoted. "Alright. We're assuming whoever dumped the truck also disappeared poor old Elmore, but it could have been some drunk kids out for a joy ride."

"Maybe, but that's a long joyride over the pass. What-ever is going on, I get the feeling it started near Buford. If Elmore is dead, and I'm prone to agree there, the only lead we have left is those two idiots in the ICU, his sister, and Captain Sherman…"

"What?" asked Javier, surprised by the pause in Landers' logic.

"They don't know about the truck yet, which means they're still looking." She paused to rub the bridge of her nose. "Did they pull the captain's service records?"

"It should be at the office."

"Let's go. I want to be back in Buford by morning."

"Can we at least get a new car from the motor pool?" he asked.

"Of course," she said. "He already knows about this one."

Chapter Sixteen

Vanessa stopped short of opening the door to her mother's house and they stood baking in the afternoon air. She paused for a moment, considering how much information was too much information.

"My mother is a good Catholic," she began.

"I won't hold that against her," Sherman replied.

"I mean, she can be nosy and maybe a touch judgmental about my choices."

Sherman tilted his head and gave her a sly smile. "Are you worried about bringing a guy over? We can go and eat somewhere else."

"No, no. Trust me, the tamales will be worth it, I just… well, you'll see."

"It can't be any worse than a conversation with my mother."

"Yeah, but Sophia doesn't remember it the next morning. My mom hasn't forgiven me for stealing her *chicle* when I was six."

"But the tamales are good?"

"The best."

"I'll brave the interrogation."

"One more thing." Vanessa hesitated again. "What happened to the gun?"

"Do I need it?" he joked.

Vanessa exhaled. "I hope not."

"It's in the car," he assured her.

Sitting around the kitchen table, everything Vanessa predicted came to pass. The tamales were fluffy and tender and delicious. The salsa was spicy and the conversation downright intrusive. Gloria battered her daughter's choices with a verbal hammer until Vanessa appeared emotionally bruised from the barrage.

"Frank, where did you say you worked?" asked Gloria, smothering another pork tamale in green salsa.

"I'm in the army."

She waved her fork about. "Ooh, and an officer too. Good men are hard to find, but Vanessa knows that. She's dated all the *tomates prodridos* in town. Not a single decent man in all these years and then you bring over an *amigo*. No offense, Mr. Sherman, but I don't know you."

"His mom is a resident at work," Vanessa protested.

"Well, at least you have a steady job. Government work never ends. Speaking of which, did I tell you the FBI came knocking yesterday? They're trying to stop some ring of car thieves."

Mention of the acronym made Sherman's head snap up. "A neatly dressed woman with shoulder-length hair?" he asked.

"Oh, do you know her?"

"We met."

"About the *landrones*?" asked Gloria, her voice sliding towards an accusation.

"Not the thieves," he replied. "Government stuff."

Vanessa knew it was an in-between answer. Not necessarily a lie, but not the truth either. He was making a connection in that twisted mind of his between the FBI and her brother. She read the name off Sherman's lips.

"Ma, have you seen Elmore recently?"

"That weasel," she scoffed. "He came around here last week sniffing for money. Told me he had something big. A spectacular profit margin or some such Wall Street phrase."

"Did you give him any?"

"Hell no! He ain't my child and I prefer to throw away my money at the slots."

Sherman interjected. "Did he say what business he needed the cash for?"

"Who knows with that boy. He got all the bad pieces from that lowlife father of yours. Why don't you go and ask him?"

"I thought he was in Vegas."

"No. He failed there too. Now he and that *puta* are renting a trailer over by the park."

"Fuck," mumbled Vanessa.

Gloria looked at Sherman. "I normally don't tolerate that sort of language in my house, except for that piece of shit."

Vanessa looked resolute. "I'll call."

"Good luck with that. He hasn't paid the cellphone bill in months. My lawyer had to track him down in person for the alimony check last month."

"We could stop by," offered Sherman.

"I'd rather eat glass," Vanessa countered.

He didn't look away but said nothing.

"Fine," she relented. "But just for one question."

Sherman stood and cleared the table. Stunned into silence, neither woman stopped him.

"Thanks for the delicious meal, Gloria."

"Don't mess up with this one," she whispered to her daughter.

"Just a friend," replied Vanessa, but not loud enough for Sherman to overhear.

"You need a good man."

"No, Mom. I don't."

Vanessa left the keys to the Honda on the table and they walked back to her house. There was a police notice glued to the front door, so they went in the back.

"Back to the motel?" she asked.

"Avoiding your father?"

"If possible."

"Will it hurt to ask?"

"Not you, but maybe me."

Unease crept into Sherman's mind. Violence, in his experience, didn't discriminate between the young and the old.

The garage was stuffy, smelling of varnish and grease. They climbed into a Jetta two decades old with stained seats and gum wrappers littering the floor. Furrows dug into her forehead as she looked down at the mess.

"Sorry," she began. "The mortgage eats up most of my paycheck."

Sherman felt at home in the tarnished interior. A few scraps of trash never bothered him. Not when there was so much to worry about on the outside of the vehicle. Flecks of a candy bar meant nothing compared to a suicide bomber.

"I don't even own a car or a house, so I'm in no position to throw stones."

"Has anyone ever said you're too nice?"

He turned the compliment around in his mind for a moment. It was such an odd turn of phrase after all the things he'd done. "No, I don't think that was ever at the top of my positive qualities."

"Oh? What is?"

"Field stripping an M4, nighttime navigation, urban combat."

"I see," Vanessa replied, looking thoroughly confused.

"Should we visit your dad now or in the morning?"

"In the morning. He'll be pissing whiskey by now."

Chapter Seventeen

The Korean businessman was unconscious on the floor when the electronic lock to his hotel door beeped. An extra strong dose of barbiturates slipped into the Pepsi of his room service order had left nothing to chance. The drugs coursing through his veins dampened even the loudest of noises and he would have slept through the attack on Pearl Harbor.

Elias Donovan stepped inside and his shadow flitted ever so briefly across the luxury suite. No detail or price tag had been skipped and the room glowed with luxury. The kind that few people ever experience, except for the super-rich and double-crossing North Korean money launders like the guy on the floor. Some people had all the luck, while others like Kang Sok Hwan had it coming.

Dressed in a concierge uniform, Elias was just another unseen member of the help. Kang hadn't even looked him in the face when he delivered the soda, bottle of whiskey, and steak au poivre. Not that it would have made much difference. The two had never met. Kang was no different from the dozen people Elias had killed before. Just another paycheck. A name in an email delivered anonymously to a free account Elias accessed through three different VPN connections.

Most people in his profession were solitary creatures living alone and hidden amongst the rest of society. Elias preferred a more direct approach to camouflage. His wife, Tiffany, liked to throw cocktail parties and was on the PTA board.

It took some effort to move Kang, but Elias got the obese Korean changed and tucked into bed. Then he tidied up the room, ate the steak, and poured himself two fingers of whiskey. No sense in letting such luxuries go to waste.

Beyond the floor-to-ceiling drapes, the neon sea of Las Vegas stretched for miles. The humming glow extended up the mountains, which contained the lights like the edge of a bowl. The immense population allowed for a wonderful anonymity, although he never came back to the same city in the same year. One of his concrete rules.

After cleaning up the plate and glass, Elias finished the task at hand. He carefully inserted a small syringe under Kang's tongue and pressed the plunger. Some of his colleagues placed it between the toes, but Elias preferred the mouth. Harder to detect.

The dose of that pharmaceutical was fatal for any adult and it faded quickly in the bloodstream. Most coroners would chalk it up to a heart attack, and given the Korean's BMI and diet, one was likely soon anyway.

By the time he reached the rental car, Kang was dead. Another successful job and another deposit in the offshore account. Elias was in the middle of confirming the contract's completion when he received a text on a burner phone reserved for emergencies. Something urgent had arisen.

Contingent offer. 3 for 6. Buford, CA. Accept?

Three targets for $600,000. It was twice his going rate. As for the location, Elias had to open a cheap paper gas station map to find it. The phone didn't have data or GPS. The name conjured a memory in the crevices of his mind— a dusty shithole on the edge of nowhere.

He typed out a quick reply: *Timeframe?*

Unlisted.

"Unlisted," he mused to himself. Every job had a time-frame, otherwise, he wouldn't be needed. Nature would take its course. Everyone dies eventually.

His wife didn't expect him back for another week and he'd planned on spending what remained with a few *chicas* south of the border. That left seven days to murder three people. Not unreasonable. Five days for recon, one for action, and one more to get home.

Accepted. Send details.

The beep arrived with an address for a rundown copy shop, not some corporate box. Elias recognized the street and steered the black Chevy sedan in that direction.

When he arrived, the clerk behind the counter looked barely out of high school and even less happy about the lot that life had dealt him. Elias kept his hat low and his head down. The kid didn't seem to care either way and kept his gaze glued to some video app on his phone while handing over a thin manila folder.

Elias leafed through the photos on the drive west. He didn't recognize the faces, but they were never familiar, not until the end. Two were classic workplace photos. Government issue. The third was a grainy still from a surveillance camera. Not the best quality, but it gave him enough to go on.

A week for six hundred grand. Besides missing some extra-marital action and cheap tequila in Mexico, Elias couldn't ask for much more.

Chapter Eighteen

Nothing unusual happened, but Sherman awoke with his mind whirring. Every sense and intuition felt charged by the morning light creeping into the room. Vanessa's arm lay draped across his chest and he slipped under the soft flesh, placing it gently back on the bed.

The inside of his thigh was sweaty from where their naked forms had come to rest after tousling through the night. He dressed in silence, taking the time to lace up his boots and holster the pistol.

Nothing of note stirred in the motel parking lot. The same cars were parked in the same spots. No one had arrived or departed. Across the street at the cafe, a few early risers were working their way through the daily special of steak and eggs.

It all looked normal. A pedestrian morning lazily beginning before the summer heat gained force. Yet, the core of Sherman's mind vibrated with uncertainty. He didn't know why, and he had stopped trying to understand the phenomenon. Years ago, he might have questioned the logic behind the sensation, but he no longer cared. Its arrival heralded ill winds of some delineation—an ambush or artillery shell buried in the road. Those were remote possibilities in Buford, but the sentiment remained.

Urged by instinct, he was halfway out the back window when Vanessa woke up.

"Was it that bad?" she asked, mostly joking.

"Pure embarrassment on my part."

"And you're climbing out of a second-story window because?"

"It's closer to the coffee."

"Frank," she said with a growl.

"A hunch," he replied. "I'll be back in fifteen minutes."

Her eyes narrowed. "And if you're not?"

"Then ask for me at the police station."

He swung himself out of the windowsill and casually dropped into the empty space below. She heard his boots hit gravel and crunch away. Then she got dressed in a hurry.

Lethargic from a lack of sleep and coffee, Agent Landers dared not look away from the motel for fear of missing something. Javier sat in a similar state, albeit slightly perkier as he'd slept on the drive back from L.A. Having upgraded their sedan to one with a functional air conditioner, he had stopped complaining about the heat, but the car was not nice by any measure.

"This feels like too many eggs in one basket," he said, breaking the morning silence.

"It took Elmore weeks to get a meeting. We can't wait

that long again. They are moving serious hardware… we've got to take a chance before they sell it all off and retire somewhere without an extradition treaty."

"If Elmore is dead, then isn't it safe to assume they're on to us?"

"Maybe," Landers answered. "But we know he didn't have the cash. If they missed out on a big payday, then it might bring them out for one more deal."

"A going out of business sale."

"Exactly," she replied. "The kind you sell anything and everything for."

Landers flicked her eyes at the rearview mirror and tried to warn Javier, but the syllables got garbled in her throat.

"*Puta madre*," he yelled as Sherman appeared next to the sedan as if extruded from the sidewalk itself.

"Good morning," he began. "I see we're still playing this game. Care to tell me why you're parked outside of my motel again?"

Javier had hit his head on the roof in surprise and was rubbing the sore spot. "You could announce yourself."

"I said 'good morning'."

"We have a problem," interjected Landers. "I think it's better to sort it out at the local police station."

Unfazed by the expected request, Sherman said, "I need some coffee first."

"I'm sure we can find some at the station," Javier added.

"There is a decent place behind the motel. My treat."

Landers studied the bearded face for a moment, wondering how much trust a shared background such as the army could engender.

"We'll buy it."

"Get in," ordered Javier.

Before Sherman could slide in the back seat, Agent Landers held up her hand. "No guns allowed in my car."

"Besides yours."

"Exactly."

Sherman nodded and ever so slowly unclipped the holster from his belt. He handed it over to an embarrassed Javier, who took it with a look of shame.

"I'm gonna need that back."

"Do you have a concealed carry permit?" asked Javier.

"Like I said," Sherman continued, "I'm going to need that back."

Stillness covered the cafe when they pulled into the parking lot. Landers kept the sedan idling and relegated her partner to pick-up man. Penance, Sherman assumed, for allowing an armed civilian in their car.

"What MP unit were you in?" he asked.

"Why do you think I was Military Police?"

"Countenance."

"That's a big word for looks."

"And your bearing."

"Oh, my bearing?"

"No nonsense. You didn't spook when I walked up on you unannounced and even had the reaction to draw your Glock the first time."

She gave a small, self-satisfied smile. One that Sherman knew was hard-earned.

"The 153rd."

"Yeah, I remember you guys were stuck in a bunch of wind-torn tents on the edge of Kandahar."

Her gaze grew distant like someone searching for the name of their first-grade teacher. "I don't think we've ever met before."

"I doubt it. We didn't spend a lot of time on base."

"Oh, what unit are you with?"

Sherman said nothing. He merely waited a beat for Javier to open the door, laden down with beverages. The question disappeared into the aroma and steam wafting up from the to-go cups. He reasoned she already knew the answer or had an inkling.

The silence continued all the way to the Buford police station, which had as much character as the barren strip mall across the street. Had it not been for the lack of a sign standing sentinel next to the road, Sherman would have assumed the building was another corporate chain store.

From the way they sandwiched Sherman between them, it was clear the FBI agents did not view him as a harmless bystander. He got to keep his coffee, but that was the only consideration granted. A local officer escorted him down the hall and shut the door behind him.

The interview room was small and cold, with peeling paint and two solid plastic chairs facing each other across the steel table. A cheap drop ceiling made the space feel even more compact. By design, its appearance invited dread. There were no windows, and a small camera in the corner was the only link with the outside world. Sherman took a sip and centered himself in a state of perpetual waiting.

Time peeled back slowly like a never-ending orange. They were sweating him, letting him stew in some perceived state of anxiety or guilt. Besides smashing the idiots at Vanessa's house, he hadn't committed any significant acts of violence in Buford. Not yet.

The door swung open. Landers stepped inside and forced a smile, revealing a single dimple on her left cheek.

She sat down and Javier closed the door but remained standing with a brutish glare on his face.

"You were asking around town about Elmore. Why?"

Sherman took another sip of coffee. "My mother is friendly with the family."

"You and the sister look a little more than friendly. Going on a date and now shacked up in that motel room," added Javier.

Sherman turned towards Javier and wagged his finger as the dots connected in his mind. They had been watching her house when the Hemet guys showed up. "You should have helped her out."

"We didn't have any probable cause. Those two could have been friends. She opened the door and let them in."

"Bullshit."

"You're right," Landers interjected. "We should have done something, but you beat us to it. By the way, one of those boys still hasn't gotten his sense of smell back after the concussion you gave him."

"They must have tripped. Hardwood can be very slippery."

"I don't give a shit about those two assholes," said Landers. "I want to know about Elmore."

Sherman waved his hands in the air. "If the FBI doesn't know, why would I?"

"Yet you're looking for him."

"A favor for his sister. She's worried."

Agent Landers hardened her gaze. "He's dead."

The news did not surprise Sherman in the slightest. He'd seen soldiers blown to pieces after giving a piece of candy to the wrong kid. Aside from his feelings for Vanessa, he could have said goodbye to his mom and found a flight back to the UAE.

"Well, I guess the mystery is solved. I'll be going now."

She put up her hand. "No, you're not. We pulled your service records... or what we could get. The redactors had a good time with you."

Sherman shrugged. His team rarely knew what national sovereignty they'd violate on any day.

"When we ran your name through our database, nothing substantial showed up. The only mention was from the metadata to a now-deleted file."

"I wish you hadn't done that," Sherman replied.

"That's an odd thing to say, Captain, because I have a friend over at the archives that owed me a favor and he tracked down the folder... and guess what?"

Sherman said nothing as they obviously had something —he was just waiting for the turn.

"This picture was in it." Landers slid over a grainy black and white still taken from a video camera. Judging by the angle, Sherman guessed it was security footage.

It showed a man walking down a hallway. Sherman bore a striking resemblance to the subject in the photo because it was him in a hallway that led to at least one dead body. Finding one would lead the agents to others. Sherman grimaced on the inside but barely batted an eye.

"Do you recognize the guy?"

"Looks average," Sherman replied.

"Or the location?"

"Carpeted."

Agent Landers smiled. "It came from Stalworth, Idaho. Does that town ring a bell?"

"I'm more of a sandy beach kind of guy."

"Senator Knight died close to there, along with several others. Including two killed in the hotel whose security camera captured that image."

"You have the tempo of a sportscaster," remarked Sherman.

"That's you in the photo, and I'm guessing that if we dig, other photos will turn up."

Sherman turned to the other agent, still standing with his arms crossed in the corner, and asked, "Shouldn't you be playing good cop in all this?"

Javier shrugged, "They don't teach that at Quantico anymore."

"Shame," muttered Sherman.

"Captain," Landers continued. "You don't want us digging around."

"Neither do the people who deleted those files. Which is why I'm disappointed with your search, in the same way that it will disappoint them. As I recall, there were some rather nasty rumors swirling about the late senator. Something about inappropriate relationships with military contractors."

Agent Landers' nose twitched ever so slightly. "Rumors are like first dates in the Capitol. I wouldn't put too much stock in them. However, I called Stalworth P.D. and they have at least two unsolved murders. Some poor saps gunned down in their truck."

Two nobodies, thought Sherman. He didn't even remember their faces, only the mistake they made in trying to run him off the road.

"What do you suggest, Agent Landers?"

"Cooperation, Captain Sherman. A little bi-partisan, across the aisle, support."

"Does that still exist?"

"A girl can dream. Or we can mail this photo over to the Stalworth Police Department. My call intrigued Chief Torres."

Sherman considered his options, which all looked like rocks. The feds made a mistake in searching his name. He hoped it wasn't too serious, but only time would tell. As for Landers' implicit threat, the answer was straightforward. Despite their difference in approach, they both wanted to solve Elmore's disappearance.

"How can I help?" he asked.

Landers took a breath and explained the circumstances of Elmore's death.

The conversation wore on until there was nothing left to say. Sherman stood up and walked out the door. An officer politely escorted him out the side exit. It was better to not be seen on a friendly basis with the local law enforcement community.

Javier took a seat next to Landers. "Are you sure this is a good idea? He's some Navy SEAL shit."

"He's in the army, Javier."

"You know what I mean."

"He's more than that," said Landers.

"What?"

"They missed a location."

"A location?"

"A FOB."

"Speak English."

"Forward Operating Base. Only one unit worthy of redaction operated from there."

"Don't leave me hanging."

"A Delta detachment. A unit within a unit. Task Force Orange."

"Sounds harmless enough," Javier said with irony dripping from the words.

"He's a killer and a spook."

"With all due respect to your shared background, he doesn't sound like someone to be toyed with. Even with that picture as leverage, the plan is shakier than my marriage."

"You're practically divorced."

"Exactly."

Chapter Nineteen

A cold, stale blast of air caught Vanessa's attention. Unwilling to wait inside the police station, she'd taken refuge in the shade cast by an oversized blue awning above the front door. Another stranger exited and another minute evaporated. Trusting Sherman's prediction felt naive and unrealistic.

Memories of the building's interior snagged in her mind like a cocklebur sticks to cotton socks. All the regrets, embarrassment, and shame of bad relationships and worse choices played louder than any dive bar jukebox.

"Thanks for waiting," said a voice to her left.

Vanessa turned towards the familiar sound with a relieved look on her face.

"Where did you come from?"

"They let me out the side exit."

"Why?"

Sherman squinted at the sun's intensity. "It's a tale. Let's grab a beer."

"Frank, it's nine in the morning."

"I know," he said with a sigh. "It's for washing down the bitterness."

Air rushed from Vanessa's chest faster than a deflating balloon as she understood the look on his face. "He's dead, isn't he?"

"They found his truck stripped for parts in Hemet."

"But not him?"

"No, but they seemed convinced."

"So, there's hope?"

Sherman stopped walking towards the bar. "No, there isn't. They told me the things Elmore had dipped his toes into and he took some serious risks. One too many, it seems."

Tears welled in paltry pools before tumbling down her cheeks. For years, Vanessa tried to keep Elmore off the same tattered path of her youth. Her brother never listened or cared to consider such hard-earned wisdom. Logic would not dislodge his own peculiar view of what the world owed him. In many ways, the news did not surprise her, but knowing that only made the pain worse.

They sat on a bus stop bench while Vanessa cried. Sherman wrapped an arm around her shoulder but offered no words of encouragement, for in that moment, none were needed. Grief had its own language and it needed space to speak.

Two buses came and went before a look of resolve hardened in the corners of her mouth.

"What kind of trouble did he get into?" The question tumbled out and Vanessa knew the answer would only invite angst.

"It was a little more than just trouble."

"Don't make me guess, my tank is empty."

Sherman nodded and took a breath. "A few months

back, Elmore got caught in an FBI sting near Hemet. It wasn't too serious, but he was looking at enough time to consider their offer."

"Did he flip?"

"Not exactly. From what the agents said, and we have little reason to believe everything, they needed someone local. Someone with connections."

"Connections to who?" she asked.

"The kind of people we talked to at the bar."

Vanessa grimaced at the mention of Ash. "Thieving assholes?"

"Something like that."

"Elmore was an informant? But those idiots are all small-time crooks, nothing more than peddling a few pills and stealing the occasional car. Why would the FBI give two shits about them?"

"They're after someone moving guns... Ash and his circle were just a means for an introduction."

"Christ alive. I should have said or done something. I felt things changing." Vanessa buried her head in her lap, trying to imagine how twisted things had been and how little she knew about any of it. She felt ashamed for abandoning their relationship.

"Don't pile on the blame too thick. He made his own bed."

She flipped her hair to one side with a confused look on her face. "Why did those agents tell you all this? You're not a cop."

Sherman glanced down the lengthy sidewalk to see if anyone was within earshot. "That's another bitter tale."

"Frank, what are you holding back?"

"Let's just say, I'm helping them out now."

"What? Why would you do that?"

"Not to be trite, but the less you know, the better. That way, they can't hold it against you."

"Jesus Christ. What the hell did you do?"

He leaned back against the metal bench while Vanessa's imagination filled in the silence. Within a glance, she knew exactly what kind of leverage the FBI had over him. Violence rolled off him like rain against an umbrella and she had no illusion that this was the first time.

"So, we're helping them. Now what?"

"I think we should have that beer."

"Damn right, but I get the feeling you have another reason why I might need one."

"The last person they saw Elmore talking to was your dad."

"Son of a bitch."

"Yeah."

Chapter Twenty

Little about the bland, sand-swept town piqued Elias' curiosity. Coming from the sparkle of Las Vegas, the barrenness of Buford irritated his urban sensibilities. Taking the main road through town, he did an out and back drive to get the lay of the land. There were a handful of cheap motels that he guessed billed by the hour. The nightlife was non-existent except for a very dilapidated strip club that looked as if it gave customers an infectious disease by osmosis.

"Caracas is better than this shithole," he said to himself.

Years before the lure of money and unconstrained violence pulled him down, Elias used to wear a detective's badge. Nowhere big like New York City, and the badge didn't mean shit outside of the city limits, but it was a crucible of sorts.

The job took a young, ambitious man and pried away the shackles of common decency. Where humanity once had an inherent value, he learned everything was transactional. The unique glory of homo sapiens disappeared into the chasm of depravity on a weekly basis. Each story stacked higher until Elias could look at the mutilated bodies of a double homicide and feel nothing but the desire for lunch.

Most cops who switched sides so blatantly did it out of greed or because another compromising aspect of their personal life left them with no other easy choice. Elias wanted the money but enjoyed the sense of power much more than material gains. Violence was the ultimate arbiter, the lowest denominator, and he reveled in using it beyond the confines of polite society.

Ten years on the circuit had not dulled his tastes or his intuition.

Circling back towards the highway, Elias found a chain motel at the edge of town and checked in under one of his many aliases. The woman at the front desk was neatly dressed but carried the same burned-out look his wife gave him on Friday nights when he slid under the sheets naked.

"What brings you to Buford? Business or pleasure?"

Elias turned and looked out at the waves of heat rising from the parking lot. "Is there anything pleasurable about it?" he asked.

The woman looked up as if no one had bothered to ask such a question in all the shifts leading up to this one.

"The mountains are nice this time of year."

"Are they in town?"

"Well, no. You have to drive to get to them."

"Then my business will stay strictly as such… unless you think of something else."

Elias gave the woman a wide, lascivious smile and she blushed.

"Here's your key. Room 231. Elevator is just down the

hall. The breakfast buffet opens at seven and the Wi-Fi password is on the receipt. Anything else I can help you with?"

"Where can I find a good cup of coffee around here?"

A frown tugged at the corners of her mouth. "There's a Denny's down the street, but most of the locals go to The Cafe."

"Does it have a name?"

"Yeah, The Cafe."

Elias smiled at his own arrogance. "Where do I find it?"

"Go into town and take the main drag west. It's just past the Sunset Motel on your left."

"Thanks."

Chapter Twenty-One

The difference was not readily observable to Sherman, but they had crossed the proverbial tracks. Dilapidated trailers spread out across the hill. Each one was within yelling distance of the next. Space, it seemed, was the only measure of privacy as a fence cost more than land.

Around the circular gravel drive they went until Vanessa recognized a battered gold Buick sedan. She pulled in behind it and drummed her fingers on the Jetta's steering wheel.

Before she could change her mind and reverse away, the trailer door opened and her father stepped out. Paul was bald save for a ring of white hair crowding around his ears that expanded out like a mushroom cloud. Burned by unending hours in the sun, his skin had the texture of cracked leather and the color of rust.

"Well, ain't this something," Paul began. "Coming by for a family reunion? Or did you see the vultures circling overhead and decide to squeeze a few bucks from your dear old dad like everyone else?"

Vanessa bit her swollen lip hard enough to taste blood. The act and her appearance did not go unnoticed.

"I see your taste in boyfriends hasn't improved." Paul pointed towards Sherman in the passenger seat. "Is that his handiwork? You hit like a pussy," he shouted towards the car.

"Have you been drinking?"

"It's a free country, of course I've been drinking. Look at this shithole." He waved his hands at the barren horizon simmering with no recourse. "Every morning I wake up to that. What man wouldn't drink?"

Listening to Paul spit upon his own slice of life reminded Sherman that his own father never complained about a thing. Not once did he raise his fist or his voice. All that emotion was long gone, lost in the killing fields of Vietnam.

"Whatever," said Vanessa with a sigh. "Where's Elmore?"

"Huh. Why do I give a shit where he makes his bed?"

"We think he's in trouble," Vanessa lied, unable to tell him the truth as she knew it and unable to believe it herself.

"You ain't too bright. He's been nothing but trouble from day one."

"Have you seen him recently?"

"Yeah, yeah. He stopped by last week singing the same old song. Digging for money like a dog digs for bones." Paul swept an arm at the singlewide. "As if I have any to give."

"Did he say why?" asked Vanessa. "I need to know."

"Does it ever change? Elmore kept running his mouth a mile a minute like it might spin some gold. A sure thing, he said. Nothing in this life is a sure thing." Paul sat down on the metal steps leading to the front door. "Look at me, I fucking damn well know. Two ungrateful kids, an ex-wife hounding me for money I don't got, and this drunken hooker who ain't turning tricks for anyone no more."

"Oh, go to hell, Paul," yelled a high-pitched voice from inside.

"She found God, if you can believe it. We went to Vegas and she found Jesus Christ, our Lord and Savior. Ain't no one prayed in that town more than two steps from the card table."

"Penance," came the voice again.

"Christ," he growled.

"Don't use his name in vain."

Paul threw his hands up towards the sky in mock protest or perhaps casting his own prayer.

"Did he say where he was going?" asked Vanessa.

"Who?"

"Elmore."

"No, and I didn't ask. That boy hit all the stupid branches on the way down. No telling what cockeyed shit he's up to these days."

"Seriously," yelled Vanessa. "I come all the way here to endure your casual indifference and you can't tell me one damn detail about the conversation."

"Hey, don't you run your mouth at me," shouted Paul as he thrust a finger in her direction. "You've got no space to be placing judgements on me."

Vanessa backed towards the car, ready to let Paul know the tidal wave of truth she was holding back. Before she could, Sherman opened the door to the car and stood there, taking over the conversation with an outsized presence.

"And what the hell are you looking at? Huh? Stay over there if you know what's best."

"It's time to go," said Sherman.

Defeated by an unchanging past, Vanessa nodded and entered the Jetta with Paul shadowing behind.

"That's right, leave. Just walk away. Again. Good work, V."

"I think you've gone far enough," said Sherman. His tone was level and dangerously low.

Paul kept coming until they were standing a few feet apart. "You can't tell me what to do. This is my goddamn property."

"Go ahead, Frank," said Vanessa.

"Yeah, Frank," mimed Paul. "Go ahead and get the fuck out of here!"

Sherman smiled, thin and slanted. Then without warning or a hint of movement, he kicked the old man in his groin. Not a schoolyard tap but a full-blown punt straight up through everything that hurt the most. There was a squeal of laughter from the trailer as Paul fell to his knees.

"What did Elmore tell you?" asked Sherman.

Vomit rushed out of Paul and sprayed onto the gravel.

"Why'd you do that?" he asked between pained breaths.

"Elmore," Sherman repeated.

"Fucking kid. He mentioned some business at Oil Valley. Now leave me alone."

Sherman bent down lower until they were eye to eye. "Some friendly advice, just between you and me," he whispered. "I've buried a lot of people for looking stupid and you've already crossed that line. Don't go and act stupid too." Sherman pointed to the nearly empty bottle of Evan Williams sitting on the plastic table in front of the trailer. "They say whiskey kills all things in time, but I'll happily jump ahead in the line."

Paul swallowed down the next round of bile and was still bent over puking onto the dirt when they left.

"What did he say?" asked Vanessa once the hill was nothing but a dirty smudge in her rearview mirror.

"Elmore mentioned Oil Valley in their last conversation."

Vanessa exhaled and her body rumbled with the effort. "I should have told him the truth. I should have just let him have it."

"Why didn't you?"

"Because I've seen the raw side of the world and I don't want to share that pain with anyone, even my asshole father. Because somewhere deep down, I don't want to believe them or you. There is this little spark of hope fluttering around and I want it to be true. I need to believe there is still a chance he's alive. If I told my dad, that would be it, and I wouldn't be able to deny it anymore."

"There is nothing wrong with a little hope."

"Frank, you don't strike me as one who peddles in white lies."

"I may be a realist, but it's important to have something to cling to. Be it an idea, a flag, or hope."

"Is yours the flag?" she asked, wondering what gave him purpose.

"It used to be."

"And now?"

Sherman's smile widened. "Let's just say I'm hoping to find it."

"Cute," she replied with a sneer.

"Can we go to this bar?"

"It doesn't open until late and there's no telling if those nine-oh-nine guys will be there."

"No harm in looking," added Sherman.

Vanessa's phone beeped, so she grabbed it out of the cup holder.

"Shit, it's work." She squinted at the phone, trying to decide if opening that can of trouble was worth it. Then she hit the green button. "Hello, oh... hey, Stan. What's up?"

Sherman tried to listen in but only caught snippets.

"Oh, shit. Um... yeah, he's with me. Okay. We'll be there soon."

Vanessa hung up the phone and cast a pitiful glance in his direction. "Your mom fell last night. She's at the hospital right now getting some scans done. Stan said she hit her head pretty hard."

The news struck Sherman like a lone train wailing in the distance. He knew it was coming for years, but its roar still sucked the air from his lungs.

"Let's go," he said.

Chapter Twenty-Two

The shrill beep of Sophia's vital signs monitor made Sherman twitch with unease. His disdain for hospitals ran deep. Many friends never made it that far and the ones who did came out the other end missing more than a few pieces. Then there was his father. He'd watched Cal wither in that plastic bed like a grape left on the vine. The life and weight ebbed away as the cancer took the last of his dignity. Then he was gone—carted off to cold storage in the night, leaving no room for goodbyes.

"How long have you been sitting there?"

Sherman looked up from the magazine he found in the waiting room and smiled at his mother. A large bruise colored the top of her forehead blue, but she had a certain glow about her.

"A few hours."

"Oh, Frankie, I'm sorry. It was just a little slip. No need for all this fuss."

"They said you lost consciousness."

"That happens every night when I go to sleep."

"Mom," he said exasperated, then stopped for a moment. "What happened?"

"I was getting a bill off the table, god damn creditors. Anyway, I put my hand down to steady myself, but it must have been on a piece of paper. The next thing I know, the room is turning on its side and my head lands on the corner of the chair."

Sherman wanted to tell her to be more careful but knew his remonstration would not reverse her aging. Blame only carried so far.

"I'm sorry, Mom."

"It's not your fault, honey."

The technicality of her truth did nothing to assuage the guilt gnawing at his gut.

"When can I get out of here?" she asked.

"A couple more days. The doctors want to keep you around for observation."

"Savages. They just want my money."

"They want to make sure your brain doesn't start bleeding from that whack you took on the chair."

"I'm fine. It doesn't even hurt."

"Mom, you take morphine every day, I'm surprised you can feel your face."

She waved off the comment and turned on the television. Sherman stood up to leave as there was no use arguing with Sophia. Dementia had not diminished her stubbornness.

"Mom, I'll be back later."

"Have fun with your friends."

He glanced back but couldn't tell if she meant it or was being sarcastic. That muddiness encapsulated the previous years.

Sherman was sitting on a shaded bench, rubbing his eyes into the back of his skull when Vanessa found him.

"Are you okay?" she asked.

"I've been worse," replied Sherman, shrugging off the question.

She'd seen the exterior scars and could only guess at the interior. "I don't doubt it, but right now, how are you doing?"

"Being honest with myself, I'm feeling like a crappy son. I haven't been there for her. Not in any way she deserves."

"You've done good by her. Far better than most. You visit and support her financially. You care."

"Visiting once or twice a year doesn't count for much."

Vanessa gave a mournful smile. "Some of the residents haven't seen hide nor hair of their family for decades. They're discarded pieces of society left to wither away out of view. People can't handle that we get old and weak and die. They don't want to deal with that inconvenient truth."

"I'm glad you care. Seriously, you breathe life into that place."

"I found something worth caring about. Have you?"

"I'm good at the soldiering."

"Hell, Frank. I'm good at getting drunk and making bad decisions, but I don't make it my life's work. At least not anymore."

Sherman laughed. "I used to believe in the cause, now I only believe in the people."

"Is that enough?" she asked.

"It keeps me going."

"That sounds noble."

"Only by half-measures. The mission comes first and then I do my best to make sure everyone makes it out."

Vanessa watched him carefully, looking for the flipside of the honorable-sounding coin. Then she found it, sitting in the open so obvious and stark, but didn't name it.

"You enjoy the other half."

"You don't have to dance around. Go ahead and say it."

"The killing. You enjoy it."

In recognition of the truth, Sherman sighed. "I enjoy being good at something, but the act brings me no pleasure."

"That's a low bar, Frank. One step up from psychopath."

"It's a big step."

"Have you thought about quitting?"

Sherman laughed and Vanessa realized the irony of her question.

She tried to rephrase. "You know what I mean. Don't re-up or whatever you call it."

I think about it every time, but I never come up with anything worth doing."

"Do you have any hobbies?"

"Drinking beer on a beach."

"Right, um, bartending then." Vanessa laughed at the thought. "You'd be a terrible bartender. Maybe the owner."

"Maybe."

"Or could it be that you're already doing exactly what you're supposed to be doing?"

"Maybe."

They sat in silence with neither knowing how to comfort the other and unable to admit it.

"How much longer does she have?"

"It's hard to say."

"Based on your experience and her condition. The truth doesn't bruise me easily."

"Four years, maybe five at most. The body knows when it's time, and once they start to slide, there isn't much left to do. We make them comfortable and then wait."

"For the inevitable."

"No one gets to avoid that, but you know that more than most."

The image of a young corporal bleeding out on the street of Baghdad swirled into focus. Sherman remembered the helpless fear and doubts that swallowed up the kid's expression.

"That I do," he replied.

"Or it could be longer," she offered. "I've seen some last decades with the same diagnosis."

He smiled at her effort to instill some hope. The same kind she held for Elmore. "Remember, I'm a realist. My hope is that the end, when it comes, is quick."

"Me too, Frank. Me too."

Sherman looked up and noticed the sun tilting towards the east. "I need to make a call."

"You can use my cell."

"It's better to leave it off your call record. I saw a payphone inside. It will only take a few minutes."

"I'll be here."

Sherman wandered off past the check-in desk and waiting area filled with anxious people. The payphone was tucked into a dimly lit corner beyond the vending machines. He dug out a few quarters from his pocket and the number scrawled on the back of an FBI business card.

He put the hefty receiver to his ear and waited until Landers answered.

"We talked to his dad."

The agent didn't miss a beat. "What did Paul have to say?"

"Nothing much, but he confirmed that Elmore was doing some business at Oil Valley. Did he mention it?"

"No," answered Landers. "We only saw him at Trotters."

"I'll look into it later."

"Captain, need I remind you of our arrangement. Time is of the essence."

"Major, you're mistaken to think I care enough about my career not to walk away and let this implode. I have my reasons for playing along, but things happen on my timetable, not yours."

Landers winced at the mention of her former rank and swallowed back the urge to dress him down, but handling Sherman was much different than her interactions with Elmore.

"Understood. Keep in touch."

The line went dead and Sherman waited in the gloom, flipping through his priorities like cards in a deck. Being toyed with while his mother was in the hospital made his chest tighten more than a hundred-pound rucksack, but Elmore's death also weighed him down. It tugged at the corners of his morality. At least what remained of it.

When he exited the hospital, Vanessa was talking on her phone, and judging by the expression on her face, Sherman guessed the conversation had not gone well.

She hung up as he approached and tossed the device onto the bench in disgust.

"What's up?"

"That was Cullen, the mechanic."

Sherman nodded in recognition of the name and the face.

"He had some unwelcome visitors."

"FBI?"

"The other side of the law."

"Let's go," he replied, but Vanessa was already walking towards the car.

Chapter Twenty-Three

All the doors were closed when they arrived and the cardboard sign in the door read *Be Right Back*. Sherman took a long look at the street and the surrounding buildings before they went inside. Trouble, he'd learned over the years, struck often and with friends. He gave Vanessa a nod when nothing set off his internal warning bells.

Cullen was sitting inside the small waiting room with a cold beer pressed to his cheek. The beer was doing little to stop the swelling and a large damp black stain covered his left shoulder.

"You look like shit," said Vanessa as she switched into work mode and collected a first aid kit from the office.

"How did it go?" asked Sherman.

Cullen pointed out the door and to a bloody tooth lying on the oil-stained garage floor. "I'll have to keep the .38 in my coveralls from now on."

From his smile, Sherman could tell it wasn't Cullen's.

"You might consider a vacation."

The mechanic's thick shoulders vibrated with laughter,

which made him wince. "With what PTO? No work. No rent."

Vanessa vanished for a moment, and when she returned, began cutting away the coveralls around his shoulder. "What the hell happened?"

"A Phillips head."

"Who stabbed you with a screwdriver?"

"Some valley assholes were looking for Elmore. I imagine the same guys who showed up at your place and gave you that souvenir."

Her chin had returned to a semblance of normal between the ice packs and makeup, but Vanessa could still feel the punch like the cells in her body retained the impact.

"Must be someone else. Those two are probably sucking on ice chips in the ICU," she said.

A look of confusion swirled in Cullen's brown eyes.

"Frank didn't take kindly to their unannounced visit," she added.

Cullen took a swig of his beer. "You did better than me."

Sherman flipped the tooth over with his boot. "I'd say you gave as good as you got."

"It's my own damn fault. They got through the door asking about an engine rebuild. I need the money, so I didn't think too hard about them. Then they started asking about Elmore and I knew shit was slipping downhill. I tried to get them out, but one of 'em cold-cocked me in the face."

"That from your fist or a wrench?" asked Sherman, still looking at the tooth.

The mechanic held up his right hand, which had a gouge in one of the knuckles. "All fist," he answered.

Sherman smiled. He liked the guy. "What did they ask?"

"'Where's Elmore?' was about all they cared about. They kept asking and I kept answering, but they didn't like what I had to say. Which was the same I told you—I don't know where he's at."

From the damage, Sherman understood what happened next. They tried to teach Cullen a lesson but learned one in the process—don't mess with a man who cranks on wrenches for a living.

"Did you call the cops?" Vanessa asked.

"Why would I do that? Those corrupt fucks aren't gonna do anything besides take my statement and drink the soda from the fridge. Besides, I don't want to get Elmore into any more trouble."

Sherman and Vanessa shared a quick glance. Neither wanted to divulge what they knew to be the truth.

"I'm sorry about all this," added Vanessa, closing off what she didn't want to say.

"It ain't your fault."

"He's my brother," she said.

"And my friend. His stupidity cuts both ways."

"We need to go to Oil Valley," Vanessa announced. "And lay claim to whatever shit Elmore got into. I can't have my friends get hurt over some shady deal he made."

"The fuck you are," replied Cullen. "Don't bait the trap and sit in it. If they did this at my garage, imagine what they'll do on home turf."

"What if they stop by my mom's place next?"

"I imagine she plugs 'em with that twelve-gauge of hers."

Even though she didn't want to admit it, Cullen was right. Her mom had lived through worse. "Fine, but you know what I mean. They could mug her in the casino parking lot or run her off the road. Who knows! My point is, it's better to find out what they want than walk around always looking over your shoulder."

Cullen had little left to say. He agreed to a point but never had the gumption she did. Not then and certainly not when they were younger.

"I've never been able to talk you down from the cliff, even when you needed to jump," he admitted.

"Good," she said with a smile reserved for friends who had stuck with her through all the muck. "Now, go and visit your cousin in Huntington Beach."

He looked at her and then at Sherman and then at the tooth on the floor. *Two guys in the ICU,* he thought. Much better than he had done.

"Fine. I'll think about it."

Vanessa smiled again, and for a moment, Cullen forgot about the puncture wound in his shoulder and the swollen cheek, then like a desert rainstorm, she was gone, headed out the door and towards the car.

Cullen pulled Sherman aside and said, "Don't make her go down that road again. It took a lot of guts to get out in the first place."

"Would you tell me what happened if I asked?"

Cullen didn't skip a beat in answering, "No."

"Good," replied Sherman, recognizing someone willing to keep their mouth closed. "Discretion is the better part of valor."

"And Vanessa?"

"It won't be a one-way trip. I'll make sure she comes back."

"I don't want to worry about two friends."

Sherman paused and looked towards the car. "She didn't want to say anything, and neither should I, but your friend isn't just missing."

Somehow, the news was not new and Cullen rubbed his shaved head mournfully. He stared at the distant angular mountains floating above the heat like broken shark teeth. "What a goddamn shame. Elmore kept barking up the wrong trees, always looking for an easy dollar. Such a noise drives people to extremes. I imagine it was a long time coming. He never had to go far to find trouble."

"Some people can't be saved," Sherman added.

"I imagine you've seen your fair share of that."

Sherman shook his head. "I was never in the saving lives business."

Chapter Twenty-Four

For a bar, Oil Valley had few amenities besides a new air conditioner and an oversized commercial cooler full of beer. The chairs were metal and folding and might have come second-hand from a church basement. A few card tables stood as the lone non-bar surfaces.

The structure itself was plain and came straight from a mobile home factory twenty years earlier. The current owner removed any non-structural walls, kept the bathroom, and called it open for business. Despite the obvious drawbacks, Oil Valley possessed one unique feature. It sat on the doorstep of a massive motocross course, and like Trotters, it was just beyond the city limits on the desert side of the pass and the county side of the law.

Vanessa parked her Jetta between several raised trucks with thick nylon straps for holding down the bikes. The diminutive car looked smaller than a kiwi among a crate of cantaloupes.

"Are you ready for this?" she asked.

Sherman counted five trucks in the lot, with room for

ten bikes. A dozen people in total, he reckoned. Not good odds, but from the sound of engines humming in the background, most of the customers were on the track.

"Are you asking me or yourself?"

"A little of both, I suppose," she answered with a nervous laugh.

"Not too late to leave," he added, but Agent Landers' threats lingered in his mind like a bitter metallic taste.

"I need to know what happened to Elmore and whatever crazy shit he got into."

"Sometimes it's better not to know."

"Thanks, Frank, but this isn't one of those times."

He nodded towards the door in understanding.

Two guys in the corner caught Sherman's attention as they entered the hollowed-out home with a neon Pabst sign instead of a welcome mat. Both cast a dirty gaze but only three eyes were visible. One had an eye swollen shut and surrounded by bright pink flesh with a streak of red that dribbled blood at the edge. The second could see fine but held an ice pack to his chin and there was part of a crimson-coated cotton ball squirming out between his lips.

"We've found Cullen's newest customers," said Sherman with a nod to the corner.

Vanessa looked around for anyone she knew, including the two intruders who forcefully introduced themselves. No one stood out, not even the bartender, and she had a history of knowing them.

The bar top wasn't much more than a fancy piece of plywood and Sherman leaned against it, waiting for the woman standing on the other side to say something.

She was in her early thirties with overlapping tattoos running up her arms while a large eagle jiggled across her exposed cleavage. The woman lowered her half-shaved head until it was even with his.

"Can I get two beers?" he asked.

"Sure," she replied. "Head back into town. There's a Chili's or Applebee's or TGI Fucking Fs. Take your pick, but this ain't the place for you."

"Why not? You have beer in the cooler, and I have cash in my pocket."

"I'm doing you a favor," replied the woman with a scoff.

"And here I thought commerce was a two-way street."

"It ain't when I refuse to service your ass. You reek of government."

Sherman felt the two guys from the corner approach. He didn't need to turn around. Two of his senses already understood the situation. He'd heard them saunter over but also smelled the sour scent of whiskey, sweat, and blood before they crossed the room. It was a familiar aroma.

They hovered behind him like wasps above a picnic as Vanessa stood off to the side, waiting for the shoe to drop.

"Tara said she ain't serving the likes of you," said the one-eyed man with a growl. "I suggest you leave. Now!"

His friend with the missing tooth tried to say something clever but it came out mumbled from the cotton ball in his mouth.

"Listen, I just want a couple of beers and a quick chat."

The two men looked at each other in surprise. Most people left when they said so and hardly anyone asked for a chat.

"Who the hell do you want to talk with?"

"Whoever you work for."

Their looks of surprise narrowed to suspicion and both men took a step to the side, freeing up space for their growing aggression. Neither had the wisdom to be afraid.

"We don't work for no one," said the one-eyed guy.

"So, you went to the mechanic's this morning on your own volition and ended up stabbing him with a screwdriver for what? A discounted price?"

"Are you a cop?" one asked.

"He sounds like a cop," added the second.

"You're outside the city limits, pig," said the first.

Sherman stood his ground and let them talk. He knew it had no place in a fight.

To Tara and Vanessa, it didn't look like a fair fight, but for opposite reasons. From behind the bar, it was two on one and she knew what harm they could inflict. Vanessa had insider knowledge too and she was already mentally switching over to nurse mode.

"What, no more fancy words?" asked the man with a missing tooth.

"Probably doesn't want to get his ass kicked in front of his girlfriend," said the guy with one good eye. "Maybe she wants a real man…"

He didn't finish the thought. Sherman swung his right fist through the guy's blind spot and snapped his chin to the side with enough force to rattle his brain. The man went slack and crumpled to the ground in an ungainly heap of bones and flesh.

Missing a tooth but not his vision, the other guy tried to swing a big looping hook in Sherman's direction. It caught nothing but air. In the space of a deep breath, Sherman moved along with his punch and crouched low. Then he sent a slicing kick straight at his assailant's ankles. The force upended the guy's balance and sent him falling to the ground. He landed on the linoleum with a crunching thud that stole the air from his lungs.

Sherman stepped forward and was considering how

many more teeth the guy deserved to lose when the bartender yelled, "Wait!"

He looked up, half-expecting to see the barrel of a shotgun, but only found a look of urgent fear and concern.

"They didn't mean no disrespect... they were just protecting me. Here," she said, opening two bottles of High Life. "They're on the house."

The man on the ground looked at Tara and then back at Sherman, relieved to see he'd met no worse a fate.

"What's your name?" asked Sherman, holding out a hand.

"Jay."

Sherman pulled the guy to his feet. "Like I said, Jay, I just wanted a beer and a chat."

"What about Charlie?" he asked, looking down at his friend.

Vanessa stepped forward and checked the unconscious heap's pulse. "He'll wake up with a hell of a headache but nothing permanent."

Jay looked at Tara. An unspoken barrage of questions and answers passed between them in a way Sherman assumed was familial. Brother and sister, he reasoned. Too platonic for lovers and the ease of their gaze underlined a shared upbringing and experiences. The same way he rarely spoke to his team when a look conveyed everything.

A few moans came from the floor as Charlie re-entered the waking world. Jay helped him to his feet but he couldn't stop staring at Sherman, who was sipping his beer at the bar and pretending he couldn't hear them.

"I could've took him if it weren't for my eye. Didn't see it coming. What did he hit me with anyway?"

"His fist," answered Jay.

Charlie looked embarrassed.

"One punch and your glass jaw went down. Then he kicked the feet out from under me like I was a kid on the playground."

"My gun's in the truck," Charlie offered.

Jay shook his head. "Do you recognize the lady?"

Charlie squinted at Vanessa, trying to rouse his foggy memory. "Should I?"

"I think that's Elmore's sister."

"No shit. Tripp will be buying us a round for finding her."

Jay nodded towards Sherman. "He asked about the boss. Wants to talk to him."

"Shit."

"Yeah, I don't want to step on no toes."

"Get my gun," said Charlie. "It sorts out all kinds of problems."

"You're not understanding me. He must have knocked another screw loose in that head of yours. Benny and Wade went to her house looking for Elmore. They left strapped down to a stretcher."

"Shit," he added, realizing the mistake.

"You said it, brother," said Jay.

"If you two are done," Sherman interrupted. "I'd like to have a few words with Tripp."

"You heard that?" asked Charlie.

"Old habits," replied Sherman.

The brothers looked at each other, then at Tara still standing behind the bar.

"Fine," said Jay. "I can't guarantee he wants to talk to you."

"Tell him we're taking over for Elmore," Sherman added.

Jay didn't say anything after that, and Sherman

reckoned it had something to do with pleading ignorance, but the silence didn't bother him. He merely turned and headed for the door.

Once outside, Jay found Tripp crouching next to a Honda 150cc, fiddling with something he didn't understand.

"Hey, boss, there is someone here who wants to talk to you," said Jay.

"And you told them I was here?"

"Well, no. He already knew."

"Why didn't you ask him to leave? Or better yet, kick his ass to the curb."

Jay rubbed his back and the bruises from hitting the floor. "We asked nicely and then…"

Tripp stood up and looked at the man. "Did you get beat twice today?"

"Charlie got it worse. The guy knocked him clean out with one punch."

Tripp smiled at the thought of Tara's brother hitting the floor and the mystery of someone so brazen. "Let's go and chat."

Sherman was standing against the bar pretending to guzzle the beer in his hand when the two men walked through the front door. Jay followed behind the other man looking smaller than when he left.

Tripp stopped short of the bar and looked Sherman over like a curious chef assessing a leg of lamb. It took a long glance for him to form a general opinion of the man at the bar. He saw a sheen of malice covering opportunity. Contrary to Elmore's soft edges and arrogant exterior, everything he saw said unconstrained ability masquerading as a booze hound.

"This is where you tell me what the fuck you want," said Tripp.

Having taken a similar glance, one honed by years of looking at warlords and petty criminals pretending to be politicians, Sherman was not impressed. "Elmore skipped town. We're taking over."

"I don't know you."

"I don't give a shit," Sherman replied. "There are facts and this is one of them."

"You've certainly got a set of balls on you." He glanced at Vanessa standing in the corner. "You too, but like I said, I don't know you. Elmore and I had a good working relationship. A rapport, if you will. And you two walk in here claiming to have usurped that relationship."

Sherman smiled. The negotiation had begun.

Chapter Twenty-Five

With the binoculars pressed to her face, Agent Landers could just make out the edge of the parking lot and the black sedan wedged between the lifted trucks. Beyond the asphalt, rising rhythmically into the air, she saw the riders.

"He's certainly efficient," Javier remarked. "Found it nice and quick. Do you think anyone is bleeding?"

"If I am right about his unit, then the chances are good."

"His record was more Sharpie than paper with all those redactions. How do you know?"

"We investigated a sergeant at the same base."

"Under Sherman's command?"

"No, he wasn't there at the time. I'd remember a soldier like him," answered Landers.

Javier gave her a questioning glance but said nothing. Her personal life was not his concern despite his curiosity.

"The sergeant had a habit of taking souvenirs," she continued. "It started small. The wallet of a dead insurgent. Maybe a blade or a pistol. Then came the heavier stuff.

Nothing new for a war zone. Lots of boys kept something in their trunk to take back home, but with the sergeant, those things never lasted long enough to go home. Our hypothesis was that he sold them to a middleman in Kabul, who then sold them back to the insurgents."

"He was helping the guys trying to kill him?"

"Inadvertently, we thought. But no matter how hard we pushed, the brass kept shielding the unit."

"Why?" asked Javier, unfamiliar with army politics.

"Body count," Landers replied, still looking through the binoculars. "Those boys were killing machines and the higher-ups would never give up on good statistics like that."

"A crime is a crime," added Javier carelessly.

"The whole affair is a state-sponsored crime."

"Sounds pretty pessimistic to me given you stayed in for so long."

"Don't be simple, Javier. The U.S. Government hunts people down. Here they have us knocking down the door and maybe a trial afterwards. Over there, someone like Frank Sherman appears and they get a bullet for their transgressions."

Javier preferred to catch a Marlins or Dodgers game than watch the nightly news, but he was not so naive to think people like Sherman did not exist. He had just never met one before.

"So, he's a killer."

"Not just a killer. We practically breed them these days. No, he's something else. Did you notice how many languages he speaks?"

"I must have skipped that section of his resume," answered Javier.

"Seven," she said in a low voice.

"Other than an overachiever, so what? I speak two languages."

"Think of it as part of the job description. Where will you need Pashto or Persian or Arabic or Russian for that matter?"

"All the shittiest of shitholes."

"Exactly."

"What happens when he tires of our little blackmail game and shoots us in the back of the head?" asked Javier.

"He won't."

"Because you wore the same uniform once upon a time?"

Landers thought for a moment and decided to leave room for the possibility. "Okay, he probably won't."

"You're banking a lot on him."

"He's resourceful, independent, and intelligent."

"And unpredictable," added Javier, interrupting her list of shiny attributes.

Landers shrugged off the addition. "I have confidence in our choice."

"In him or his type?"

"Elmore came close to those guns. Maybe Sherman gets us to the source."

"Or he'll disappear too," Javier suggested.

"I'm more worried about him being recalled for a mission."

"Or shooting us while we wait."

Landers laughed at her partner's morbid consistency. "Or that."

"We could drive over to the base," he suggested.

The agents were not fools. Military-grade weapons only come from a few places. The map had twelve near Los

Angeles and they circled them all. Not that it mattered. Access was strictly forbidden.

"Unless the director kissed some serious ass, you know they'll tan our hide for asking questions. The Marines love nothing more than a pissing contest," said Landers.

"Government bureaucracy never ceases to baffle me," Javier mused.

"Remember, catch 'em outside their wire. That's the plan. Not ruin the surprise by asking questions."

"Detective 101," Javier replied. "Beat the bushes and something inevitably runs out. Get them all paranoid and they're likely to make a mistake."

"If we have the right place," added Landers.

"You know we do. Your gut is telling you so right now."

"No unauthorized visits to the base," she reminded him. "That came straight from the director."

Javier frowned sarcastically. "I should have stayed in Miami."

She handed him the binoculars. "And miss this?"

In the heat-smudged distance, he could see two figures shaking hands. It took a moment for his brain to believe the image.

"That's Tripp."

"Still doubting the captain?"

Javier said nothing. It took weeks for Elmore to make his proposal to Tripp Cross. Sherman got a handshake in sixty minutes. He watched in silence as the Jetta bumped down the dirt road and back into the city limits.

To his surprise, the sedan pulled into the gas station parking lot and the captain surreptitiously looked him in the eyes as he walked into the attached convenience store.

Landers elbowed her partner as she opened the door and headed inside. "I told you so."

She found Sherman near the three cooler doors piled high with Miller products. He crouched down looking for something, anything, other than that. Landers circled a shelf of corn chips, acting like she had trouble deciding between nacho cheese and ranch. They danced around each other for a few seconds before speaking.

"That went well," she began.

"The man certainly likes big words."

"Did you come to an agreement?"

"Of sorts. We can have the same deal as Elmore."

"You're in," she added with a smile.

"Not exactly. He wants a trust-building exercise of sorts. His words, not mine."

She grabbed the same six-pack as Sherman was reaching for and their arms hung together, clasping the small plastic handle.

He let go. "I need to torch a car."

Landers turned away from the beer section and picked up a bag of barbeque potato. "Do I need to run interference with the locals?"

"Maybe, but it's petty stuff like kids on the playground."

Landers looked over his shoulder at the cashier who was more interested in the pixels on his phone than any actual customer. "That's it?"

"It's a slippery slope, but he seemed intent on humiliation more than harm."

"Who's the target of this juvenile prank?"

"Ash. I met him at Trotters."

Landers nodded her head in understanding. The locals hadn't filled her in on the dynamics of their criminal underclass, but she understood there a general dislike between the locals and those from the valley. "They have an ongoing beef over the pill trade. Not a Hatfield and McCoy situation, but there is some serious money to be made or lost."

"I feel like a high school senior on prank day with this piddly shit."

Landers stood up to pay for the chips and beer. "I can't imagine you as a teenager."

Sherman couldn't remember much more than flashes of cheaply painted walls and the occasional burning trash can. A few teachers stood out as particularly competent while others were blundering idiots. There were girls and booze and drugs, but what he remembered most was the desire to leave as soon as possible and to go as far away as possible. In retrospect, he couldn't have gone much further than where the army sent him.

Vanessa was waiting inside the Jetta uneasily watching the FBI's sedan disappear down the road.

"What did she say?"

"I let her know about Ash."

"You admitted to a crime."

"I haven't done anything yet," he countered.

"But you are going to do something."

"Yes," said Sherman.

Vanessa nodded and glanced off into a memory. "We should do it tonight. Wait until he is good and drunk, puncture his gas tank, and then..." She stopped upon seeing the grin on Sherman's face. "What?"

"Not your first rodeo."

"My misspent youth," she admitted.

"Mine was never so exciting."

"I can't imagine you as a teenager."

"Agent Landers just said the same thing."

"Be careful with her. She's a shark for sure."

Sherman flashed a momentary grin to hide a growing fondness for the FBI agent. "My gut says she is far worse than that."

Chapter Twenty-Six

The strange geometry of light refracting off broken glass cast an otherworldly glow and Trotters appeared like a glittering disco ball abandoned in the sand. Alone and stilted in the surrounding darkness. Vanessa and Sherman parked down the lonely road watching the lights dance across the fractured facade.

"You know, I used to come here a lot," said Vanessa. Her words broke several minutes of silence, and she found the sounds of her own admission startling.

"It's none of my business. Pasts are best left as such."

"You're sweet, Frank. But I've seen the sideways glances. You don't hide curiosity very well. It sort of crinkles in the corner of your eyes like crumpled tin foil."

"It's your secret to tell."

Vanessa laughed softly. "If only. Hell, half of the town probably knows. Telling you doesn't make it any worse."

Sherman nodded but said nothing.

"Years ago, I dated Ash. Back when I was the girl egging him on, all drunk to high heaven in a too short mini skirt with my ass hanging out. We used to do all kinds of stupid shit. Somewhere between, oh, fifth grade and high school, I misplaced my path in life and started dating guys like him. Type-A dickheads, I know, but they were confident and strong and didn't give a damn about what normal people thought. It felt good. Hope and belonging are powerful forces, you know."

"I know," agreed Sherman. "I'm in the army. 'Be all you can be' and other such lies."

Vanessa turned to face him, and Sherman could feel a certain warmth wafting in his direction. "Tell me something, Frank. What is the most rebellious thing you've ever done?"

"Some friends and I broke into a country club once. I was probably in tenth grade and dumb enough to think it was cool. We snuck in through a ventilation grate in the ceiling, opened the garage doors, and drove the golf carts out."

"Grand Theft Cart," joked Vanessa.

"Something like that. We planned on driving them all back in and sneaking out like nothing had happened, but I crashed into one of my buddies and the cart started sparking like crazy. After that, it wouldn't budge, so we pushed it into the lake to hide our crime."

Vanessa was laughing hard enough to rock the sedan back and forth. "That's amazing and so innocently sweet. Was that the zenith of your high school rebellion?"

"No. That would have been me going to college."

"Father issue?"

"My dad did not approve. He wanted me to join the Marines and follow in his footsteps and his father's and his father's and so on and so forth. You get the picture."

"Oh, I'm in touch with familial disappointment," added

Vanessa. "Couldn't catch a break from my mom when I was young, and now my father wants nothing to do with me."

"Seems like a mutual feeling," he added.

"I keep hoping for something to change but it never does."

"I've felt that way with my mom for many years. Hoping that somehow she'll escape this long and slow decline."

"Facing the inevitable is tough," said Vanessa.

Sherman languidly scratched his beard. "It's not death that I fear. I've seen plenty of that in my life and I've accepted it like a fisherman accepts the water or a fish the current. It usually comes quickly and painfully, but it is not years in the making. It is not the slow decline where you lose yourself in the process. You're here and then gone. It is all wrapped up and done in a matter of minutes, if not seconds."

"Are you afraid that one day it might be you in the nursing home?"

He stopped scratching. "If I'm honest with myself, that hits pretty close to the truth. Although, I don't think I'll ever get that old."

"Why not?" she asked. "Your father made it out."

"He was a different breed. Built from the bowels of the Great Depression and World War Two. Guys like him don't catch a bullet."

"You haven't."

"Nothing fatal," replied Sherman.

Vanessa shifted forward and started the car. "I thought I left this all behind, but to be honest, I'm almost giddy."

"Payback?" asked Sherman.

"Yeah," she answered with a grin. "I want to see some tears on that asshole's face. For all the shit he put me through, it seems like the minimum payment on that debt."

The thump of an over-amped sound system carried over the parking lot and into the sprawling darkness. It pulsed and echoed off the cars and gave the night an electric tinge, filling it with possibilities.

Emerging from the field, Sherman led Vanessa to a garbage bin on the edge of the lot. They stayed low and peered towards the dilapidated racetrack.

"Which car is his?" asked Sherman.

Vanessa strained to see any detail in the tessellated lights. "It's a Mustang. A new one."

There were several muscle cars in the lot and they all looked alike to Sherman. Hot-wiring a Toyota Hilux in Syria was no problem, but back home, they all looked the same. "What color?"

"Gray, I think."

"That's not very flashy."

"With red rims," she added.

"I can work with that. Stay here, I'll be back in a few minutes."

"You want me to hide in the dark on the edge of a bar where the guys would just as soon slap me around and have their way?"

Sherman got the point. "Okay, stick close and stay low. We're headed for the closest truck."

Vanessa nodded and silently thanked him for not leaving her behind. They threaded their way between a few stationary tumbleweeds and arrived at the truck unseen and unheard. Sherman checked the back to make sure no one was sleeping off an early and heavy start. It was empty.

He pointed at the next target and they crouch-ran towards it. The density of cars grew as they approached the building, and so did the noises—drunken yells, slurred speech, the sound of guys pissing in the field, and a few hoots from outside the bar.

Sherman checked his watch. A few minutes after midnight. Nowhere near closing time, which didn't happen until the sun came up.

"I think I see it," whispered Vanessa. She pointed towards a Mustang several cars up, close to the building and the people milling about outside.

There were a few other vehicles nearby and Sherman mentally mapped out a route in and out. Nothing complicated. He'd take far riskier paths in the mountains of Afghanistan, but he could always fall back upon overwhelming violence if discovered. He had no plans on shooting a bunch of strangers in rutted parking in Buford over a damn car. Even if it was his ticket into the good graces of Tripp.

"What now?" she asked.

"We wait."

"For what?"

"Some privacy."

She looked at the small crowd. "There's always people coming in and out. The bathrooms there are disgusting and barely work."

Sherman circled to the side of the truck they were hiding behind and rummaged around the bed until he found a large, discarded Slurpee cup and newspaper.

"Thirsty or bored?" she asked, confused by the sudden need for a cheap plastic container and broadsheet.

"Poor man's Molotov."

"You could just throw in a burning towel."

"Speaking from experience, I see."

"Remember that path of life I lost... well, I was lost for a while."

"I'm hoping to speed up the process," explained Sherman.

Vanessa understood. It wasn't her first arson attempt, and if events continued apace, it might not be her last. "Good idea," she agreed.

"You think the car is locked?" he asked.

"Would you leave a brand-new car unlocked in a place like this?"

"I've never owned a car, let alone a new one," Sherman admitted.

"What a strange life you've led."

"I'll assume that is a yes."

"Honestly, it could go either way. No one here would fuck with him, so arrogance may be on our side."

Sherman dug around in powdery dirt until he unearthed a softball-sized chunk of asphalt that once covered the parking lot. The noise level had died down and he craned his neck around the front of the trunk. The group nearest to the front door had dwindled and no one was standing near the Mustang.

"Time to go."

They ran low and fast, sliding the last few feet like a baseball player stealing second base. Vanessa was breathing hard from the excitement and the exertion, but she noticed that Sherman looked no different than a man considering the options on a burger menu.

After weaseling under the rear of the muscle car, Sherman wasted no time in slicing through a rubber section of the fuel line and filling up half of the Slurpee cup. The liquid sloshed about and the fumes made his eyes water. He stuffed the newspaper inside and slid back to Vanessa who was waiting near the passenger door.

"It's unlocked," she whispered and nodded towards the cracked-open door.

Sherman dropped the chunk of pavement and shook his head. He had seen a good deal of humanity in more ways than he cared to recall, but its proclivity for stupidity never ceased to amaze him.

"Open it up," he instructed and Vanessa obliged.

The Mustang still had that new car smell of industry and opportunity. The scent of freshly spent money. It was a nice car, even by Sherman's less-than-discerning standards. In the dancing lights, the leather interior shined like a pair of buffed loafers.

From his pocket, Sherman retrieved a cheap lighter he'd bought at the gas station hours earlier after Tripp related his pompous plan. It took two clicks for ignition and he held the flame under an ad for the local strip club. The newspaper burned fast and he quickly tossed the gasoline-filled cup onto the carpeted floor mats. Physics and chemistry took over after that, and in seconds, the passenger seat was consumed in sickly green and orange flames.

As they ran away, a voice cried out from a nearby van and a naked couple stumbled out into the flickering light and stale heat. Sherman caught the look of recognition on the man's face.

"Hey!" yelled the exposed figure, struggling to find his footing. "What the fuck! Help!"

Vanessa and Sherman ran hard for the Jetta parked off the side of the road. The car wasn't more than a quarter-mile away, and by the time they reached it, the flames were dancing in the still night air above the parking lot.

Giddiness rippled down Vanessa's body as she started

the car and sped towards town. Her hands were white-knuckled and gripping the steering wheel. "That was amazing," she said.

"They recognized us."

She turned and studied Sherman's face. "How do you know? It's blacker than tar out here."

"I knew him."

"Who?"

"The guy who grabbed your arm the other day."

"Colt," she said.

Sherman shrugged. He wasn't much for names unless they were distributed at a pre-mission briefing, and those usually came with a picture and an authorization of force. "If you say so."

"And you're sure he saw you?"

"Yeah. Hard to miss that look of recognition on his face."

"Shit," she replied. "What do we do now?"

"Get some sleep. They'll be looking at your place, not the motel."

"This ain't L.A., there are less than a dozen motels."

"That should buy us a few hours. We'll find someplace else tomorrow."

Vanessa had not considered anything past the morning, let alone an entire day. The thought of more of the same made her stomach twist into knots of excitement and dread. "I hadn't considered tomorrow."

"We need to figure out who Elmore was buying from. I don't think Tripp has a clue. Otherwise, he would have just done it himself."

A sudden wave of sleep swept over Vanessa's mind like an avalanche. It took all her concentration to make it back to the motel without crashing into a light pole.

Chapter Twenty-Seven

As flames swept through the parking lot, Elias knew the night had taken a sudden and interesting turn. He was five drinks into a decent evening and had even found a lovely young thing willing to follow him around for free booze and a place to sleep.

Earlier in the day, he asked the birdish woman at the front desk for a bar recommendation. Her frown told him nothing good was forthcoming, so he changed tactic.

"Where would you never go?"

She looked confused. "What do you mean?"

"What is the worst bar around here? The place you'd ground your daughter for a year if she patronized."

The woman eyed him disdainfully. "Trotters."

"Why's that?"

"Full of drunken criminals."

Elias tilted his head in interest. "How do you know?"

A blush of embarrassment burned her cheeks. "We just do. Everyone in town knows. It's a well-known secret, of sorts."

"How do I find said establishment?"

The woman was nonplussed and struggled to find her voice. "Why would you want to go there?"

"Curiosity, I suppose," answered Elias with a devilish grin that belied his placidly normal exterior.

"That killed the cat," she quipped.

"So did too many questions."

Elias took it upon himself to start the search. Tedious work, he knew, but everything starts from something, and he only had six days left until his wife expected him back in their bland suburban home. So, he cast his net wide that morning. Doing what he'd done years ago as a detective.

He circled past trailer parks and half-built suburbs, through desert washes and newly minted chain restaurants with unpeeled paint on the signs. The city followed a certain clock-like pattern, with the newest buildings clustering toward the freeway at twelve o'clock and the tattered remains of the past sagging down towards six. Each hour away from the top brought with it a certain layer of grit. Trotters was well down at the bottom—a fact that Elia enjoyed.

From that initial pass, he spiraled in towards the city center and found himself parked one block from the police station. Despite his ongoing criminal behavior, Elias did not fear the police. His insider experience made them too familiar for genuine fear. There were moments of angst and the occasional heart-pounding lapse in judgment, but Elias was careful enough to feel comfortable in his occupation.

Often, it was the disgruntled sergeant stuck at the front desk or the recent naive hire that gave Elias the information he needed regarding a target. He considered trying the same approach, showing the photos to whoever got stuck with desk duty and making a show of being a member of the law enforcement fraternity. Then he thought otherwise. The direct approach was risky for many reasons, but chief among them was bureaucracy. Local police don't like federal agents sniffing around, and Elias had quickly determined two of the three targets were working for one acronym or another.

He recognized the dark gray shades of an upmarket but still off-the-rack suit and the industriousness in the woman's eyes. The Hispanic guy, who Elias pegged as Dominican or Puerto Rican or Cuban, appeared worn at the edges but not too disillusioned. A lifer, for sure.

The third picture piqued his interest and elicited an old detective tingle at the top of his spine. A blurry monochrome still from a hallway showing a bearded man intent on ensuring the camera didn't get a decent image. Elias knew enough to dodge the surveillance or wear a disguise, but the beard looked real enough, so he was left considering the man was someone in a similar line of work.

Killing the eager beavers in the nice suits was unremarkable, not because it was commonplace, but rather, it made sense in his deviant brain. So too did culling the competition, which was what his gut labeled the bearded stranger. Neither plan was original or interesting by itself, but killing all three made for an intriguing story. The timing was too close to be coincidence, like some cosmic alignment of marks, which meant that all three were connected. Elias enjoyed puzzles, especially the entwined and convoluted kind.

For the hottest part of the day, Elias drove the streets of Buford until it emerged in his memory like a layered oil painting. Each street added another brush stroke, building up a mental map and sense of place. Poor people clinging to a faded prosperity, propped up by government money and a dying industry.

Finding someplace like Trotters did not surprise him. Most places humming with a certain level of desperation had a similar establishment. The place where all those constrictions of everyday life could be burned in the fifty-five-gallon drum along with most anything else, from bourbon to boredom.

Fringes of the sun still wavered over the horizon like orange fingers when Elias found a bar stool. Benton opened the doors minutes before, and Elias had his pick of seats. He took one near the end, slid across a twenty-dollar bill, and pointed towards a bottle of rye.

"Keep 'em coming until I run out."

Benton reached up and retrieved the bottle of Bulleit, getting a measure of the stranger's appetites. Neat, no ice, no water, and certainly no mixers. The bartender slid over two fingers and added it to a mental tally.

"Cheers," replied Elias, congratulating himself for finding such a gem.

"No offense, man," said Benton. "But I'm not sure this is your kind of place."

With a receding hairline, chalky complexion, and a Panama shirt, Elias came off somewhere between detective and soccer dad. Both were truths in their own ways.

"Oh no, to the contrary, I think this is exactly the kind of place I need."

Benton raised an eyebrow, but he'd seen plenty of middle-aged men trying to reimagine themselves or blow off steam.

"Suit yourself. It gets rougher as the hours turn."

Elias took a sip and savored the gentle burn. "I'll be on my best behavior."

"I don't give a shit if it's your best or worst, just don't break anything inside. That's the rule."

Elias finished the drink and slid the glass across. An understanding passed with it and Benton poured two more fingers and took the money. Elias replenished the Jackson and continued to do so for several hours.

As his wallet thinned, so did the open seats to either side. Elias had always enjoyed a certain shade of woman, usually over a bottle of tequila when his wife was blissfully unaware. His bar-top largesse that night left little doubt over his ability and willingness to pay. The collared shirt added an impression of stability. It brought him a fair share of attention from both sides of the gender aisle.

"Care to share?" asked one woman who showed more leather than skin.

"And what would the two of us late-night revelers have in common besides a taste for whiskey?"

The woman giggled at the stranger and his vocabulary. "It's gonna take more than a glass of rye to figure that out."

Elias slid Benjamin's face across the bar and Benton left what remained of the bottle. He filled an empty glass and placed it resolutely between himself and the woman.

"I'm not one for foreplay, but let's see where this gets us."

The woman's glance ricocheted between the whiskey and Elias before her afflictions took root. "Cheers," she said and downed the glass.

A happy ending seemed all but wrapped up when a flickering glow caught his attention. Fire. Not just any fire, but a car. Not his either, which made the spectacle worth watching.

Beyond the blaze, a naked man was shouting and

pointing with wild urgency. Elias grabbed his bottle and followed the crowd outside.

"My car!" yelled a man that Elias recognized from inside. "They torched my fucking car!"

"Ash, I saw 'em," replied the naked man.

"Who?" asked Ash. His voice was low and determined.

"Your straight and narrow whore of an ex-girlfriend and that bearded prick who sucker punched me."

Ash stepped in and sent a right cross through the guy's chin, which sent him sprawling onto his bare ass.

"Don't talk about her like that! Now, stand the fuck up and let's find them." Ash reflexively reached into his pocket for car keys and yelled in disgust upon finding them useless.

Having watched the events unfold with increasing amusement, Elias handed the bottle over to the leather-enclosed woman, who took it greedily. The description of the mystery arsonist elicited more interest from Elias than any liquor-fueled tryst. A bearded man willing to burn a car next to an assailant he'd already punched. The third picture glowed in his mind.

"Who is he ranting about?" asked Elias.

The woman lowered the bottle from her lips. "Ash's ex-girlfriend turned nurse, Vanessa."

"No, the guy."

"Colt there got throat-punched the other morning," answered the woman with a laugh. "V roped some serious-looking dude into coming with her. Colt grabbed her on the way out and ended up drooling on the dirt."

As several men in various stages of inebriation piled into a van, Elias walked to his car. When they left, he followed. There were too many intersections of the absurd not to see the outcome.

Chapter Twenty-Eight

When Sherman awoke, all his senses snapped on in a wave of awareness, but he continued to lay there in the dark and listen. From the corner, the air conditioner buzzed, and beyond that, an ice machine two doors down rattled against the still-present heat. Somewhere below in the parking lot, he heard voices. Three or four distinct lower octaves. A small group of men discussing something that he couldn't make out. Not through the wall and the rattle of machines.

Two doors closed with a pop and the talking stopped. Sherman sat up and grabbed Vanessa's arm, applying as much pressure as possible without inducing a scream.

Her eyes opened with a start, but not a scare. "What is it?"

"Listen closely," he began in a low tone. "You need to go and lay in the tub. Take the blanket with you and stay under it. Don't say anything and don't move until you hear my voice. Do you understand?"

Despite her lack of sleep and delayed adrenaline release, Vanessa didn't say anything. She nodded and took the blanket into the tub. Then made the sign of the cross and waited for what might be the last few moments of her life. Images of fire still danced in her eyes.

Sherman grabbed his father's old service pistol and stood in the corner of the room against the wall facing the parking lot. The window looking out onto the exterior walkway was small and thin. He stayed away from it, not wanting shards of glass in his face.

Muffled footsteps sounded on the walkway. One set, then two. The consequences of stirring up a pot of crazies with no sense of restraint. Local outrage used to arrive with pitchforks. Sherman doubted he would be so lucky.

The steps stopped and a shadow flitted across the blinds. He raised the pistol towards the door and hugged the wall. At least the tub was metal. All he had was stucco and drywall.

Retribution arrived with a bang. The first shotgun blast tore apart the door handle and the lock, showering splinters through the air like tiny arrows. A man heaved his heavy boot against what remained, and the door swung open and crashed into the wall. Sherman stayed still and hoped Vanessa didn't dare breathe.

Two shapes stepped inside and turned the small room into a display of raw power and carnage. They pumped through shells in a whirlwind of propellant and pellets.

The two queen-sized beds fell apart in giant chunks and wispy threads of stuffing hovered in the air, illuminated with each new blast. Sherman stayed still and watched. Each flash brought about the briefest of glimpses. A momentary spark of information.

Of the two men, he recognized one. The name didn't materialize, but Sherman remembered the face. Those bulging eyes hungry for oxygen right after he caught the guy in the throat. It stuck in his mind from the immediacy, but he had forgotten far worse acts.

Sherman counted the shots. One for the door, then thirteen more in quick succession. After the fourteenth shell came two barely audible clicks. The shooters looked down at their guns and then bolted back out the door, down the walkway, and into a waiting van.

Even after their footsteps receded into the night, Sherman still didn't move, but not out of fear. That kind had long since disappeared from his system. He could have shot them both. Two trigger pulls with nothing but splattered remains to show for it. But he didn't. *Best to let them have a pyrrhic victory,* he thought.

"You okay?" he shouted.

"No," came Vanessa's weak reply.

"Are you hurt?"

"No."

"Good. We need to go."

Her head appeared around the bathroom door and surveyed the scene. It sent a chill across her back. The air conditioner was hissing and spewing some sort of liquid into the air. The mattresses were mangled corpses of springs and foam. Even the walls had tiny craters that reminded her of close-up images of the moon.

"Grab your bag," instructed Sherman as he did the same.

"Where are we going?"

"Out."

In the distance, the squeal of sirens grew. They hurried down the steps to the parking lot. Vanessa headed for the Jetta, but Sherman stopped her.

"We need to leave it."

"Why?" she demanded.

"It's how they found us. That and Harold at the front desk."

"Frank, I'm losing my shit right now," she said, holding back tears. "What are we going to do?"

"I need to have a word with our friends from the FBI. They'll be here soon enough," he answered while scanning the surrounding area. The open sign on the coffee shop caught his eye. "You're going to wait over there until they arrive."

"I suppose a coffee couldn't hurt."

"Give me your bag. If they ask, tell them gunshots woke you up."

"They won't ask," she replied and headed towards the blinking neon sign.

Sherman watched from the shadows until she was safely ensconced in a booth before turning his attention to the descending swarm of law enforcement. First came the local police and SWAT unit, followed by ambulances and fire trucks. It all unfolded in a prescribed order despite the chaos and unknowns.

It took time for SWAT to clear the building and the surrounding area. They moved haltingly, despite the copious amounts of military gear and training. Sherman watched with a mixture of amusement and indifference. He held nothing against the locals but thought they could use a few pointers. Maybe there was something he could do on the outside after all, assuming he survived long enough to retire.

Strobing emergency lights bounced around the motel parking lot as Sherman watched from across the street. He was standing near the alley entrance with a few other onlookers. Locals who never missed a show of force by Buford SWAT. Most expected some modicum of action, but nothing happened, and the crowd thinned.

Having spotted the FBI sedan some minutes earlier, Sherman was waiting for the inevitable. Landers would spot him. *A tangible fact*, he thought. As iron-clad as finding an apple in the supermarket. Even his waiting spot was purposeful. The same alley he snuck up on them from days earlier. It carried significance.

Four more minutes, he thought to himself.

It took only two for Agent Landers to figure it out.

She motioned for Javier to stay put and met Sherman in the darkened cocoon of pavement and stale beer where the lights turned bits of broken glass into rubies.

"Glad to see you're still in one piece. Is the sister okay?"

"She's fine," he answered.

Landers nodded and glanced back at the motel. "Anyone on a metal slab?"

"No, but they made a good show of trying. Came in blasting with shotguns."

"People don't take kindly to arson around here. How did they know it was you?"

"We were seen."

Landers tilted her head ever so slightly to one side. "You or her?"

"These things happen," replied Sherman, feeling the weight of the question.

"Captain, with all due respect, I know you work better solo. We could move her to a secure location for a few days until things calm down."

"Until you get what you want," he countered.

"We both want to find Elmore's killers," she added as a reminder of their solidarity.

"No. I want to give Vanessa some closure. Maybe find a body for the casket."

Agent Landers kicked a flattened soda can off the pavement and gave him another off-kilter look. "I don't pretend to know you, Captain, but I know of you. I called around the few friends still on the inside. They gave me the cliff notes. Rough sketch stuff, since no one wants to acknowledge what you do, but everyone said you have a reputation for seeing things through. Impossible things, if the stories are true. All this to say, I don't think you give a damn about closure as much as putting those responsible in the ground."

Sherman didn't reply right away. She spoke the truth and it always took longer to respond to that. "Maybe I'm softening in my old age."

"Or deflecting."

"I let those two idiots walk away."

Landers let out a muffled chuckle. "And I don't believe altruism factored into that decision."

"I do hate paperwork," he admitted.

"Especially the kind with your name on it," she added.

"Can't slip anything by you," said Sherman.

"Don't be an ass."

"You need to keep my name out of this."

"Is your name on the registry?" asked Landers.

"Yes."

"Why would you do that?"

"I'm visiting my mom, not hiding from the mob."

"Your choice of motel indicates otherwise," she retorted, but knew the assumption was wrong as the words left her tongue. Landers doubted he'd spent more than a few weeks a year on a real mattress and remembered the strange sensation of re-entry into civilian life and the American emphasis on comfort.

Sherman smiled at the embarrassment flitting across her face. "It's the closest thing to the nursing home."

"I'll do my best," she said.

"You have a badge with big federal letters. Dictate what happened. Use your imagination."

"I don't need the pep talk, Captain."

"I didn't think so, but my track record with your agency is dismal."

"Do I want to know?"

"No, Agent, you don't," Sherman answered and turned down the darkened alley.

In the faint flashes, Landers made a mental note to check the Idaho case files again. There was no mention of agents on the scene—local or otherwise. She held the thought for another minute before crossing the street and wading through the police tape lines with her silver badge held high.

Around the block, Vanessa fought back against her drooping eyelids and the inexorable pull of sleep. Coffee had failed to do anything but act as a diuretic and she had almost given up hope of finding a bed when Sherman slipped in through a side door.

He didn't sit down.

"Have you paid?" he asked.

Vanessa looked down at the empty mug and shook her head. "No."

Sherman put a ten on the table. "Time to leave."

"To where? They'll check my house too."

"I have an idea."

"Am I going to like it?" she asked.

"I hope so. It requires your help."

From the darkened interior of his rental car, Elias watched the entire incident unfold. The bungled shooting, the occupants fleeing unharmed, and the meeting between two of his targets. It was better than any movie and miles more exciting than the leather-wrapped regret he left behind at the bar.

Elias smiled as the puzzle gained size and complexity. He couldn't help but try to unravel the connections. It was in his nature and training. No different than his propensity towards violence or his egocentric disregard for others. Pulling at the strings until something unraveled brought him satisfaction. If people got killed in the process, it was not his concern, unless someone paid him to do it.

Six more days, he thought. *More than enough time to see things through.*

Chapter Twenty-Nine

"What the hell are you two doing here? I'm not on death's doorstep."

Sherman opened his eyes and found an apparition from the past looking back at him from the hospital bed. Gone was the cognitive haze and milky opioid gaze. Sophia was alert and commanding.

"It's a long story, Mom."

"You think I have somewhere else to be? Your father's dead and the pope ain't coming for a visit, so spit it out."

The conversation woke Vanessa, and she stared blankly from beneath a blanket. "I know a nurse, she let us stay."

Sophia smiled, her eyes alight with curiosity. "How you got in those chairs is less interesting to me than why you're invading an old woman's hospital room?"

"You could say it's a matter of convenience," Sherman answered.

"Don't be vague with me, Frank. Your father shared two stories with me for thirty years of marriage. I won't allow my son the same leeway. And don't tell me it's classified or of national importance. This is Buford, not Baghdad."

Sherman knew the look and the tone of voice. He relented and said, "We ran afoul of some local boys."

"Friends of your brother, I presume."

Vanessa nodded hesitantly, enamored with the older woman's radiant authority.

"Elmore had a deal with some folks who wanted to continue the business arrangement. Since his disappearance, I've taken his place in said arrangement," said Sherman.

"Why would you do that?" asked Sophia, who then took one look at Vanessa and understood her son's motivations. "Never mind, I get it."

"Things took a twist last night and my motel room was repurposed."

"As a firing range?"

It was Sherman's turn at surprise, and it spread across his face in an unexpected smile.

"Please, I lived with your father long enough to recognize that acrid smell. You know, he tried to lie to me once and said it was just a navigational exercise. I called bullshit. After that, he never said another word about where he'd been or not been, but at least I knew it wasn't a lie."

"Shotguns," Sherman admitted.

"They really don't like you."

"No, I hit a nerve."

"We burned my ex-boyfriend's Mustang," clarified Vanessa.

"On behalf of his rival," said Sherman.

"Didn't they teach you better in the army?" asked Sophia.

"Meth dealer politics wasn't high on the list."

"You should have followed your father into the Marines."

"Not this again," said Sherman with a sigh.

"Well, they would have given you more structure. You always needed structure."

"I had plenty of structure at home."

Sophia shook her head in a slow rhythmic movement. "No, you didn't. Your dad was gone more months than I can count, and I wasn't exactly the ideal mother."

"You did fine, Mom, all things considered."

"That's nice, Frank. I appreciate your confidence in my parenting skills, but I carry some regrets over your childhood."

"I don't," replied Sherman. "I recall it being pretty good. Lots of time outside, exploring whatever looked worth climbing, and I usually found friends at whatever base Dad got shuffled to."

"Except for Bret," she added with an accusing outstretched finger.

"Who's Bret?" asked Vanessa, who had been silently enjoying the exchange between mother and son.

"Frank here got into a scuffle with a major's son named Bret when he was in high school."

"It was sophomore year. He was a senior."

"Well, don't keep me in suspense. What happened?" Vanessa asked.

"He was an asshole, and I made my feelings on the matter very clear. We exchanged some harsh words. He shoved me, I shoved him back."

"Did you beat him up?"

Sherman and Sophia laughed aloud in a familial chorus. "No. I slipped on a discarded baked potato and he kicked the crap out of me."

"Why are you laughing at that?"

"My dad was so pissed that his son got whooped by the major's boy that he didn't speak to me for a week. Just gave me the cold shoulder. He could really telegraph disappointment with a single look or the lack thereof."

Sophia nodded. "Your father could be a hard man."

"Looking back, it was his way of teaching me a gem of a lesson."

"Don't fight bigger kids?" Vanessa guessed.

"No, that's how you get better. It was a lesson on planning. A month later, after all my bruises healed, I snuck up on Bret while he was smoking a cigarette in the parking lot after school and put his head through the car window."

"What!" exclaimed Sophia. "I never heard about this."

"Dad called in a favor and they swept it under the bureaucratic rug. Later that night, when he got off duty, he sat down at the kitchen table while I was doing my homework and handed me a beer. Didn't say a word, just slid the bottle across the table. We drank longnecks on the porch and watched the stars."

Sophia sniffed and a tear traversed her cheek. "He wasn't always so tough, you know that. Cal had a softer side. He buried it under all that macho bullshit, but it was still there. I said he only told me two stories, but that was a lie. There was one more that I never told you."

Sherman sat up a little straighter.

"You were only a few years old, and he was off somewhere in the Middle East. One night, he came tromping through the front door looking tired in a way I'd never seen before, and I knew something had gone wrong. Something he couldn't leave behind at the front steps or drown with a few beers. We sat on the couch in silence for a while before the words tumbled out in a torrent. It was the first time I saw the little boy inside of him."

"What happened?" asked Sherman.

"I don't know when or where, but your father orphaned a boy about your age while the kid watched. Pulled that trigger and severed the connection, the bond between father and son. He did it because that was the mission, but it hurt his soul to do it. Cal said the boy reminded him of you. I don't think he slept at all that night or the one after."

"Wow," muttered Vanessa. She looked at Sherman, but he had a distant look in his eyes like they were focused beyond the horizon.

"You okay, Frank?" she asked.

"I'm sorry if that upset you," said Sophia.

Sherman rubbed his face and tried to shake away a ghost from his past. "It's okay," he replied. "You're right. I hadn't heard that one before."

Sophia looked at her son leaning back in the chair with his eyes roving through his own past. "You and your father faced some hard choices over the years. Part of me wishes you'd stayed in college, got a degree, and moved to the suburbs. I could've had some grandkids."

Sherman moved over and patted her hand. "Can you imagine me in the suburbs?"

"No," his mother replied with a crooked grin. "You were never cut out for a normal life."

"I was a pretty good baseball player in high school."

"And your father was an All-American safety, but he bowled over Viet Cong rather than go to college."

"I tried the college thing," retorted Sherman, but the words felt hollow.

"That you did," admitted Sophia. "I thought Cal was going to drop dead of a stroke when he heard the news. I even put away the good china before telling him, just in case he needed to break something."

The image of his enraged but helpless father made Sherman smile. "Yeah. I felt pretty good that day. It was a short-lived rebellion, but still."

"Oh, please," his mother quipped. "You joined the army. That stung almost as much."

Again, Sherman smiled at the memory.

"You could have picked something different," said Vanessa.

"You can't just wake up one morning and decide what you want to be. It doesn't work that way," said Sophia.

"I did," replied Vanessa. "I woke naked, in my vomit, on some random dude's couch, and thought to myself, there is more to life than this."

"I woke up to the Twin Towers burning. Nothing mattered much after that."

Sophia nodded, "Sometimes you can't ignore a calling."

"I don't know about that, Mom. I woke up that morning, saw the smoke billowing and the people jumping, and knew I couldn't stay. There wasn't much point in choosing after that."

Sophia glanced over at the clock on the wall, "You better get going."

Sherman looked towards Vanessa with a confused look. He didn't see any reason to leave, not yet.

"She's right. The shift change happens soon."

"And the head nurse is a real ball-buster, let me tell you. Nurse Ratched in training. She won't let me swap out these goddamn peaches. Each morning I ask for something else, and each time she blows me off like I'm some old crazy lady."

"Mom, you are an old crazy lady."

Sophia feigned injury for a long moment that made Sherman wonder, before smiling. "I know, but they could at least switch up the damn fruit."

"I'll check in on you tomorrow."

She held his hand. "If you're going to do stupid things, be smart about it and don't take any half-measures." Looking at Vanessa's retreating figure, she added, "And don't let her get hurt."

He squeezed her hand one last time. "I'll do what Dad would have done."

"God help them."

Vanessa was waiting in the hall, trying to look like she had just arrived for visiting hours.

"Are you okay? That story about your dad, well, it seems like it spooked you."

Sherman didn't know where to start, but it needed to come out. That much he knew was true. "I didn't want to say anything in front of her, but there's a lot more to that story."

"I've got two good ears. Tell me."

"I'm pretty sure I killed that kid."

"What do you mean? She said you were only a few years old."

"Not back then," Sherman began. "It was a few years ago, on the other side of the world. I did some things for the mission that still burn to think about. That story she just told... it is the same one I heard then, just from the other side of the rifle. From the kid's perspective."

Vanessa felt something akin to disgust mixed with acceptance. She had always joked with Sherman about classified missions and clandestine trips, but she never considered the outcomes. The sum was always missing from her equation, and it had suddenly been revealed.

"Like your mom said, you've made some hard choices. I don't envy that kind of burden."

"The aftermath," said Sherman. "Sometimes it leaves a long trail, and today, I felt it again in vivid, gory detail."

"Where to now?" asked Vanessa, exhaustion rooting into her gaze.

"Oil Valley," replied Sherman. "We need Tripp to front the money for what Elmore was buying."

Chapter Thirty

Before they arrived at Oil Valley or left the hospital, Sherman stopped at an isolated payphone to call Landers. Their conversation lasted only a minute. The language was a clipped and precise amalgamation of government dialects. Part military, part federal, all business.

When he hung up, Sherman knew his name was not in the police report, and Landers knew the plan was advancing. All he needed to do was connect to the middleman and get a meeting with the sellers. Assuming Tripp gave him the cash with no other trust-building exercises. One angry drug dealer was enough.

"This place gives me the creeps," said Vanessa as they sat in the Oil Valley parking lot listening to the audible onslaught of motocross engines. "And I was a regular at Trotters."

The solitary and stark nature of the establishment reminded Sherman of a West African shebeen more than an American bar, but the differences were narrow. Both had booze and loud noises, but Oil Valley had more weapons per drunk than anything in Ghana.

"You can stay if you like," offered Sherman.

Vanessa shook her head with the weight of a bowling ball. After leaving the hospital, they'd borrowed Sophia's old Ford Taurus from the retirement home. The state had long ago confiscated her driver's license, but Stan graciously started the car once a week to keep it running. It was a faded gold station wagon smelling of decay.

"I'm coming," she added with an emphasis that betrayed her own fears.

"Don't say anything about Elmore's connection."

"I don't plan on saying or touching anything. The less contact I have in there, the better."

The air conditioner was running full blast when they walked inside, like a preemptive attack on the coming heat. Tara, the tattooed bartender, had several cases of beer on the bar and was restocking the coolers from the night before. Her brothers were in the corner and Sherman couldn't tell if they'd gone home or were still wearing the same stained clothes. It all looked the same from their previous visit.

"I thought your goose was cooked last night," said Jay. His lip was swollen and blue.

"Yeah," echoed Charlie. "I heard you caused quite a ruckus over at Trotters. Ash is a shitty shot if you made it out alive."

"Don't mind them," said Tara. "They're just jealous not to have lit the match themselves."

"We would have done it if Tripp asked."

"And ended up as a pile of pulp in the parking lot."

"Like this straight-backed asshole is any better," said Charlie, looking in Sherman's direction but not at his face.

"You're five-nine, a hundred and eighty pounds," Sherman began. "And couldn't run a ten-minute mile if lions were nipping at your heels. You favor your right too much and that left knee of yours took a beating in high school. Probably football because you're much too fat and short for basketball. And don't bother standing up because I will sit you down for a long, long while."

Jay started laughing. His face still remembered what the stranger could do, and it gave him some relief to see the fear in his brother's eyes.

"Like I said, don't mind them. They've been sitting there drinking all night like a couple of hyenas tearing at a carcass."

"Where's Tripp?"

"Not here yet. Give it another hour."

"You got any coffee?" asked Sherman.

Tara placed a Keurig on the counter and handed him a plastic pod. A moment of self-reflection trickled in his mind, but Sherman wanted the caffeine more than the taste.

———

Thirty minutes later, they were still waiting when the sound of tires crunching on gravel filtered through the flimsy bar walls. The brothers gave Sherman a lopsided grin as he walked outside.

Tripp climbed down from his truck. He wore black jeans and a Metallica shirt. He was clean-shaven and had the look of a startup CEO waiting for a morning briefing.

"I want to be there for the meeting," he began. Tripp's jaw was set and expression unyielding.

"Not a chance," replied Sherman, glad to be past the trust exercises and small talk.

"I'll pull out. No money, no deal."

"Your loss," replied Sherman as he turned to walk away.

"Hey!" yelled Tripp. "I'm not done talking."

"I can see that, and I don't give a damn."

Tripp started laughing and slapping his legs. "Elmore said something similar when I asked him the same thing."

"Smart," said Sherman.

"All I got from him was some stupid phrase. 'Follow the signs,' he said. Whatever the hell that means."

Sherman shrugged and said nothing because he knew less than Tripp. The connection was everything. Without knowing who to call, he was flying blind in some damn treacherous mountains.

"Just remember, those guns are mine. Bought and paid for by me. Not you, not Elmore, or that little piece of ass you got. It's all mine. Save for your fee, which I'll take from what Elmore owes me."

Guns were nothing new. Sherman had been around them since childhood, and he couldn't count how many had been discharged in his direction. Legal and illegal, the country was awash in firearms of all types. A guy such as Tripp wouldn't concern himself with a load of Saturday night specials. Sherman guessed only something serious would grab his attention. A crate of old Kalashnikovs or maybe a worn M60 from Vietnam. Everyone wanted the gun of Rambo.

"You're not getting anything without the cash," said Sherman, pointing towards a backpack in Tripp's hand.

"There is fifty grand there. I want proof your guys have something worth buying. I've heard Elmore's stories and they'd better be true. I wouldn't want for something to happen to you or that sweet sister of his."

Threats came and went like the wind in Sherman's world. Some were omnipresent, while others lurked unknown in the shadows. None of it bothered him anymore. It was a fact of life, no different than changing gas prices for the average American. He took Tripp's word seriously—the guy was dangerous, but it didn't churn up any panic. Talk was always cheap. Consequential, but cheap.

"I'd prefer to keep this civil," replied Sherman.

"It will be if you deliver. I can be a very unpleasant man when people don't follow through on their promises."

Sherman didn't make promises. Never had and never would.

"I'll be in touch," he said with a wave and turned towards the station wagon.

Vanessa was already standing there ready to leave. The place and people did not agree with her constitution.

"Are we done here?" she asked, casting an uneasy glance towards Tripp.

"For now, but this kind of cash must come with some strings. The kind that follows you around town."

"Keep him out of the frame," instructed Landers as her partner maneuvered the telephoto lens.

"It feels awkward to be the one reminding you of the regulations, but we need photographic evidence of both parties."

"I gave him my word that we'd keep him out of this."

Javier said something under his breath that Landers couldn't understand.

"Do you have a problem with that?" she asked.

"You're bending pretty far for this guy. Is this one of your brothers-in-arms things?"

Landers waited for a moment to reply because she was unsure why stretching the rules felt like the right thing to do. Maybe it was a shared institutional past or just a gut feeling about the guy. "Call it a two-way street," she said. "We leveraged the photo to get him this far. A little flexibility is worth it if he gets us to the seller."

"And if he doesn't?"

"You saw that motel room. It's his risk right now, not ours. And this from a guy who used to hand out sandwiches to the working girls down on Wilshire."

"They're good sources," replied Javier with a sheepish grin.

He focused the camera and kept Sherman out of the frame while snapping photos of the exchange. Across the shimmering distance, the two figures were brown smudges in a sandy sea. Javier could make out shapes, but not much more without the camera.

"Alright, I will give this guy some credit. Tripp just handed over something looking a lot like a backpack. I doubt they're exchanging schoolbooks."

"Solid start to a RICO case. We've got the cash and intent to purchase. If the captain can get a meeting with the seller, we'll have a trifecta."

"What did he say about that?"

"Nothing yet," answered Landers.

"He better get a move on. If Tripp figures out he doesn't know, that backpack will turn into a bullet."

"The captain has dealt with worse."

"Warlords and wizards?" asked Javier, jokingly.

Landers drummed her fingers along the steering wheel.

She liked Javier as a partner, but his narrow slice of experience wore down her patience. "A friend told me a story about his unit."

Javier paused and put down the camera. "The captain's unit?"

She nodded. "He couldn't give the time and place, but I filled in the blanks. The CIA used to run guns between the ISI and the Northern Alliance. One of those strange little love triangles war brings about. We'd buy Kalashnikovs from Poland, move them through the Suez Canal and up through Pakistan, then hand them off to the Northern Alliance in Afghanistan. The ISI would take their cut and pass them off to the Taliban. And guess who drove the trucks across the border?"

"No shit."

"One guy, no drones, no flag on his shoulder. Him in a truck across the wilds of Pakistan and Afghanistan."

"Christ," said Javier, and his jaw stayed open after the word came out. He slowly took up the camera again, but with an increased appreciation for the captain's capabilities or insanity.

"I think he can manage Tripp," Landers added.

Vanessa pulled out of the gravel lot and steered the ungainly Ford towards Buford. She glanced in the mirror, half-expecting a truck or two to appear. "You think they'll follow us?"

"Not them. Someone else in the city limits. They know what we're driving. Easy enough to call ahead."

"I'm still shaking from last night."

Her expression was strained as dark bags sagged under

her eyes. Sherman understood the harrowed look—when the adrenaline is all gone and only fear remains.

"Tripp's not a threat unless we skip out with the cash or he figures out who is selling the guns," he added.

"I still can't believe Elmore got mixed up in this. Drugs I get, but this is way worse than the shit he used to do." She raised her hands as if suddenly remembering a missing fact. "We don't even know how to make this happen!"

"Take the main road west out of town," instructed Sherman. "I have an idea."

"Care to share?"

"Something that Elmore told Tripp. Follow the signs."

"He was probably drunk or high or both."

"Or he was trying to be clever," offered Sherman.

"That sounds like my brother. Using twelve words when two will do."

Chapter Thirty-One

The gold station wagon swayed down the road, taking up more than its fair share of asphalt. Buford slid past looking like the color of undercooked bread.

"Where are they off to now?" asked Javier from the passenger seat of their sedan. The camera still sat in his lap, ready for whatever came next.

"Not sure," replied Landers. "But they seem intent on getting there quickly."

"Do you think she knows the seller?"

Landers eased off the gas as the Ford's blinkers flashed up ahead. "Maybe. Maybe not. She and Elmore didn't seem particularly close."

"What does that have to do with family?" asked Javier with a joke lurking in his voice.

"Maybe in your dysfunctional family."

"Oh, please," he retorted. "No family is perfect. I reckon most are broken in one way or another."

The station wagon pulled into a gas station followed by a doddering Toyota once painted like the summer sky, now faded to a shade of silvery-gray. Landers eased their sedan into a restaurant lot down the block and waited.

They watched as Sherman exited his vehicle and approached the Toyota parked on the far side of the filling station. He closed the gap with quick, confident strides. Javier got out the camera, expecting something incriminating.

"What now?" he wondered aloud.

Landers already knew. She could see the outcome written in concentration across the captain's face. "Don't bother," she said.

"Why not?"

But Javier didn't have to wait for his partner to answer. Sherman reached the Toyota, bent down to say a few words to the lone occupant, and then did something Javier should have expected. The captain grabbed the driver's head and slammed it into the steering wheel. It bounced back and forth like a tetherball from Javier's elementary school days.

"Jesus," he muttered.

"It was following him since the city limits," said Landers.

"One of Tripp's guys? Or maybe the guys from the motel?"

Landers didn't reply as she pulled back onto the road. The answer had little impact on the investigation or their safety. The risk rested on the captain and they both knew it.

Vanessa struggled to say anything when Sherman slid back into the Ford. The driver, who looked a few years shy of drinking age, was clutching at his face. Blood streamed out of his pimply nose, covering the green shirt he wore with splotches of red that turned copper-brown as they dried.

"He's just a kid."

Sherman glanced back at the aftermath of his actions. She was right about his age. The driver was young and inexperienced, but swimming in the deep end of life where the consequences cut deep and fast. He'd given a lesson worth learning early when the damage only amounted to stitches.

The kid was lucky, Sherman thought. He'd killed younger people for far fewer reasons. In some parts of Iraq, any boy over fourteen was considered an enemy combatant by the very nature of being able to shoulder a rifle. A time when puberty could get you killed.

"A broken nose is a learning opportunity."

"For what?"

"Not to follow us. Better he learn it now and live to regret his mistakes."

Vanessa sighed as they headed west across shimmering puddles of heat. "I'd like to plead ignorance and say I don't know what you're talking about, but you've met my father. He's a grade-A asshole, so I learned to think on my feet and fend for myself."

"And you deserved better," said Sherman. "All kids do."

"But not him?" she flicked her thumb back over her shoulder.

"He's old enough for the draft. That's old enough to learn the hard way."

"One of Tripp's guys, right?"

"He was waiting by the A&W as we came back into town. Too interested in us to be anything but a tail. Not very original either. Could have rotated cars. Maybe three or four staggered down the road with overlapping coverage."

The dip into tradecraft amused Vanessa, who felt she'd bridged an invisible gap in his world. "Is that what you do?"

Sherman smiled at her probing question. It was a good try. "No," he answered. "We'd blow him up with a drone."

"Oh."

"Not a lot of room for company over there."

They had passed the city hall and the low-slung police station resembling a muffin with no top. The west side of town beckoned. Vacant lots lay covered with scraps of trash and pieces of dead vegetation like beige sores upon the urban landscape. The notary and accountant came and went in a garish display of hand-painted billboards. Beyond that stood the overlapping arrows of development, pointing toward the unbuilt subdivision, with each amount barreling towards zero. A history of desperation.

"Follow the signs," said Sherman, pointing towards the office they'd visited days earlier.

"Seriously?" asked Vanessa. "You think it's Jones?"

"Call it a gut reaction."

"He's my real estate agent."

"You said he had fingers in all the little pies."

"Not guns."

"Why not? Drugs, guns, or stolen cars. If you're after money it doesn't matter. One isn't better or worse than the next."

His point was valid, and she nodded silently at first. "He does like his money. Maybe you're right."

The BMW sat resolute against the ebbing economic tides of real estate. Vanessa eased the wide card into a spot in front of the sales office. The junker truck from a few days prior was gone, and they could see Jones through the blinds, leaning back in his chair like the world needed to slow down with him.

He gave a congenial wave as they entered but made no effort to stand. Sherman noticed a wastebasket full of empty cans under the desk. *Celebration or commiseration,* he thought.

"Hey, V. What brings you back? Looking to upgrade?" Jones flicked his thumb towards the partially constructed subdivision.

"Elmore," she replied, trying to inject casualness into her words.

"He still hasn't turned up?"

Having spent years listening to lies about the war, Sherman had an ear for dissonance. The mouth said one thing, but the body could not follow. Brains only handle so many lies at once and the guy's body was telling another tale.

"In the wind," answered Vanessa. "Maybe drinking away his good fortune in Vegas or TJ."

Upon the whisper of money, Jones sat up a little straighter.

"You wouldn't know anything about that?" she asked.

Jones slunk back down and crossed his arms. "No. Why would I? I told you I haven't seen him for, well, days."

Vanessa took a seat across the desk while Sherman lingered. He'd learned there are several ways to induce a conversation, but fear and greed often worked the quickest. Standing tall and looking angry worked with a certain subset of the population susceptible to intimidation. Jones looked the type.

When she spoke again, her voice was soft, almost silky. "Because you know all the hustles going on in town. Don't tell me you didn't know about Elmore's. You mentioned a side project last time we spoke."

Flattery worked too, thought Sherman, loosening his stance.

"Your brother tried a lot of different honey pots," added Jones.

"Well, Frank and I… you remember Frank, we are looking for a real specific pot. One I'm hoping you can help us with. For a finder's fee, of course."

Flattery and greed. Sherman liked her approach.

"I charge six percent, but for you, I'll drop it to four."

Vanessa gave a curvy smile and leaned in radiating feminine charm.

"What are you looking for?" asked Jones.

"Guns," she answered.

What openness for discussion existed snapped shut like a screen door, and Jones leaned so far back in his chair that it almost toppled over.

"I don't know anything about that," he mumbled.

Sherman felt the urge to step forward. He was not against using force to gather information. Not torture, at least, but the application of pain loosened lips. Even if the results weren't always accurate.

Before he could change course, Vanessa continued. "Listen, Jones. I want out of this dump, but I need cash. Frank has a friend who wants to buy. The bigger, the better."

Sherman nodded. "He's willing to pay a premium for quality hardware."

Greed softened the real estate agent's sour expression, and his brow creased with consideration. "I might know someone, but they only take serious offers."

"I have fifty grand for a preview order and another two hundred and fifty if it's worth my time."

They watched Jones tumble through the mental math,

carry zeros and new BMW models. His pupils widened as the dollar signs grew.

"Five percent," he announced.

"You said four," countered Vanessa.

"I changed my mind. Take it or leave it."

"Deal," said Sherman. It wasn't his money and he could care less about the cash. He wanted to know who killed Elmore and exact a little revenge, even if he didn't admit that part to himself.

Jones flashed a smile filled with bright white teeth and opened his desk drawer. Inside were a dozen different phones. Cheap ones. Each had a sticky note on top with a phone number. He picked one out like a child selecting their favorite chocolate from a Whitman's sampler. Sherman took it and placed the small piece of plastic in his pocket next to the extra pistol magazine.

"I'll call you on that number with a time and place, but I'll need some earnest money before we proceed."

Vanessa scoffed at the brokerage term but Sherman had seen such a request coming. Not even friends acted without incentives. He tossed over the backpack.

Jones unpacked the money and gave it a quick count. Ten neat stacks of Andrew Jackson's face sat on the wood surface. Twenty-five in each pile. Fifty thousand dollars in total. His eyes gleamed with a yearning for more.

"That will get you a meeting," said Jones.

"When?" asked Sherman.

"I don't set the schedule. Maybe tonight or tomorrow."

"Hurry up and wait," mused Sherman.

"Exactly."

"I expect that call," he said tersely.

Jones stashed the money in a small safe and waved away the concern. "You'll get it. Don't worry about that."

They stood and left without another word. Waiting often took a good deal of time.

Landers had scarcely set down the binoculars before Javier started fidgeting in his seat like a kid who drank too much Kool-Aid before getting in the car.

"That's him," he exclaimed upon seeing Sherman and Vanessa leave the real estate office. "He must be the seller."

"Supposition," she replied, only half-believing herself.

"Don't tell me you think this is some kind of coincidence."

"Did the background check come back yet? This guy looks more like a hyena than a lion."

"Don't shit on my good vibes."

"Don't get your hopes up."

Javier shrugged and started making calls. Even if he was wrong, he guessed they were one degree of separation from whoever had direct access to the weapons.

Chapter Thirty-Two

The day unfolded with a tedious crawl that Deet loathed. Nothing about it resembled the adventure he imagined when enlisting two days after his eighteenth birthday. He'd tried to sign up the day after, but his father talked him into sleeping on it. The vain attempt to change his mind failed, but looking back, Deet wondered what might have been. He wasn't one to dwell on things he couldn't change, but boredom was a slippery slope leading to a great pool of unanswerable questions and a churning tide of what-ifs.

"Did you finish Lot 3-4-7?" asked a voice Deet knew all too well.

He looked up from his clipboard and caught the eye of Colonel Wakefield. The prick had only been outside for two minutes or fewer, only from his office to the loading dock, and was already sweating through his uniform. It was off-putting. Deet couldn't understand a man who couldn't take a little heat.

"The corporal and I are finishing that one now, sir."

The colonel gave him a stare that laid bare a contempt for Deet's work ethic and efficiency.

Deet straightened to his full height, towering a few long inches above his commanding officer. Neither man blinked, each knowing they held a different sort of power. One could end a career. The other could stop you from walking, permanently.

"Is there something wrong, sir?"

"I expected that batch on the truck hours ago."

Deet looked down at the manifest—electronic hardware bound for Jordan. High-dollar stuff, which made the colonel's impatience understandable. It was the high-tech items that brought in the most money, and Deet was sure the prick was getting a hefty kickback somewhere along the line. Everyone did, or at least that was how he rationalized his own side business. The great War on Terror was over in name only, and that meant everyone was scrambling for a piece of the smoldering pie.

"My apologies, sir. The last work order took longer than expected and the forklift broke down."

The colonel glared. "Excuses do not make an officer."

This was one of those nonsensical responses Deet expected from those in power. He nodded, but the comment made less impact than a pebble hitting the moon.

"Understood, sir."

"Good. I won't hold you up any longer."

"Thank you, sir."

Deet smiled long enough to see the sweat-stained colonel disappear into the air-conditioned office.

"Prick," he muttered, knowing the colonel couldn't hear.

The long shadows lingering behind him rustled and Hadz appeared drenched in sweat as if someone had poured a pitcher of water over his head. He was dirty, tired, and irritable.

"What was that about?" he seethed.

Deet looked over his shoulder towards the colonel's office. "The bottom line."

"His or ours?" asked Hadz.

"His. It's always his."

"Are we still good?"

Deet nodded and whispered, "They ain't giving two shits about the small stuff as long as they get paid."

A glimmer danced in Hadz's eyes, and Deet knew something extravagant was brewing. "What if we went bigger?"

Although the thought occurred to Deet before, he shook his head emphatically in wide arcs as if such an idea was unfathomable.

"Why not?" hissed Hadz.

"They'll notice," Deet replied, only half-believing the answer.

"So what? We could be in Mexico before they figured it out."

Deet drummed his fingers on a nearby crate, entertaining his friend's outlandishness. "It don't make much of a difference without a buyer. We could nab an A1, but it would just sit in the shed. We have what they call a demand side problem."

Hadz nodded in understanding, but his face said otherwise.

"There ain't no demand," Deet reiterated.

"I get it," Hadz blurted out and then waited a beat before adding, "I could call my cousin."

"I'm not selling to the cartel," whispered Deet. He wanted to keep what few morals remained intact.

"He's local," added Hadz, as if that mattered.

"Shit rolls south, it always does."

"At least let me reach out."

Deet stood up to his full height for the second time in twenty minutes and looked down at his subordinate. "No means fucking no."

Hadz backed away. "Alright, man, it was just a suggestion."

"Keep it shelved."

Behind them, a door opened and the two men separated for fear it was the colonel looking to stir the pot. It wasn't, but Deet didn't turn back. He kept going about the day like it mattered.

It didn't, but admitting that Hadz was onto something or that he'd even consider the offer provided more than he could face. So, he kept busy, just like every other day of his life because busy hands meant a busy mind, and his mother always warned him about the lurid evils of idleness.

Only after the colonel left for his tee time privileges did Deet put down his clipboard and take stock of what remained of the day. The sun hovered over the mountains with the angry red glare of a lit cigarette. The heat remained stifling as if the entire base was trapped in a car stalled out on the road to Baghdad.

Deet sat down in front of a dented box fan in the bowels of the warehouse and chugged a bottle of tepid water. The thought of one good payday had stayed with him like razor burn. He couldn't shake the need to get out. It lingered longer than his shadow.

Unable to hold back his own desires, Deet reached for the burner phone taped under a shelf on the furthest wall. A place so deep inside the Marine Corps logistic base that he knew the colonel would never find it.

He powered up the phone and waited.

The synthetic ding that followed made his heart beat faster. The text was from Jones. It read:

Got something big! Tour at 9.

At under thirty characters, the message was a model of brevity, but Deet felt like he could see the end of an interminable road. It was hazy, but there, only just beyond reach.

The beach, the *mamacitas*, endless beers, and freshly grilled fish. One more job, he told himself, and there it was. Something big, with an exclamation mark. Jones had never used that before. He'd probably want a bigger finder's fee, but Deet didn't mind, as long as the man delivered. If he didn't or it proved to be like the last asshole... well, Deet had a 'two strikes and you're out' policy. Anything more wasn't worth the heartache.

He found Hadz exactly where he always found him— two beers deep at the cheapest bar within walking distance. Deet took an empty stool but said nothing.

"I'm sorry about earlier," Hadz began.

Deet waved away the thought. "Like piss on sand."

Hadz smiled, toothy and broad.

"Besides," Deet added. "We've got another offer in the wings. Meeting at nine to discuss."

The bottle of beer stayed up, but Hadz eyed Deet with apprehension swirling on his lips.

"Substantial," Deet assured.

"How big?"

"Big," replied Deet, trying to convince both in the process.

"Will it be enough?"

"Maybe," answered Deet with almost enough hope to will his retirement into existence.

"What time again?"

"Nine."

"I'll be there," Hadz added while tilting back his beer.

"And sober?"

The younger man waved his hands towards the town. "Sober enough for that asshole."

Deet stood but didn't say another word. He still needed to wrangle up Boot from whatever honkytonk cesspool had claimed his cousin for the night. There were only two nearby, so his odds were even.

The oversized *For Sale* sign came and went as a thin stream of dust danced in the headlight's yellow blaze. Dipping beyond the dunes, the road descended away and out of view. The ragged truck jostled and creaked over ruts and rocks. Inside, the three men swayed with the movement, impervious to the discomfort of a worn suspension. They stopped at a lone sales trailer abandoned after the market crash, when no one could even give the land away.

Deet had always liked the spot for its seclusion and cool air clinging to dips and grooves. He turned off the ignition but didn't move.

The men waited a beat and listened.

Nothing existed out there, not even the faint hum of insects or a coyote's howl. Not at that hour of night when life was just beginning to shake off the shackles of a summer's day.

They were early. They were always early. Deet made sure of that. It minimized surprises and unwanted guests. They would see anyone coming down that road well ahead of any action.

Hadz and Boot hopped out and disappeared into the shadows while Deet moved the truck behind the trailer. He believed Jones could deliver, but didn't trust the man, and never would. The real estate agent was a criminal—a vulture willing to do anything for his share. Opportunism was something Deet could understand, but naked greed stepped beyond his moral boundaries.

As usual, Jones was late. Not much, but still late.

Deet recognized the LED lights and European growl of the BMW, but he stayed in the shadows. Only after Jones exited the coupe did Deet emerge into the moon's faint glow.

"Jesus Christ alive," yelled Jones after seeing a figure detach from the darkness.

"You called this meeting," said Deet.

"For once, could you park out front like a normal person? You just about gave me a goddamn heart attack."

"You're still breathing."

"No thanks to you," muttered Jones.

"I don't have time for chit-chat. Tell me what you've got."

Jones shuffled on the hard-packed dirt as Deet watched his movement with cold brown eyes.

"Someone came to my office looking for some hardware."

"And?" asked Deet impatiently. Lots of people bought guns, but his customer segment was a narrow slice of the American population.

Jones hesitated and the words caught in his throat when he spoke.

"Spit it out," growled Deet.

"It's Elmore's sister. She wants to take over the deal."

"Elmore?"

"The... uh, the last guy."

Deet scoffed. "The liability."

"Yeah, well, he got the short stick on the family tree. His sister is playing with a full deck and the guy she's with has serious cash."

At the mention of another stranger, Deet's eyes narrowed to thin creases. "What guy?" he asked.

Jones flapped his arms nervously and forgot to lie about the total. "The guy with the money. He gave me fifty grand as a deposit like he was dropping off dry cleaning."

The number did not assuage Deet's suspicion, and his expression hardened.

"Look, I don't know much about him, but he looks kinda like you guys. Well, not all trimmed and proper, but his eyes have an edge to them."

"What the fuck does that mean?"

"I don't know," Jones huffed. "Just that they remind me of a mountain lion I saw out hiking as a kid. Like he might pounce at any moment."

Deet chewed over the newest information. They needed a serious buyer with serious cash. Fifty thousand was not chump change and it indicated deep pockets. Judging from the realtor's jitters and sudden nervous disposition while describing the stranger, Deet guessed the man was no joke. After the last debacle, he wanted someone committed. Before he could reply, the connection his mind whipped into focus came crashing down.

"You said Elmore's sister. Does she know what happened to her brother?"

"Half-brother," replied Jones. "And no. She thinks he ran off to Mexico with the cash and is living large with some *putas*."

Deet glared.

The realtor backed up a step. "Sorry, no offense."

"I'm Puerto Rican, not that you'd know the difference."

Jones tried his best 'this is so worth the money' smile.

"Did the sister or her banker say anything about what they're looking to buy?" asked Deet.

"Serious hardware," answered Jones.

"Home Depot has hardware," yelled Deet.

Jones took the hint. "He wanted something mil-spec and not left-over Vietnam shit or Kalashnikovs."

Deet nodded. "And his total budget?"

"At least three hundred grand. Maybe more."

The stars suddenly twinkled brighter above them, and Deet swore he heard Hadz's mouth drop open in the shadows.

"Set up a meeting," ordered Deet.

"Okay."

"For tonight."

"Tonight?" repeated Jones.

"Give them the directions here. Tell them they have thirty minutes."

"You sure?" asked Hadz from the walls of night surrounding them.

Jones jumped and muttered an obscenity under his breath.

"Yeah," replied Deet. "I want to know if he's for real. Besides, this is home turf."

Hadz grunted and slid away with his rifle, saying, "Let's do this."

"Make the call," added Deet.

"Text," whispered Jones, but he got out his phone nonetheless and scrolled through a sizable list of burner numbers.

Chapter Thirty-Three

The cold remains of a half-eaten Reuben sat alone on an oversized plate smudged with red ketchup streaks. Sherman kept his eyes out the dirty window at the front of the diner. A thin layer of grease covered every surface such that future archeologists might have confused it with a strangely human permafrost. The plasticized menu consisted of a single page with pictures. Under different circumstances, Sherman would have enjoyed the indifference to health codes and haute cuisine. As it stood, he was waiting for the other shoe to drop… because it always did.

Vanessa spun her water glass around like a ballerina and looked up from her empty plate.

"He'll text, but it might take some time," she said.

While Sherman agreed with half of her answer, he knew time would not be an issue. The almighty dollar flowed through Jones like a river carves a canyon. Greed was etched so deeply, it could not be separated from the rest of him. He'd call soon enough—Sherman was certain of that.

"Eat something," added Vanessa, filling the silence.

"I ate the fries."

"That's not real..." she began but trailed off. "I'm just saying, you should take care of yourself."

Sherman smiled at her sincerity and the absurdity that cholesterol would be his demise. A thousand things would kill him before that.

"You want some more coffee, hon?" said a voice cracked with age and too many late nights.

The cup was half-empty, and Sherman slid it in her direction. "Thanks."

"You want a to-go box too?"

He glanced up at the tired eyes and stooped shoulders looking down at him and nodded for no other reason than it seemed the polite thing to do.

The waitress returned with a Styrofoam box and the bill. Her uniform rustled like aspen leaves as she walked away.

"Are you actually going to save that?" asked Vanessa, clearly skeptical of his choice.

He didn't answer her. Not out of spite, but because the phone Jones had given them vibrated to life. Sherman checked his watch—9:30 PM. Not desperation quick, but the sellers, whoever they might be, were motivated.

Sherman looked at the text long enough for the screen to dim to conserve the battery.

"What does it say?" asked Vanessa.

"They want to meet in thirty minutes."

"Isn't that good?"

"Yeah, but never agree to the first offer."

Vanessa shook away her confused expression and scoffed. "I'd like to see you buy a used car."

Sherman hadn't owned a car, let alone haggled with some sleazy guy in a half-barren parking lot.

"We usually just steal them," he replied, skipping over a substantial chunk of his own history.

"I see," she said but had the look of someone very much in opposition to understanding.

Taking up the phone, Sherman tapped out a response.

One hour. Where?

Then they waited for a conversation in parts unknown to run its course to some conclusion. Sherman continued looking out the windows while Vanessa's fingers danced across the greasy Formica table.

A vibration ended the interlude and Sherman showed her the address.

"How far is that?" he asked.

"Twenty minutes, it's on the other side of town."

More instructions arrived and the phone trembled in his hands.

Stay on the dirt road until the trailer.

Park in front.

Turn off your lights.

Get out slowly.

Hands visible.

"Oddly specific for Jones," Vanessa observed.

"He's just the middleman," replied Sherman. He could almost hear the instructions passing from one party to the other.

There was a cold, methodical calmness to them that he appreciated. Such orchestration took a particular type of mind—one attuned to tiny details. An attempt to contain unknowable outcomes.

Three minutes later, they were in the car having over-paid for the meal but not caring in the least. By changing the timeline, Sherman gained nearly forty minutes of recon-naissance time and he planned on using every second.

The town passed in a droll smear of beige homes and jittering neon lights. Beyond the commercial strip, they passed more failed developments. One billboard after another fell into their wake, each with lower prices and less hope until they reached an expansive red sign rising above the road. White lettering flaked away, and the faded color blended with vast slabs of rust.

Sherman read aloud, "Whispering Winds."

"That's it," said Vanessa, unable to conceal her disdain for the name.

"Keep going another hundred yards and then let me out. Circle back after another couple of miles and wait out of sight."

"For how long?"

"How long does it take to get to the trailer?"

"Ten minutes or so. The road is pretty rough."

Sherman checked his watch. Thirty-five minutes remained of the hour. "Wait twenty minutes and then head down. I'll meet you on the road somewhere out of sight."

Vanessa didn't look convinced but nodded, and Sherman watched the taillights disappear around the next tumbleweed-clotted bend. He stood listening to the fading engine and little else. A smattering of bugs chirped along the road and a small rodent crackled its way through the desiccated vegetation. The quiet of a desert made him feel at home.

Picking through boulders and cacti was no easy task, but Sherman slipped into a different mindset that activated the caveman instincts passed on by his forebears. The ones that saw him through grueling nighttime marches in sweltering Iraq and the cliffs of Afghanistan, past Islamic State fighters in Syria, and Al Shabab ambushes in Niger. Some called them gut reactions, but he knew it was not so simple. The brain grows stronger with repetition and Sherman had over-exercised that part for fifteen years.

He counted off the time.

Ten minutes to reach the bottom, plus five more to circle back. That left a small window for snooping on whoever was waiting.

The moon's bluish glow revealed a wide, shallow valley spreading out from the dirt road. Circumstances aside, Sherman saw the natural beauty of the area with its sweeping views of the mountains and relative seclusion. Someone far smarter than him would have created an alluring sales pitch with a slick brochure touting a spacious natural wonderland not fifteen minutes from downtown. Maybe there was even a now long-forgotten golf course in the plan.

A hundred yards beyond the intersection of valley and road sat an abandoned construction trailer. The kind where a foreman with unscuffed boots worked in air-conditioned splendor while everyone else sweated a lake. The windows were broken and the door leaned against the grungy exterior, having lost its original purpose. From his angle, Sherman saw two vehicles.

The BMW he recognized… it belonged to Jones.

Parked behind the trailer was a domestic truck of much older provenance. Early nineties, Sherman guessed, but he was no car guru. Not by a long shot. They were a metal-clad means to an end from A to B, nothing more.

Hidden by the inky shadows and cream-colored rocks, he moved closer until that buried core of intuition told him to stop. Two people were waiting next to the BMW. Jones and someone else Sherman couldn't quite see, but who towered over the realtor by six inches. In the buttery velvet sheen of moonlight, the guy looked tall and thick but not defined.

Sherman scanned the area and found only shadows and smudges. Sight was but one of many tools, so he closed his eyes, listening to Jones anxiously whispering to the other man who said little in response. Down the valley crickets pined their lonely tune, while further out, coyotes howled on a hunt. Then slowly, as if matching a puzzle piece that had been right in front of him, Sherman heard other noises.

The crunch of a boot on rocks as someone shifted their weight.

The swish of a hand and the scratching of skin.

A deep nasally inhale.

A joint cracking from standing for too long.

Two more accomplices existed in the darkness. Sherman was certain of it. They would be sitting back in the deepest of shadows. One on either side, creating a V with the BMW. Ready for whatever foolhardy adventurer came their way. On another night, in a different place or another continent, he would have found them in their hiding spots and got his hands wet, but that was over there, and he was back home.

Satisfied and running short on time, Sherman moved away from the trailer and towards the road. It didn't take him long.

Vanessa slid the car to an abrupt stop as he stepped into view. He hopped in before she could exhale.

"Frank, you scared the Holy Spirit right out of me. Christ alive," she spluttered as the car stole into motion.

He said nothing.

"Well, did all your sneaking around pay off or is my near heart attack the only outcome?"

"Jones is down there talking to someone."

"That seems friendly," she added, but hesitation ruffled her voice.

"There are two more hiding."

Her upper lip twitched. "And why are they hiding?"

He remained silent but cast a hard glance about the facts of life in his world.

"Armed and dangerous, got it. Story of my life."

Sherman gave a sniff, and Vanessa's face scrunched tight.

"Sorry," she said. "Story of your life too. Actually, way more of your story than mine."

"Everyone is entitled to their own. It doesn't make mine any more real than yours."

"That's nice. You're nice. A better friend I've not encountered, so thank you for that."

"You can buy me a beer when we find your brother."

"What's left of him," she added softly.

Sherman thought to say something uplifting, but she was right. The FBI thought Elmore was dead, and he saw no reason to doubt Landers or try to counter Vanessa's statement. It was the best truth they had in the moment and that can hurt more than any weapon.

He finally settled on some realistic encouragement. "Focus on driving. We might need to make a quick exit, and I don't want your mind wandering off into the land of what-ifs."

Vanessa clutched the wheel tighter and her knuckles turned white. "I'm fine."

"Remember the instructions. Park. Lights off. Exit slowly with hands up."

She nodded while dodging a tire-sized rock protruding from the washed-out road. The BMW was in sight with

Jones standing off to the side, looking every bit the sleazebag.

"Frank," she began. "Do you think these guys killed Elmore?"

Sherman knew the question must have been brewing in her mind for hours since Jones arranged the meeting, growing in intensity and urgency since they left the diner. It was the same question he'd asked himself. The answer would determine the next few minutes, if not hours and days, but Sherman didn't want Vanessa to jump ahead in line and demand retribution. Not when the odds towered against them. Not when he was walking unarmed into an unsprung trap.

"I don't know, but we'll find out," he replied, then opened the door and raised his hands.

―――――

No one moved. The three of them stood motionless in the sallow glow as the sedan's engine burbled back to the ambient temperature. Vanessa and Sherman kept their hands up, waiting for Jones to say something. Leaning against his gleaming imported sports car, he was a model of inaction.

"You're late," boomed a voice from the shadow's folds surrounding the trailer. The owner was destined to be heard but not seen.

Sherman made a show of looking at his watch but didn't care about the time. They were in a dance of sorts. The tango of power and trust. The unseen stranger hoped to establish a power dynamic. Sherman understood the tactic because he'd used it before. An off-balance foe can be easily toppled, or so they said.

"We're here," he replied.

"You're wasting my time," came the voice.

"Then leave."

"Respect is the cornerstone of good business relationships," admonished the voice.

"Then show me some respect and step out into the moonlight."

There was a deep chuckle and the sound of boots tamping down gravel. Then a hulking mass of muscle and bone swarmed into focus. Sherman guessed the guy was six-foot-six and over two hundred and thirty pounds. Hispanic origins of some delineation, although the moon kept some secrets more than others. Despite the size difference, Sherman was not impressed. In his experience, big guys just hit the ground harder.

"Satisfied?" asked the stranger.

Sherman wanted the other two shooters to step out and lay down their rifles but knew such a request was irresponsible, so he merely nodded.

"Our realtor here says you're interested in a specialty order."

"I'm particular about my gear," answered Sherman.

"Don't make me play twenty questions, Frank."

Sherman grinned at being on the back foot, but names mattered little. He said, "I see we're on a first-name basis now. What should I call you?"

"D."

"Fine by me, D. Look, I'm going to name some items. Nod if you have it in stock."

The man put a volleyball-sized hand up to stop the oncoming slew of questions. "Jones vouched for your partner over there, which is good enough for me, but neither of us knows a goddamn thing about you."

"Other than my name and the fifty-grand deposit I gave your realtor," corrected Sherman.

He'd expected pushback on his credentials. After all, he barely existed within most federal databases. More of a statistical whisper than a taxpayer. For all they knew, he was an FBI informant. Which was true. Although, he planned to omit most details to Landers until he was confident these were Elmore's killers. Once he knew that, then only the outcome mattered, and Sherman felt sure Landers would see them serving long prison terms.

"Money doesn't buy everything."

"Spoken like a man who doesn't have any," replied Sherman, trying to rattle a cage or two.

The comment cut deep enough for the man to pause, and Sherman knew they'd reached a deal.

D said nothing. The corner of his eye twitched and Sherman knew a robust inner monologue echoed through the behemoth's mind.

"Ask your questions."

Sherman smiled, thin and tight, and squinted into the darkness, hoping to catch a glimpse of the two other men.

"HK416?"

A head shake.

"M4A1?"

A nod.

"M249?"

A slow side-to-side reply.

"M27?"

A nod, almost imperceptible in the moon-cut shadows.

"MP5?"

Nod.

"M17?"

A shake.

"Glock?"

Another shake.

"M18?"

A hesitant nod.

"Night vision?"

More nods.

"Ammo?"

"That costs extra," said Jones, who had inched towards the conversation.

"I didn't expect it *gratis*," replied Sherman without looking over his shoulder.

"Send the details to our realtor. He'll get you a quote. Fifty percent upfront. Fifty percent after delivery."

"And if you don't deliver?" asked Sherman.

"We always deliver."

Sherman gave his best 'what a bunch of shit' face and waited.

The man pointed at Jones and added, "Take it out on him."

The realtor swallowed hard, and his fear carried across the windswept valley like a thunderclap.

"How long?" asked Sherman.

"Depends on the order. Expect two to four days."

"Drop-off?"

"To a locale of my choosing?"

Playing on home turf didn't surprise Sherman. It made sense.

"Transport away?" he asked, playing through the steps even though he had no intention of taking possession of any weapons.

"Buyer's responsibility but get something big."

Sherman glared at the tall stranger and then flicked his gaze towards the armed men hiding in the darkness. He held it there longer than needed before saying, "We'll be in touch tomorrow."

The man leaned forward, "Tell your partner's brother it was good doing business with him. Assuming he ever comes back from Mexico."

A solemn bell of confirmation tolled in Sherman's mind, and he knew more than needed. All the ends were tied together. The only thing left was to burn it down.

"I'll pass that on," he replied and turned to leave, hoping he hadn't misjudged the situation. Hoping that a bullet wouldn't find him on the way out.

Nothing terrible split the silence, and Vanessa started the car but left the lights off.

"Can we go?" she asked softly.

"Please."

The four men amassed around the trailer and watched red taillights dissolve to dust over the hills.

"Well?" squeaked Jones.

Deet didn't answer but continued gazing off into the distance.

Jones opened his mouth to ask again, but Hadz cut him off.

"He heard you. No need to push your luck."

Jones hung his head and said no more.

No one spoke as Deet gazed on like a statue, motionless and implacable.

"He looked right at me," said Boot, breaking the silence. "Like he knew I was there, but no shot he saw me."

"Me too," added Hadz. "Dude practically made eye contact through the dark."

"He was fishing," Deet concluded.

"What?" asked Jones.

"The list. He was fishing for what side of the fence we're on. I should have seen it earlier. He started with an army pistol and ended with a Marine one."

"Do you think he's a cop?" asked Hadz.

"Nah," answered Deet, unable to take his eyes off the horizon. "Not a cop. He's a soldier—past or present."

"He don't look like one of us," Boot observed.

"Not on the surface."

"Should I pull the plug?" asked Jones. He spun a cigarette in his fingers like a baton twirler during a Fourth of July parade.

"No. Clear the money now. I don't want a paper trail. If he's serious, we'll get a request soon enough. If not, well, you know where she lives, right?"

Jones swallowed. "I helped her buy the house."

"Then it's settled. And, Jones, don't pay over five percent. That last place was a scam."

Jones nodded and mumbled, "I got the family discount. He's my uncle."

Hours later, in a hotel room on the edge of town, the reflection looking back in the mirror gave Sherman pause. His eyes still swirled with orange and green. His hairline had held its line against the years, even the few gray hairs didn't feel out of place. Stress came with the job. Yet lurking behind all the familiarity, muscle tone, and scars was something old and tired. It weighed on him like some invisible yoke, leaving a strained pall with its passing.

Vanessa caught his gaze for second-guessing. "Frank, you okay? What's on your mind?"

For the first time in years, Sherman didn't have an easy answer—deflection or otherwise.

"Feeling my age, I suppose," he answered.

"You're not that old," replied Vanessa, but her eyes traced the jagged white lines across his back. A history etched in flesh. They told a story not of youth but of long years of pain and sacrifice.

"I'm not that young either. Somewhere between the two in a state of limbo. Too young to quit. Too old and broken to feel good about it."

"Did you ever feel good about it?"

"Sure. I walked into that recruiter's office without an ounce of doubt. It all made sense to me at eighteen. Being young is like looking through a pinhole camera. You don't get much depth of field, but what you see is clear enough."

"If you're saying we were myopic, I couldn't agree more."

Sherman turned and slipped on a clean shirt. His last. "When did it stop for you? That feeling of anything being possible and the future still not yet starting."

Vanessa sat down on the edge of the bed and smoothed out garishly colored circles on the comforter. "I was twenty-four. I woke up naked on a couch that was not my own, reeking of vomit and sex. A naked stranger, who I couldn't remember, had his hand on my butt. I'd never felt so exposed in my life and it wasn't just the missing clothes. It was like all my missed opportunities got piled up and lit on fire, and I worried there weren't going to be anymore. I remember thinking that this is my life. All the next steps were gone, permanently over the horizon. I'd never experienced panic like that. It hurt deep enough to change things, to change me."

"You went back to school?"

"Yeah. I finished my Associate's degree and started building credits for nursing school."

Sherman, who had been standing, lay down on the other bed. "Why nursing?"

Vanessa smiled. "It felt right... like you said. I needed to give something good back to the world."

A stark difference clung to their stories, but Sherman knew they weren't altogether different. They were two people doing what they considered right, yet only Vanessa seemed to still believe in her choice.

"You're wondering about what Sophia said, about the great what-if," Vanessa added.

"I am," Sherman admitted. "Without 9/11, I would have stayed in college. No army. I might have finished my degree, got a job for some corporation making six figures, found a wife, had kids, bought a house. That long, drawn-out story of the American dream."

Vanessa gave him a curious look. "Have you ever wanted that?"

Sherman let the images and feelings wash over him in a wave of possibilities. "No," he finally answered. "I didn't then, and I haven't budged since. My mom's right, I'm not cut out for white picket fences."

"I don't think that is a bad thing, Frank. If we all lived in cul-de-sacs, the world would be pretty fucking dreary. We both know there is a need for people like you. Things aren't so simple or nice or clean."

Sherman bobbed his head in agreement. He'd seen plenty of ugly things. "I'd like to think it stops at some point."

"And do you?"

"No, I don't."

"Then continue being you and stop worrying about the past or the future. Believe me, it isn't worth living in either of those worlds."

"You would have made a fine therapist."

Vanessa laughed. "I'm too fucked up to seriously help someone else."

"Well, I feel better."

"Please, I've never seen anyone more comfortable in their skin than you. If you're having doubts, I know they're temporary at best."

"Thanks, I think."

"Shut up and turn off the light. I'm exhausted."

———

As the lamp clicked off, Landers took off her headset and stopped listening.

"Anything useful?" asked Javier from across the room.

"Nothing pertinent," she answered, but it felt like a lie. Much of what Sherman had said resonated with some latent sensibility, and her mind vibrated with possibilities.

Chapter Thirty-Four

The hotel's complimentary continental breakfast was in full swing when Sherman arrived. Their room had cost the same, but indirectly. It was a small concession from Agent Landers and came out of Uncle Sam's pocket via the FBI, which felt like free, but it still cost Sherman somewhere along the line.

Outside the narrow windows, angled shards of sunlight fell over the valley but it felt early and he was still tired. Aromas of cheap coffee and pre-cooked bacon mingled with boisterous conversation and clinking plates. There was a certain claustrophobia to the large, albeit crowded room.

He started with caffeine.

Two cups of the stuff because they were small, and he didn't want to wait in line again.

Nearby, people jostled over the waffle station like hyenas over prey, and Sherman wondered how the hotel was at full occupancy. From what he could tell, Buford held little cultural or commercial interest. A highway stopover was the only thing that made any sense, but his idea of vacation rarely included roadside hotels, even ones with fancy signs, new carpet, and Wi-Fi.

A secluded beach with a case of beer. Now that was a vacation he'd endorse. Not extra points on the rewards card and a reheated meal.

He was working through a plate of protein and starch when Vanessa arrived looking exhausted but clean. She glanced down at his food, then up at the line still snaking through the common area, and stole Sherman's half-finished cup of coffee.

"At least the water pressure is good," she said.

Despite the joke, recent events were wearing on her. Sherman could see as much in her furrowed brow and burgeoning lines of stress stretching out from her mouth. He knew it took hard work to escape the piles of shit and heartache she endured. What life she'd built was falling apart or sucking her back down into the muck.

"I think we've taken this far enough," he said.

"Frank, I've barely had any coffee. Spell it out for me."

They were sitting away from the crowd in an alcove towards the back of the room looking like two tired lovers after a long night.

Sherman glanced over her shoulder before adding, "We've helped out enough. The feds can make a case. Maybe it's time to leave town."

Vanessa brought her cup down hard and the coffee sloshed over the side. "They killed Elmore. He practically admitted as much. The only person I told that bullshit Mexico story to was Jones. He must have told them. I want his body back, and they damn well know where it's at."

"The FBI can make it part of the plea deal," suggested Sherman.

Vanessa downed what remained in her cup and stood

up to get more without another word. He had tried and that counted for something, although Sherman knew it would do nothing to assuage his guilt if something happened to her.

She returned with three coffees, two muffins, and a sulky look on her face.

"Sorry," she began and slid over one cup like a peace offering. "I didn't mean to explode like that."

"No worries. I just don't want to ruin your life, or worse, over this."

"Frank, I dragged you into this fucking mess. It wouldn't be fair for me to duck and run."

"I came under my own volition and without reservations or expectations."

She smiled, thin and tight. "I can handle myself... I don't need hand-holding or coddling."

"Trust me, I believe you, but this isn't some macho 'women can't handle it' speech, and for the record, I held the hand of a friend for thirty minutes while the corpsman tried to stop the bleeding. I held it until they loaded his corpse into the helicopter."

Vanessa sniffed.

"I don't want to lose another friend," he continued. "But if you want to keep going, I'm right here to help."

She blew on her coffee, steam wafting over her face, and looked content enough with the option. Sherman thought about getting up for another plate when he spotted two suits enter the foyer.

Vanessa watched his expression sour. "Trouble?" she asked.

"The devil doth appear, and they don't look up for small talk."

Agent Landers circled the room, grabbing a glass of orange juice and a cherry Danish before sitting down at a nearby table. Javier did the same but loaded up on potatoes and bacon before taking a seat.

"Late night?" she asked, eying the six empty paper cups of coffee on their table.

"Not really, but you already knew that. It probably wasn't hard to get the keycard timestamps from that lady at the front desk. She seems like someone impressed with that badge of yours," answered Sherman.

Landers gave a thin smile of recognition. "Magnetic strip technology is old but reliable."

"So is GPS," added Javier, between mouthfuls.

"You tracked the car," Sherman conceded, although the move did not surprise him.

Landers shrugged like tracking a car came more naturally than visiting the grocery store. "With all due respect, Captain, I didn't expect the unrestrained truth from you. I figured you'd leave out a few details like clandestine meetings."

The coffee cup in Vanessa's hand shook as she laughed. "Shit, she's good."

Sherman made a show of frowning, but neither woman was misinformed. "What do you want to know?"

"Details, Captain Sherman."

"We met with someone last night regarding the illegal sale of military weapons. Happy?"

Landers sipped her juice but didn't look away. "No," she said sharply.

"Jones set up the meeting, but you already connected that dot, so I'll spare you the details."

She said nothing and the only sound was Javier lapping up the last of his eggs.

"We met his contact," Sherman began, but Landers interjected before he could say more.

"Describe them."

Sherman took a slow sip and continued with what he had planned on saying next. "About six-foot-six and proportionally large. Hispanic or Caribbean by history, although his accent was mild."

"Big brown guy," added Javier.

"If you say so," replied Sherman.

"Did you come to terms?" asked Landers.

"Not yet, I'm sending in an order today."

Landers pulled apart her Danish like it deserved corporal punishment until only the ruby center remained intact. "Do you know where they're getting the gear?"

"Inside job," replied Sherman.

"What side of the fence?" asked Landers with an eagerness in her voice that Sherman recognized as trouble.

"Not sure," he lied.

Truthfully, he knew from first sight the guy was a jarhead. No doubt about it. He'd been raised by one, spent his childhood surrounded by creed and ethos. If not for a youthful rebellion, he might have become one. Sherman knew a Marine in day or night, uniform or jeans.

"Don't bullshit me," hissed Landers under her breath. "I recognized you from first glance. There is no way you don't know."

"It was dark," countered Sherman.

Landers turned to Vanessa like a lion switching prey. "Did you recognize them?"

Vanessa shook her head. "Nobody I know."

The Danish was nothing but sticky residue on the plate, which Landers turned like a Lazy Susan.

"So, you two don't have any inkling who these people work for?"

"The system leaks like a sieve," replied Sherman without answering the question.

Landers glowered across the table like smoldering coals but said nothing. All the while, Javier shoveled food into his mouth in great messy forkfuls.

"I want to know everything you know when you know it. Is that clear?"

Her commanding authority responded in the small alcove, and Sherman nodded—not out of fear but because he believed the agent carried the noblest of intentions. She wanted to do good for the world. For that, he saluted her drive, even if her goal was nothing more than a shimmer of heat pooling like water over the asphalt.

"Good," she said and motioned for the door.

Javier sighed at his empty plate and followed her out.

The guests continued with their morning, not noticing the two suits or the tense conversation with the tired lover types in the corner. All except one man in the opposite corner. His eyes lingered for a second too long, and Sherman felt it like a cold splash of water.

The stranger wore a floral-patterned dress shirt paired with an off-color tie. The combo reminded Sherman of a professor he knew from his short-lived college career. There were other similarities, too. Both were mostly bald and wore round eyeglasses.

Despite the loud colors and playful pudginess of the man, Sherman caught the unmistakable whiff of decay as they exited the common room. Nothing strong, not like the other killers he'd known, people not unlike himself, but still identifiable. Something about the man stuck out like a rose hidden in a vegetable garden.

"Are you alright?" asked Vanessa as they walked back to their room.

"Did you see the guy in the corner by the exit?"

Vanessa shrugged. "No, sorry. Do you know him?"

"Not directly."

Vanessa stopped in her tracks. "And indirectly?"

"I'm not sure, but we're changing hotels."

"Why? This one is nice and clean."

"There are others across the freeway."

"Yes, but the water pressure…" she grumbled.

Sherman said nothing. He just cast a glance over his shoulder, wondering how long the stranger would pretend to read his newspaper and ignore their departure.

Two minutes passed. Nothing happened. Vanessa flitted about nervously.

"I'll meet you in the room," he said.

She shrugged again and set off down the long, newly carpeted hallway.

Sherman turned back in time to see the edge of a floral pattern retreat from the doorway and back into the common room. He took a mental note of the stranger and texted Landers to arrange different lodging for the night. He doubted they would accept the request without haggling or direct challenge. That was just how procurement worked in the U.S. Government.

When Elias finally set his newspaper down, he could scarcely contain his primal joy. Not one or two, but all three of his targets in one room built more excitement than any sexual conquest of sleek call girls in New York or leather-clad groupies in cheap dive bars. The tinge of possibilities cascaded down his spine and left him giddy.

For ten minutes, he'd forced himself to read the news

while the excitement built like flood waters behind a dam. Yet, he was not sloppy. People who acted on urges alone got caught by people like him. Well, the type of person he'd once been.

Elias knew better and held the warm glow of anticipation, focusing it on the task at hand. Solving two-thirds of the problem appeared straight-forward. The suits were government types from the alphabet soup side of the house, some delineation of the FBI, CIA, NSA, etc. The department made no difference. Killing them was merely an outcome of planning. It took little skill—just timing and circumstance.

The bearded man from the grainy still image was different. Elias understood that indisputable fact. He'd only looked for a few seconds before the stranger spotted him, and he hid behind the L.A. Times, pretending that world affairs meant something besides background noise.

During his decade behind the badge, Elias had never been made so quickly. Although his backstory would hold up against scrutiny, Elias felt the sands shifting beneath his feet.

His burner phone buzzed softly atop the newspaper. It read:

An associate brought another local opportunity to our attention. A hat trick at 20 per.

Elias sat with the request, slowly sipping his tea and imagining all the drugs and women he could buy with an extra sixty grand.

He replied: *Timeframe?*

Concurrent. They appear connected.

The ex-cop leaned his chair back until it creaked and contemplated the offer. Twenty thousand per was good money, but a pittance compared to the other three. The new targets were bit players at most, unwanted flotsam at worst. Either way, they'd be dead soon enough. Elias cherished the idea of a neatly constructed story. He was once a detective, and the legal system loves a tight story.

He typed back: *Details?*

Do you accept?

Yes. Details?

Coming in person.

Elias frowned at the request. *No face-to-face.*

Impossible. It must be.

His frown deepened into fleshy waves. *No.*

Too late. Details forthcoming.

Coordinates popped up and he followed the map to a golf course past the Marine Annex, near some industrial buildings.

5 pm. 13th hole. South of the green.

Elias chewed through a soggy piece of bacon and wondered what strangeness would come next. Such an event felt inevitable, like the tide.

In the meantime, he let his excitement grow unbridled.

The ride back to Vanessa's house felt short and direct. Ten minutes. No more. No less. Sherman enjoyed the simplicity of her life and the ease of Point A to Point B. A small-town life. Except, he knew things weren't so simple, not for her. A tough life leaves scars, and Sherman knew enough about trauma to recognize it in her attitude and demeanor, in the instincts for preservation, and the indelible marks it left on her flesh. But he also saw something else—a spirit of hope. Grit, they used to call it, as if that one word could sum up a person.

Shimmering curtains of heat swarmed the street outside of Vanessa's house by the time they arrived, but it wasn't the temperature that stood out. Painted across the garage, in the neon red of spray paint, was the word 'cunt'. Each letter stood six feet tall, and the slur stretched across the length of the retractable door. Thin rivulets of paint ran down from the end of each letter like tiny exclamation marks.

Vanessa's voice caught in her throat somewhere between a road and a whimper, and she tried to hide her tears when Sherman looked over.

"I'm sorry," he began, but she shook her head.

"It's just a word," she sniffed.

Sherman, who had seen enough suffering to fill a century, knew that everyone had a breaking point. The longer he watched her quivering lip and shaking hands, the more he knew Vanessa had reached her own limit.

Had it been just the graffiti, maybe she could have buried the anger and fear, but the violations did not end there. Broken glass and furniture covered the floors, and they stepped over the shattered remains of her once-normal life as they entered through the front door.

Sherman swallowed hard.

Everything lay broken or slashed, down to the condiments thrown and squirted against the walls. Red and yellow lines traced great arcs across the kitchen cabinets and a solitary mound of mayo sat on the coffee table like the peak of a snowy mountain.

Having held back the tears outside, Vanessa broke down into shoulder-heaving sobs. Sherman sat down with her as the grief tumbled out. All he could do was be there, but he guessed that made up more support than she usually got from her feckless brother, self-centered mother, or asshole father.

When all that could come was gone, Vanessa stood and took in the sheer magnitude of the vandalism.

"Do you know who did this?" asked Sherman.

She nodded her head and wiped snot on her sleeve because all the tissues were stuffed into the sink.

"Ash did it."

One burned car for one ruined home. *An odd retribution,* thought Sherman, but he'd seen stranger things in parts of Afghanistan where the laws of Hammurabi still ruled. Except the scales still tilted out of balance. Insurance would pay for the car. Ash's retaliation cut a deeply personal note.

"What am I going to do now?" asked Vanessa. Her eyes were bloodshot and hollow.

"Call Cullen. Tell him you need a ride to the coast. Tell him to pack for a few nights."

Vanessa didn't fight the suggestion of leaving anymore. That reserve had long since evaporated. She made the call and they sat outside, waiting in silence. Cullen, being a reliable friend, didn't leave them waiting for long.

She forced a smile as Sherman walked her to the truck. "1075 Sycamore Street," she added.

"What?" Sherman asked. He didn't need an explanation but wanted some tacit confirmation that she knew the outcome of giving up such information.

"It's the address I know you want to ask for."

Sherman nodded and repeated it to himself.

"Take care, Frank."

"I'll see you on the other side," he said.

She sighed. "I hope you mean the mountains."

"Me too," he replied and watched as they drove away into the heat and dust and blood of Buford. He hoped they'd be safe.

Chapter Thirty-Five

Agent Landers turned on the sedan's air conditioning, slouched into her seat, and wished the hotel coffee cups held more than three ounces of liquid. She hadn't been sleeping well, not for the last few days, and all she could do was caffeinate.

They were parked down the street from Jones' office. Being the best lead they had, it seemed fitting to stay close. Maybe the sellers would show up or they'd witness something incriminating. Leverage for any future negotiations with the realtor.

"I need a favor," said Sherman.

Landers grimaced. A favor was the last thing she wanted to grant. "After you place the order with the sellers. We need to move this operation forward."

"Fine, consider it done."

She paused. Something was wrong. Men like Sherman don't just give in so quickly. "What do you need?"

"To be sure no one is watching Ash's house at 1075 Sycamore Street."

"Why would someone be watching his house?" she asked before understanding he didn't want witnesses.

"Because."

"Never mind. Don't tell me. I don't want to know."

Plausible deniability felt better than an actual denial, at least she thought it did.

"Smart," replied Sherman.

"I'll make some calls. Place the order now."

"I will."

She paused, considering her words and what little impact they could have on the captain. "This doesn't end well, you know that."

"No, it never does."

She hung up and turned towards Javier to see what he'd overheard.

"What's he up to now?"

She drummed her fingers on the steering wheel in contemplation. "I don't know, but make sure the locals steer clear of 1075 Sycamore Street. The last thing we need is Sherman getting arrested."

"Why would he get arrested?"

She threw her partner a don't ask kind of look, and Javier made the call. A back-and-forth ensued with some laughing and sharp words.

"The locals laughed at me, which means they know who lives there and want nothing to do with the mess. What is your boy up to?"

Landers rubbed the bridge of her nose in frustration. "It's best if neither of us knows."

"This," replied Javier with a twirl of his fat finger, "is playing with fire. And you know what happens with that."

"You get burned?" she asked incredulously.

"No, the whole building goes up in flames."

The sun felt like a heat lamp from a fast-food joint strung over the state, almost close enough to reach up and touch. It burrowed into the back of Sherman's head like tiny pieces of white phosphorus. Parking out front brought attention, so he'd walked the last few blocks marveling at the few differences between Baghdad and Buford. Both were hot, violent, and apathetic.

He didn't see a soul outside, and all of the neighbor's curtains were drawn shut, trying to maintain what little coolness sprang from the overworked air conditioners. At least until he arrived at Ash's address.

Some form of music rumbled from the backyard of a ghostly white ranch house paler than the salad dressing and equally nondescript. The whole neighborhood looked identical, and it took a moment for Sherman's mind to cope with a continuous sense of déjà vu. Without the bass and horrid lyrics, it would have been just another home, but some people cannot help but stick out.

Ash was one of those people

Sherman slipped around the side unnoticed and edged towards the backyard. In addition to the music, he heard at least four voices—three male and one female. He recognized Ash, Colt—the guy he'd hit in the throat—and two randoms.

Four versus one. Not great odds, but not terrible if he played it smart. Groups create a false sense of security through sheer numbers. Experience had taught Sherman the best way to overcome a numerical disadvantage was to act quickly and mercilessly. Anything less failed with catastrophic consequences.

He waited at the corner of the house like a lion in the

grassland, biding his time for the opportune moment. That split second when all the variables line up and some long-buried inner voice screams, "Now!"

The opportunity came quickly when Ash announced he needed to take a shit. Four against one became three, and Sherman's core lizard impulse propelled him around the corner, scooping up a broken chunk of concrete paver on the way.

Years of practice gave Sherman a keen sense of space and what he saw in the backyard matched his own mental image. Three people sat in cheap plastic chairs brittled by the sun, all facing an empty fire pit, which was nothing more than a hole in the ground. Empty beer cans littered a nearby table while a triangular shade cloth flapped over-head in a languid breeze.

The only thing different from his version was the gun. Colt had it stuck in his waistband like some two-bit gangster of yore, while Sherman figured he'd be smart enough to keep it on a flat surface and not point it down at his manhood.

A can of something domestic dangled in the idiot's hand while three more lay crushed in the dirt under his feet. Colt saw Sherman first, but his reactions were slow and damp-ened by alcohol. Recognition flickered in his eyes, but he didn't move, not until Sherman stood behind the other two. Only then did the fool try to pull the pistol out of his waistband.

He fumbled the draw.

Sherman heaved the chunk of concrete.

It hit dead center with a horrid crunching, squirting sound that made the guy flinch and then spasm. Then the gun in his hand went off, with its barrel still stuck in his pants and pointing downward.

A dull thud echoed around the yard before dissolving into the nothingness beyond. From the angle and shocked look, Sherman knew where the bullet hit, the anatomy it damaged, and the probability of survival. He turned to focus on the other guy, while Colt fell backwards, shorts soaked through with blood and a face whiter than chalk.

The second guy survived because he was too drunk and too slow to know better. Sherman dropped his elbow into the soft connecting tissue between shoulder and neck. The lights went out faster than a switch and only one remained outside.

Not as drunk as the other two, the woman put up her hands in surrender. Sherman considered it a smart move, but taking prisoners wasn't on the cards. His real priority was inside the house and he felt anxious to attend to it.

Only when Sherman stepped forward did he realize the woman had no intention of taking it easy. In a great glittering flash of stainless steel, she almost sliced clean through his jugular with a knife that seemingly materialized in her hand. Anything longer would have killed him, but he backed away with only a nasty shaving cut.

The woman maneuvered for another attempt. Her short black hair danced with staccato bursts at each step, and a jingling sound swirled out from her jacket like a jostling bag of coins.

Sherman's grave error in judgment gave him a sneering, snarling smile. He felt blood trickle down his neck. The woman was capable and confident, but she hadn't capitalized on his mistake and he wasn't going to make another.

When she swung again, Sherman caught her wrist with one hand, pulling the arm straight, and sent the other straight through the elbow joint, snapping ligaments and tendons like worn shoelaces. Bone bulged unnaturally under flesh as the joint crumbled.

The woman's eyes faded from shock and she hit the ground with a muted thud. Sherman checked his throat and came away with bloody fingers. Not a small amount either, but not enough for concern. Had the knife connected, he wouldn't be standing, that much was clear.

He stepped over the unconscious body and past the other two idiots, only one of whom was still breathing, and into the house. It was dark and smelled of piss, stale beer, and sex.

A toilet flushed and Ash wobbled out of the bathroom reeking of booze and shit.

"What the fuck was that?" he asked, bellowing towards the sliding glass door leading outside.

Then he stopped and stared at the three bodies lying motionless around the fire pit and the blood pooling on the ground and the pistol covered with dirt.

Ash mumbled, "Oh, fuck."

He might have said more, but Sherman smashed a bottle of tequila over his head and that ended any chance of immediate conversation.

When the call came, and Agent Landers knew it would, she reluctantly answered the phone. The man spoke loudly, quickly, and with great disdain for her organization. Details and threats flew about for anyone to hear.

Landers took several deep breaths, trying to contain her rising ire at the man's tone and unprofessionalism as the conclusion came and went.

She said nothing and placed the phone back into her jacket pocket.

"Who was that?" asked Javier.

"The Buford Chief of Police."

Javier dumped what remained of his lukewarm coffee out the car window and tossed the empty cup on the floor.

"Let me guess," he began. "Multiple casualties at a house on Sycamore Street?"

Landers shook her head, although Javier's guess dovetailed with her own imagined outcome of Sherman's foray.

"One DOA, self-inflicted from the looks of it. Two in the hospital and one having a mental breakdown."

Javier looked confused. "What's the big fuss then?"

Landers fidgeted in her seat, digesting the question into a slow of answers. None of which sat well with her. She couldn't help feeling like they'd missed a crucial piece of information.

"I'm not sure, but something lit a fire under the chief's ass. Run a check on the department. See if there are any complaints or violations and see who owns that house. I'm gonna find the captain and make sure he holds up his side of this cluster."

She dropped Javier off at the motel and started the search for Sherman. It didn't take long. The GPS tracker still worked, and it placed his car not far from Buford's commercial strip. She took one look at the map and started driving.

The lunch rush had come and gone when Landers arrived at the shiny steel door under a neon sign spelling out *Diner* in great curly letters. It was old by American standards. A child of the post-war boom called the fifties. The white subway tile walls were mostly clean despite their age and the waitress smiled when she entered.

"Over there," said the young woman without waiting for Landers to ask or explain.

Following her outstretched arm, Landers found Sherman sitting alone in the corner with an empty plate to one side and a full cup of coffee in front.

She sat down.

He said nothing.

The waitress stopped and deposited another cup of coffee, again, without being asked.

"Did you place the order?" asked Landers.

Sherman nodded.

"And?"

"Waiting for a reply."

"What did you list?" she asked with dwindling patience. The captain's evasiveness gnawed at her already raw nerves.

He sipped his coffee. "Enough to get you what you want."

She snorted. "And what do I want?"

He matched her gaze. "A way out of this dump. Proof of where the weapons are coming from. Although, I imagine you already have that figured out, otherwise, you wouldn't be sweating it off in this place."

Landers laughed and wondered how much of his answer was bluster or if the captain had feigned naiveté.

"What else do you know, Frank?"

"That you got a call from the Chief of Police."

Landers paused. "Why would I get a call from him?"

"I had words with his son earlier today, which is why you're sitting here and not calling me to discuss."

The meaning of the chief's call sunk in like the last shot on a long night of drinking, and Landers felt queasy. Meddling so blatantly in a local affair was a career-ending mistake and she cared for little else in life. She had no family or partner, only work.

"Frank," she hissed, looking over her shoulder to see if anyone was listening. The place was empty. "What the hell did you do?"

"I had a little chat with Ash."

Landers did not look surprised. "And what did Ash do to earn such a visit?"

He took another sip of coffee. "He ransacked Vanessa's house and painted *cunt* across her garage door."

Landers paused and said nothing but felt a bright spark of rage flicker to life. Then she tamped it down like she always had when the words and actions cut deeper than she could admit, when it hurt too much to say otherwise, and when the risk of retaliation remained too high.

"That was stupid, Frank, and you don't strike me as the unintelligent type. Now I have the Chief of Police up my ass and they're no doubt looking for you too."

Sherman's face lightened and he gave a thin smile. "Ash won't be pressing charges and ruining your little operation if that is the concern."

"Right now, he's babbling nonsense. The doc called it a complete mental breakdown, except his language was much more colorful."

The captain scratched his beard and Landers leaned in. Curiosity always got the better of her in the end, and the soldier before her was the oddest mix of mystery she'd seen in years.

"Fine, I'll bite. What did he say?"

"Nothing admissible," Sherman began. "But he painted a rather bleak picture of law enforcement in Buford. Criminal, if you ask me."

Landers rubbed her temples. They ached with stress and lack of sleep. "Anything I can actually use?"

He slid across a scrap of paper with a twenty-digit number written on it.

"I don't do codes," Landers replied.

"It's a bank account worth looking into."

She frowned at the idea of another case. "Why?"

"Leverage or proof, take your pick, but the Chief of Police might shit himself if he knew you had access to his personal drug-fueled slush fund."

Landers knew the playbook. She'd seen it before in Afghanistan a dozen times. Corruption didn't stop at the border. "You've been deployed too long, seeing nothing but forest and no trees."

"Maybe, or perhaps the difference between there and here isn't as big as everyone wants us to think."

Sherman stood to leave but Landers grabbed his arm.

"Don't get caught up in this David versus Goliath shit. Keep the bigger issue in focus. We need to stop those guns from reaching the streets. That is the greater good. Not revenge for Elmore or dirty cops or sunburned meth-heads. The guns—only the guns."

"Goliath should have worn a helmet."

"Where are you going?"

"To visit my mom."

Then he walked out the door, leaving Landers with a queasy knot in her stomach.

Chapter Thirty-Six

Only the vestiges of visiting hours remained when Sherman arrived at the hospital. Metal carts filled with bland food and wobbly Jell-O crisscrossed the hallways as he entered. Dinner time for those unlucky enough to suffer through another evening meal.

A thick antiseptic stench grated at his senses and long repressed memories danced at the fringes of awareness. Chaotic field hospitals and helicopters smeared with blood. Flight crews hosing off the sticky remains of lost lives and forgotten dreams. Caustically white lights of operating rooms in Germany. The smell clung to personal belongings like spilled soda, dragging the aroma of loss back home with the bodies.

Sherman knocked on his mother's door before slowly opening it. She was asleep and he sat down, leaving her to a world of dreams.

He had a text to send. The one he lied to Landers about at the diner. He never placed the order but knew it needed to happen. With Vanessa gone and his flight back to Qatar only a few days away, only a narrow window for action remained.

FBI threats aside, Sherman knew his motivation for staying did not shine on the hill, free of mud and muck. He wasn't fighting for freedom or country, but neither for money or greed. Nothing so grandiose compelled him to write the text to Jones. Anger fueled his message.

Anger against those who hurt Vanessa, who killed her brother, who trashed her house, and those seeking to ruin her life. It wasn't love or lust, but an affection for those helping others that elevated her cause. Anyone willing to care for the many faces of Sophia deserved support.

He wasn't one for saving the world—such naiveté fizzled after his first tour—but doing good didn't always happen on some late-night infomercial for the Red Cross or on the backs of aid workers in Sudan. Sometimes doing good meant getting dirty, breaking bones and eschewing any moral justification. In his experience, doing good was an awfully violent endeavor.

Sherman punched out a short but expensive list with enough hardware for an African coup or a street war in Mexico. Not that either place needed more weapons, but he had no intention of taking delivery. Knowing those behind Elmore's death would languish in prison was enough, he hoped.

The phone beeped as he hit send and he stared intently at the screen like a pool player visualizing all the different angles and outcomes of his turn.

"You know those things will give you brain cancer," said a crackly voice.

Sherman glanced up at Sophia and smiled. "So I've heard. How are you doing?"

"Itching to make a run for it. Most people my age don't

make it out of places like this. Do you remember Aunt Phyliss?"

Sherman nodded at the name and the story to surely follow.

"You knew she went into Saint Agnes to remove a mole and ended up dead on the operating table. No one could explain why and she was younger than I am now."

"She had cancer, Mom."

Sophia waved her hands as if swatting away a fly or an inconvenient truth. "That's what they said afterwards. Damn doctors covering their tracks and making up stories rather than taking responsibility."

Sherman changed the subject. "They said you're getting released tomorrow."

She shrugged. "That's just trading Jell-O for peaches."

"The Desert Rose is better than here, right?"

Sophia looked at him but said nothing for a long minute before adding, "Frank, I don't want to die here."

"You're not gonna die, Mom. They're releasing you. The doctor said you are doing fine."

"Not now, but soon enough, and I don't want it to be here. This place is so hot and dry and filled with lost hope."

Sherman had never heard his mother more morose and honest. Buford held no magic, save for an ability to ensnare its inhabitants.

"I thought you liked it here."

"Your father liked it, and I loved him, so we stayed. Hiding here helped him cope."

"Cope with what?" asked Sherman.

"All that death. Your father didn't show it, not in front of you or me for that matter, but I don't think he ever got past it."

Sherman scratched his beard, growing scraggy over the

last few days, and realized he had more in common with his father than he wanted to admit.

"I've seen that look before," continued Sophia. "Something is chewing you up."

Her sudden and penetrating lucidity made Sherman smile. It reminded him of bygone years when she sniffed out the slightest trouble in a single glance. Knowledge like that didn't always end well for her son, and Sherman found himself on the wrong side of her wrath more than once, but he'd always known she cared.

"Things are messy right now," he replied, choosing his words carefully.

Sophia motioned for him to close the door as if sensing his unease. "With Vanessa's friends?"

"Among others."

She frowned. "Are you over your head?"

"Not yet," he answered.

"Soon?"

Sherman considered the question. Running away didn't bother him, not the way it might a younger man. Reputations were nothing but words, and he had the unassailable trust of his team. Besides, biology dictated fleeing as one of the three tenets of the human experience. He was still alive because his brain knew better than to take a hopeless fight.

Hopeless.

The word tumbled around his mind until it became smoother than a river rock.

"No, there's still plenty of rope left," he answered, borrowing a phrase from his father.

Sophia smiled, her eyes twinkling in the past. "To pull yourself up. Not for hanging."

He nodded.

"Is Vanessa alright? I've grown quite fond of her over the years."

He nodded again. "She's over the pass until I get this sorted."

"Frank, be careful. Don't do the wrong thing for the right reason."

Sherman squeezed her bony foot sticking out from the thin hospital sheets. "I'll see you tomorrow at the Desert Rose. Stan arranged for pick-up."

Sophia waved in his direction and poked at a bowl of neon green Jell-O. "Thanks. Oh, Frank, will you let your father know. I don't want him to worry."

Her lucidity vanished in a terrifying flash, but Sherman merely smiled and walked towards the rear exit. The ending aside, it had been a remarkably normal conversation, and it hurt to realize how much he missed them.

The burner phone in his pocket buzzed before he reached the pavement outside. Sherman stepped under the shade of a bus stop awning to read the text.

$300K. Order will be ready tomorrow, pending the first install-ment and a meeting.

Sherman typed out: *No more meetings.*

Not negotiable. Tonight @ 10. Same place. Bring the first half.

Another face-to-face meeting made Sherman uneasy, especially when they were expecting a hundred and fifty grand in cash. Money that he did not have, nor did he know if Tripp did either.

Fine.

He put the phone away knowing two things needed to happen in short order. First, he had to call Landers and let her know about the meeting. Second, he needed to acquire a lot of money in the next six hours.

There was a payphone in the Greyhound station down

240

the street and Sherman ducked inside the battered doors, passing rows of grimy benches sparkling under the harsh fluorescent light.

He fished out some quarters and waited for an answer.

"Special Agent Landers speaking."

"Meeting at ten. Same place as before," he replied, not bothering with an introduction.

She didn't miss a beat. "Will there be money and goods exchanging hands?"

"Money, yes. Guns, no. But you might get a look at the trio."

"No guns, no case, no arrests," she replied in an over-simplification of the judicial process.

"I know that already."

She paused. "We'll be there."

"Stay out of sight," added Sherman, although he knew she didn't need a reminder.

There was a beep, and the line went dead. Task one was done, only the financing remained. Sherman slipped into the car's stifling interior, rolled down the windows which only moved the hot air around, and headed towards the Oil Valley.

Chapter Thirty-Seven

Elias kept to the speed limit as he drove out of the scorched town and onto the highway. His phone lacked GPS and he navigated by means of a cheap map he'd bought from a gas station with cash. It struck him that such a skill, let alone the physical article, would disappear within a generation or two. His grandkids, whenever they appeared, would probably never read the printed word. Everything, he imagined, would be digital. Ones and zeroes floating around, waiting to be manipulated for fun or the highest bidder. Elias pitied their yet unknown life, knowing he was too visceral a person to survive in such a virtual world.

The shabby entrails of Buford receded into the rearview mirror as he headed northwest. He turned the radio up and soaked in the icy air blowing full blast from the vents.

A smattering of trailers came and went like long-forgotten Legos left to wither in the sandbox. Abandoned by their owners, reasoned Elias, but still used for cooking meth or other illicit activity.

Further on came the Marine Logistical Annex. It

reminded him of an open-air Walmart but filled with ordnance and not the ordinary everyday crap of life. Bright green splotches caught his eye, and he double-checked the map. The golf course he was going to remained miles away and didn't use Astroturf.

"Poor bastards," he muttered to himself as the lime-colored excuse for fun passed by.

Nothing of interest existed between the base and his next turn. No gas stations or rundown motels. Even the exits petered out into sunbaked dirt after fifty feet. The asphalt just stopped and the road became a lone brown streak cutting across the endless wasteland of California's guts.

When he finally exited, there wasn't even a sign, but new pavement indicated activity and development. In the distance, sparkling like an oil spill in the ocean, lay a dozen sprawling buildings. Elias paid little attention. He focused across the road at the rolling lawns that had once been scrubby hills.

The golf course was large, immaculate, and completely out of place. He'd thought the same about those in Las Vegas, but at least there were tourists and retirees there. This place had no such customers within fifty miles. The closest town was Buford, and he doubted anyone there played more than mini-golf. A corporate retreat was the only thing that made sense to him.

Easing the sedan between two towering pillars tall enough to support the Parthenon, Elias parked in front of a sumptuous steel and glass clubhouse.

He checked his watch.

Ten minutes to five.

Not much time to spare and he wondered how far he'd have to walk to get to the thirteenth hole. Not the full distance, he reckoned, but close. Nine out and nine back was how he imagined it.

A dapper-looking young man met him at the front door and Elias suddenly felt under-dressed and ill-at-ease. It happened to him at fancy places, where snobby people turned up their noses at his ilk and paid too much to too little.

"Can I help you, sir?" asked the well-dressed man.

Elias chuckled at his British accent as it seemed to fit the surrounding extravagance.

"I'm meeting a business partner."

"Ah, do you have a tee time?"

Elias frowned. "No, I was told hole thirteen."

The young man nodded so low, it looked like a bow and gestured outside. "Take the right-hand path. It's impossible to miss."

The word impossible stuck on his tongue like a taunt as if Elias couldn't find beer in a liquor store.

The man nodded again, and Elias found himself sweating his way across the well-irrigated grass towards the thirteenth hole.

To the young man's credit, it was impossible to miss it. Large signs indicated the way and the numbers were even written into the grass by the greens.

Elias passed one group filled with tan but pudgy men on the sixteenth hole, but he was alone approaching the thirteenth.

Having seen no one, Elias took shelter under a lone acacia tree and waited. It wasn't long before he heard the soft thump of balls landing nearby and watched as two men approached. They were thinner than the previous lot, but not outdoor types. Desk jockeys of some delineation, and judging by the course, Elias guessed they were at the executive level.

The duo stopped upon seeing him and they met in the shade. Introductions were not needed, nor offered.

"I thought you'd be younger," said the taller man with closely cropped hair.

"I thought you knew better than to request a meeting," Elias replied, keeping his gaze on the speaker.

The insult hit ever so deep and the guy's brow furrowed with anger. Elias fleshed out his story from there.

"We have a personnel problem that needs a solution."

Christ alive, thought Elias, he hated all the cloak-and-dagger nonsense. Death was the only truth in life, he just helped speed up the process.

"Who? When? Where?"

The officer-type frowned at the directness of the questions but produced a small envelope from his back pocket and handed it to Elias. Inside was a single piece of paper with three pictures.

"All three require immediate termination."

Elias nodded. It mattered little who crossed his list. Rich or poor, young or old, he accepted all jobs, save for children. Women were fine, just no kids.

"Where can I find them?"

"They come and go from the base. I'll be in touch when they're outside the perimeter. Nothing can happen to them until then. Understand?"

Elias waited for more information like the location of the base, but nothing else came.

He added, "Kill them off-base, I got it."

The officer glowered and moved towards his ball on the putting green. The conversation was over, and Elias knew he was no longer welcome. He wasn't fond of those who couldn't face what they ordered.

Back in his car, Elias replayed the events. Something about the stranger stuck in his mind like a cocklebur. He couldn't get rid of the irritation. The two men were smartly dressed but wore it casually like only those of privilege and money could do. The silent partner had longer hair and a softer build. Elias pegged him as a corporate man, someone accustomed to moving pieces of the chessboard without remorse for the outcome. A profit first, people last type.

The point-man wasn't far removed, but he gave orders and probably felt entitled to that authority. Elias considered him middle management. A major or colonel in the armed forces. Someone accustomed to barking orders, but also used to the pull of a leash from higher up the food chain.

He looked at the sheet of paper with the three faces. It was from a copier and in color, but the paper felt cheap. Faint edges were visible on the page, probably from folders, and Elias assumed they came from personnel files. The men's joyless expressions confirmed it. No names were listed, only faces, but Elias liked it better that way. His line of work was dirty enough, personalizing things only created complications.

The faces were enough, and his detective mind began to place the pieces, starting with the edges. All three were soldiers, their uniform and haircuts suggested as much. The officer mentioned a base, but not where, so he concluded it must be the Marine Logistical Annex he'd passed on the way.

"Killing your own men," he said aloud. "Fucking coward."

Elias drummed his thumb against the paper for another moment, thinking the way he used to, looking for motive in a maze of opportunities. An officer ordering a hit on his own soldiers. Someone with authority could have the three offenders transferred or disciplined if they were making trouble. Only something serious would make an officer step outside the chain of command. Elias knew of only one thing that would drive someone like that to do such a thing —greed. Money made sense as the motive. Money was always the motive. Elias couldn't make the next connection, but he knew it somehow related to the silent corporate accomplice on the golf course.

He started the sedan and caught the dapper young man looking at him through the clubhouse's glass facade. Elias thought better of glaring and reversed away, reminding himself to scope out the annex on the way back to Buford.

A pleasant sensation washed over him like someone who was about to make a lot of money, which he was. He'd already seen the big dollar targets up close at the hotel, and now with the three soldiers, everything was falling in place for a windfall payday.

Chapter Thirty-Eight

Of all the many competing priorities in Sherman's mind, getting the money for his meeting that night was at the top. Without one hundred and fifty grand, the whole deal would fall apart. The FBI would have no case, Vanessa no closure, and Landers might even follow through with her threat by looking into events in Idaho. Sherman could walk away from many things, but his gut said this fight was not one of them. Maybe Sophia was right... maybe he'd gone too far.

When he arrived at Oil Valley, there were only a few dirt bikes motoring around the course. Six o'clock on a summer evening felt no cooler than three in the afternoon and the parking lot was almost barren. Sherman reversed into a spot, facing out towards the road as a precaution against an early exit.

Looking at his father's pistol, Sherman debated with himself over its efficacy if the moment required persuasion. He decided against it and stuck the gun in a small space under the glove box.

A bell over the door announced his arrival and Sherman wondered how it must sound on a busy night with thirty drunks stumbling in and out. Perhaps it was drowned out by the jukebox full of heavy metal and Schlitzed arguments.

Jay and Charlie were still sitting in the same corner like fleshy statues stacking up beer cans. Tara, the bartender, eyed him up with all the suspicion of a prison spotlight and kept her hands beneath the bar. Judging by her wiry frame, he figured it was a sawed-off double-barreled shotgun. Two shots were more than enough to end most unpleasantries, and it had the bonus of scaring the devil out of anyone standing in range.

"Is he here?" asked Sherman.

All six eyes latched on to him and stared in union. Regret over the gun left behind trickled out from Sherman's subconscious.

"He's in the back," answered Tara.

"You better have something juicy," said Jay.

"Some fat worth chewing," added Charlie.

Sherman glanced at the men, who were still recovering from their last encounter, but kept his attention on Tara. The bartender's hands hadn't come up from beneath the counter and the detail snagged in his mind. She was either washing glasses or fingering the trigger. He hoped it was the former.

He pointed towards the office in the back. "Can I go back?"

"Door's unlocked."

Sherman walked past the two fools and their tilted tower of cans, entering the small office in the corner of the bar. It still had the original wood paneling, brass fixtures, and carpet, which reeked of booze, mold, and long-forgotten sex.

Tripp glanced up as he entered with an amused expression on his face and leaned back in an old green leather office chair. It squeaked and groaned in the process, but Tripp didn't seem to notice or care.

"Well, lookie here. About time you came back."

Sherman surveyed the claustrophobic space, crammed with files, mail, and empty bottles of booze. Stacks of cash rested on Tripp's desk, right next to a few topo maps and a Smith and Wesson .357 Magnum revolver glowing in the evening light. Sherman regarded the gun with casual indifference like a surfer might regard a pelican. They existed in the same world, but neither cared for interactions. There was no fret or worry, just an observation of fact.

"The deal is in place, but I'll need another two hundred and fifty to secure it all."

"Secure what?" asked Tripp. "I gave you fifty large and I haven't seen shit. There is no way you're walking out of here with a quarter-mil on your word alone. Hell, I'd be laughed out of town for stupidity. 'Here comes Tripp,' they'd say. 'That dumbass gave away three hundred large for some chump's solemn promise.' No way."

Sherman said nothing. He sensed Tripp had not finished his tirade.

"You know what, Elmore gave me his word too and look what it got me. Bupkis. Nada. Nothing. No proof, no money. I'm not a fucking charity."

"Fair enough," replied Sherman. He placed the phone on the table with the text containing the order. "This is what you're getting for that quarter-mil."

Tripp's eyes sparkled with interest for a moment as they examined the extensive order, but quickly narrowed. "This could be a conversation with your grandmother for all I know."

"She's dead, and if you want the guns, I need the cash now. I'll deliver tomorrow night."

"So, the deal is soon," said Tripp.

Sherman ignored the comment. "Cash now. Guns tomorrow."

Tripp crossed his arms in defiance. "No proof, no money."

"That's not how it works," said Sherman. Having seen a few arm's deals up close, he knew trust and reputation mattered more than examples.

"I don't care about how it works in your world. You're in mine and I want proof."

As the conversation wobbled, Sherman eyed the money on the desk, arranged like a giant taunt. If the bands wrapped around each stack were accurate, Tripp barely had enough for the first installment.

"Is that all you have?" he asked.

Tripp appeared insulted as if his honor had been besmirched. Acting tough, he stood up and stuck out his jaw. Sherman didn't flinch. He needed the money and was willing to take steps to secure it.

"What I have or don't have ain't your business."

"I'm afraid you're wrong about that. You asked for guns, I need that cash to make it happen."

Tripp's eyes bounced about looking for meaning. "Elmore started this train, not you. I don't know you and I don't see his sweet piece of ass sister standing beside you. Hell, for all I know, you put both in the ground. Maybe that was the plan all along—just milk the townies for money. I heard someone crashed Ash's party. Was that you too? Are you closing out accounts?"

Chairs scuffed against the floor as Tripp raised his voice. Jay and Charlie appeared behind Sherman, leaning on the doorframe and acting larger than they were. He'd over-played his hand and came across as desperate. Men like Tripp gorged on desperation and could smell it from across the room.

"I guess I'll take my guns somewhere else."

Tripp laughed. "Not with my fifty grand you won't. Jay and Charlie here will drive you to get my money back."

Sherman sighed as any chance of negotiation ended. "I don't think so."

"I stopped caring what you think, stranger."

"Let's go, asshole," said Jay, reaching out to grab Sherman by the shoulder.

His grip was strong and fingers dug into Sherman's muscle, but leaving empty-handed never crossed his mind. As Jay pulled him back, Sherman reached across his body, grabbing the man's wrist and, in one fluid motion, ducked under his assailant's outstretched arm. Jay tried to escape, but it was too late. Sherman took what was given and twisted hard until he felt the tendons strain and a high-pitched squeak leaked out of Jay's mouth.

Before Tripp or Charlie realized the horrible potential of unfolding events, Sherman sent his right elbow into Jay's temple with as much force as physics allowed. The results were immediate and significant.

As Jay hit the ground, Charlie gulped and stepped back.

Tripp lunged desperately for the revolver resting on his desk.

With the bottom of his boot, Sherman kicked the old piece of metal furniture hard. It slid fast across the moldering carpet and hit Tripp just above the knees, knocking him backward into a tower of cardboard filing boxes stacked haphazardly against the wall. Papers and receipts spewed into the air, covering Tripp in a brief shroud of white. Somewhere in the mix, Sherman heard the distinctive thump of the revolver hitting the carpet.

During the chaos, Charlie made a bold decision and flung himself on Sherman's back. He was not a light man, and for a brief second, Sherman's knees buckled under the strain and he felt Charlie's arm wrap tight around his neck. Panic flickered in the deepest kernel of his mind.

Then, like a bicyclist finding their balance, it all changed. Sherman bent forward and flipped Charlie's beer-sodden bulk onto the metal desk. There was a loud crack, followed by a deep, guttural moan, and Sherman knew Charlie had broken something structurally important. The man looked back at him with wild, pain-drenched eyes.

Papers rustled in the corner as Tripp frantically searched for the revolver. Sherman pounced on top of him just as Tripp found the rubberized grip. Leverage won the day, as it always did, and Sherman kept one knee on top of the wrist holding the gun. Anger and rage briefly got the better of him as he proceeded to shatter Tripp's face into bloody shards of bone. When Sherman finally stopped, Tripp didn't have much of a life left to live.

The room came back into focus and Sherman grabbed the revolver, keeping it trained at the door. He hoped that Tara stayed well enough away. Under a pile of liquor receipts, he found a plastic bag and filled it with fifteen stacks of cash. He could only hope the count was accurate.

Taking stock of the aftermath, he glanced around one final time before edging towards the door. The map from Tripp's desk caught his eye. It was a map of the border with Mexico. Routes into the country, but the arrows went south. Not routes in here, but routes into there. A smuggling route south. Sherman realized why Tripp wanted the guns. He was selling them south and the cartels were the only buyer of note south of the border.

He kicked the map aside. It landed next to Charlie, who was alive and moaning over ragged breaths, while Jay's chest moved in rhythmic unconsciousness. Only Tripp looked critical as he let out a gurgling sound in the corner.

Sherman checked his angles and stepped out into the bar with the revolver leveled. Sticky bits of Tripp's face clung to his hands and wrist, while blood trickled down towards his elbow.

Tara was still standing behind the bar, her hands unseen beneath the counter, with a mixture of fear and anger scribbled across her face. Each emotion fought for control as the inevitable fight or flight debate raged inside.

Sherman paused but kept the gun pointed at her chest. Tara's tan face paled at the sight.

"I'd appreciate it if you would let go of whatever scattergun you got under there and put your hands up."

Tara's eyes drifted towards the office. "They alive?" she asked.

"They're kin, right?"

She nodded.

"Alive, but in need of a doctor," answered Sherman.

Tara slowly raised her empty hands above her head. Thankful, Sherman kept the revolver steady but moved towards the front door.

"And Tripp?" she asked.

"Best if you found a new place of employment," he replied and left through the front with a somber ding of the bell.

Sherman crossed the parking lot with a hurried purpose, careful not to run or glance too much over his shoulder lest there be someone watching. Reaching the car, he tossed the cash onto the floor next to his father's pistol. Red streaks shimmered on the plastic and he examined his hand. It was incriminating in the least. He found one of Vanessa's old scrub tops on the back seat and helped himself. Remnants of violence remained, but the obvious bits came off. Anyone looking close could still see his crime, but now was not the time for a deep cleaning. There was time to ditch the gun and burn the top—maybe even the whole car.

Hidden behind a pump at the gas station down the hill, Landers set down her camera and nodded for Javier to start the engine.

"What happened?" he asked, trying to see the photos she'd taken on the small screen.

"He's got a bag he didn't go in with."

"The money?"

"I don't think it's a change of clothes."

"That's good," said Javier.

Her partner was right. Sherman's actions kept the case moving forward, but what she'd seen flipped her stomach over and bile lingered on her taste buds. Bending the rules was one thing, and she had no qualms about playing on the fringes of legality, but the captain worked on the fringes of humanity and that frightened her. Landers realized they'd not only let the wolf out but fed and encouraged it. Whatever control she had—or thought she had—over Sherman was long gone. The guardrails had burned away. Only their tattered plan and the captain's resolve remained.

"Are you okay?" asked Javier.

"Yeah, good," she replied before deleting the images she'd just taken.

"Now what?" he asked, pulling into traffic.

"We get our hiking boots and find a good place to watch tonight's meeting."

Javier frowned. "Are we gonna grab dinner first?"

"Fine. Food, then hike."

Chapter Thirty-Nine

Deet and Hadz arrived at the abandoned suburb earlier than they had before. An old-timer in Iraq once told them, 'The early bird gets the worm while the late one gets ambushed.' With those words in mind, they hid the old truck behind the dilapidated sales trailer and prepared to sweep through the surrounding area.

It wasn't so much the heat waves as much as all the sand that bothered Deet. He had tolerated it during deployment because they were too busy fighting and dying to care. Stuck on base, driving forklifts and suffering under the colonel's oppressiveness changed his mind. Suddenly, the landscape became more than a view, it was a prison just like the tall chain-link fences and razor wire surrounding the annex. He loathed the area and the people. The place dried you up, leaving a desiccated and broken shell of your former self. If someone had asked for the polar opposite of Florida, where he grew up, he would have placed his thick finger on top of Buford, stabbing the map for emphasis. He missed the humidity, the ocean, and even the alligators.

He nodded towards Hadz and the two started a perimeter check. Paranoia did not carry a negative connotation in their vocabulary. Vigilance was good... extreme vigilance, bordering on paranoia, was better. If they always thought someone was out to get them, they would never be surprised.

Having left Boot on base for fear of attracting unwanted attention, Deet felt acutely aware of their slender numerical advantage. Two was better than one, but not by much, not after what he'd learned.

Over the long night, he'd done some digging into Frank Sherman and found almost nothing, which as digital finger-prints go, was nigh impossible. Such a slender past worried Deet about who they were dealing with. Only people living in the shadows had no online trail, and Sherman's was so barren, it must have been obfuscated.

Deet had even gone so far as to call an old Gunnery Sergeant from Iraq, who still called the Corps home and asked if the name Sherman ran a bell. The guy fell into a long silence like he was weighing the risk of speaking.

Finally, he'd said, "I wouldn't put my foot into that hornets' nest. Stay clear of those boys."

"What boys?" asked Deet. "I'm only talking about one guy."

"Leave those ghosts alone. Nothing good comes of it, believe me."

Having never backed down from a fight, his friend's words chafed against Deet's sense of self. "Gunny, you can't be serious."

"Listen here, I'm only gonna say it once. If he is who I think he is, and I'm pretty sure on that account, then what-ever business you have best be conducted swiftly and accu-rately, or better yet, not at all."

The call ended, leaving Deet swimming with curiosity and apprehension. Three points stood out.

First, and most important, Sherman was not a cop.

Second, Sherman was dangerous, but Deet already knew that from their first meeting when the stranger practically vibrated with a capacity for violence.

Third, he had no idea why such a person was in Buford buying guns on the black market.

That final thought stuck in his mind on replay and he kept rehashing the question from different angles and not coming up with a plausible answer. If Sherman was who the gunny suggested, then he wouldn't need to go to some backwater Marine annex to get guns.

Of course, Deet kept the call to himself and lied when Hadz asked about it. Like a toddler listening to a scary story, it would have spooked the younger men. They were already prone to conspiracy theories and flights of internet fancy, and Deet didn't want to add fuel to that particular fire. Although, he suspected that Hadz already knew. The man was intuitive like that.

Night lingered above, waiting for the vestiges of light to sink below the horizon. Deet and Hadz finished their sweep and settled in for the waiting game. The two had already decided it would be the last time they used the abandoned subdivision as a meeting place. In preparation, they'd left a gas can by the truck and planned on burning it before humping out on foot.

Deet drank coffee from a thermos and watched the first star appear from behind the sun's veil. He was pensive. The gunny's call left him second-guessing the operation. In desperation for more information, he'd searched for Sherman's name on the base's personnel computer. It came back with nothing, not a single result, which only raised his blood pressure.

Sherman also arrived early, but not before stopping by Bob's Ironclad Storage to grab a few items of interest. His father's stash was legendary, and it took a few minutes to decide. In the end, Sherman went with the only classic he knew worked.

The Arisaka Type 99 was a relic brought back by his grandfather from Guadalcanal. The bolt-action rifle had a six-times optic, which was all he readily wanted, but having the rifle didn't hurt. If something felt off, he could always end the meeting or the sellers from five hundred yards. That was four hundred yards short of his father's best shot, but Sherman hadn't inherited that particular ability. He was an average marksman by army standards, but mediocre compared to others on his team. It suited him just fine as he tended to operate within smelling distance of the opposition.

Driving Sophia's car with his father's rifle, wrapped up in oil cloth, sitting on the seat next to him brought out a strange longing for family. It was something Sherman hadn't felt or allowed himself to feel in years. Home had never been a physical place, they moved around too much when he was a kid, and the army never stayed still.

He was a nomad.

Still, family bridged any geographic boundary, and he realized the only person left was slipping away with each passing day, and with her went the memories and connections he suddenly felt attached to. A sense of shame for not having done more to help his mom weighed heavily on his chest and it took a dozen long breaths to focus on the task at hand.

He parked the station wagon four miles east on the shoulder of a rarely used dirt road and hiked in with the rifle and a backpack full of water bottles. Using a dried-out wash for concealment, he approached with deliberate caution. Alone, on the edge of nothingness, brought out a certain joy that towns and cities could never match. He felt alive and oddly at home.

Sherman picked out a group of rocks and cacti six hundred yards east of the trailer. It offered cover from three sides and good sightlines. He crawled the last few feet to ensure that no one saw him enter the hide.

Dusk had settled over the forgotten development before he spotted any movement. An old Ford truck rattled down the washboards and stopped behind the trailer. In a sudden burst of memory, Sherman made a connection. He had seen it before at the realtor's office, the day they asked about Elmore. The truth had been right there under his nose. They'd walked a giant circle through town only to come back to Jones and his connection to the Marines.

Two men exited the vehicle and Sherman recognized them both but wondered about the third. They were smart enough to come early and set up a perimeter, but did they have the foresight to drop off a shooter first? The question rattled about because he didn't have a good answer.

As he watched the Marines patrol the area, his apprehension evaporated quicker than the sweat on his brow. There was no third, not this time. The others were too cautious, almost paranoid. With overwatch, their movements would have been more relaxed and less fearful.

Nevertheless, the Marines did fine work in sorting out a safe space for the meeting. They checked a good three hundred yards around the trailer and Sherman had to stay very still for fear the tall soldier might spot him.

Night swept across the sky like a curtain opening to a starry wonderland. Sherman lay hidden, marveling at the expanse above. Nothing bested a clear night's sky in the desert. Something about the majesty of harsh places made looking up all the more satisfying. A gift for surviving the heat and sand, maybe even the day itself. Sherman made a point of enjoying the view when the opportunity arose, and it certainly had over the last ten years. He'd watched stars twinkle over Iraq, Afghanistan, Syria, Pakistan, Chad, Niger, and even Somalia.

In those wildernesses, there was always someone lurking in the darkness who wanted him dead, be it warlords, militias, or angry hicks. Sherman wondered if retirement might allow him to gaze up unconcerned by those on the ground.

Then he heard the distant, yet distinctive crunch of boots behind him and all thoughts of a life after melted away in the lingering heat. He detected two sets of steps— one louder and heavier than the other, but both were together. Two people walking in a group, in the night, stumbling a bit over the terrain, but moving in his direction.

To conclude that the heavy, plodding footsteps belonged to Javier was not a stretch. Sherman assumed they would be watching the payment from somewhere close. The opportunity was too great. If some weapons appeared, the case would make itself, book closed, game over. If not, they would at least have proof of money passing hands, although he hoped they would keep him out of the frame or out of focus.

Sound carried over the sand like an echo in the mountains and Sherman hoped the two agents would stop soon. Javier made more noise than an overladen pack mule crossing the Hindu Kush mountains. Finally, some hundred yards from Sherman's position, they stopped and settled in. The glowing hands on his watch read nine o'clock. One more hour until the meeting. One more hour until he handed off more money than his annual salary, but he still wasn't sure why.

If avenging Elmore mattered, he knew taking the shot was quicker and more effective than any trial. As for the FBI's case, justice didn't hold much water in his world.

Sherman contemplated the absurdity for a moment. It was not the first time he'd questioned his own motivations and likely not the last. Healthy skepticism was part of his survival strategy, yet Sherman didn't feel unsure or uneasy. A calm certainty radiated from his gut and he knew he was in the right place.

He just wasn't built to sit on the sidelines watching the other guy get destroyed. Something in that genetic code or his father's frenetic stare had made inaction impossible.

As for waiting, that was a different story. Even the most driven person had patience. At a quarter to ten, Sherman slipped out of his makeshift blind and maneuvered towards the trailer. He'd memorized the route in the preceding hours easier than most people remember their computer passwords. Navigation of inhospitable places in complete darkness was a routine and the outskirts of Buford felt peaceful in comparison.

Snaking between rocks, brush, and cacti, Sherman made easy time. He even heard a faint obscenity from Javier as he crossed into their field of view. It must have been a shock for the agent when he materialized out of the shadows.

When Sherman reached the road, he started whistling whatever tune came to mind and purposely shuffled his feet, trying to be loud. Appearing from nowhere in front of two jittery Marines would likely end in him bleeding out in the dirt from a few new holes.

Enough moonlight remained for Sherman to see the big guy who went by a single letter. The other one was hiding off to his left, probably aiming at the newcomer through the night sights of an M4A1.

Sherman slowed and held up his hands. The rifle was still at his rocky hiding spot, but his father's pistol was holstered behind his back. Arriving unarmed amounted to a suicidal risk—one he wouldn't take.

"That's close enough," said a voice in the night.

The voice wore body armor over a t-shirt and had an M16 slung across his shoulder. It dangled there like a miniaturized toy, silhouetted against his bulk.

Sherman stopped.

"You alone?"

"Yup."

"You armed?"

"Yup."

The man paused as if not expecting an honest answer, but pressed on. "Keep your arms out and slowly walk on up."

Sherman did as instructed. The tall Marine remained calm and collected with no detectable hint of malice. There was no reason to worry, not yet.

"I'll be needing that first installment now."

Assurances were useless and Sherman didn't ask for any. This was a game of blind trust and terrible outcomes. The bullets kept people in line.

"Do you have my gear?"

"Tomorrow."

"When and where?" asked Sherman, trying to gauge

the seriousness of the man and if they planned to let him walk out alive.

"In the afternoon. Jones will text you the location."

A smart move, thought Sherman. The Marine was maximizing his advantage. If he didn't know the location, then he couldn't do any planning and would walk in blind.

"Money," insisted the soldier.

Handing it over without proving his own seriousness was too much for Sherman. He looked through the darkness at the other man, still hiding behind a sandstone boulder.

"Have your friend come out. He's making me nervous."

The Marine paused and scrutinized Sherman with one eyebrow raised like he was trying to remember the face. Then he gave a little nod to himself and whistled.

When the other man arrived a minute later, he did not look surprised. The guy was shorter and wider. He reminded Sherman of a corporal he'd known back in the early days of the war when the newcomer roamed the halls of middle school.

"Speaking of nervousness... you're a ghost," said Deet. "A figment of someone's imagination. I searched through all the databases, hit all the servers, and you ain't nothing."

"I'm standing right here," Sherman countered. "Feels solid enough."

"You don't even have a legend," Deet said with a sigh.

"He's probably wearing a wire and working for the feds," added Hadz.

"Come, take a look. I'm not modest."

Hadz looked over at his friend but D shook his head.

Sherman sensed a growing unease between the two. They wanted to know who he was and finding only what the army declassified had spooked them. Their service experience was filled with structure and documentation. Everything followed a pattern. Uniformity, down to haircuts and hats, was how the Marines functioned as a fighting force. It was part of their success. Even Elmore's checkered history would have jived with their understanding of the world and Sherman wondered if the truth behind his death might ever be told.

He tossed the money over, not wanting them to back out over his missing past and before he changed his own mind about keeping the pistol holstered.

The tall Marine clicked on a small red flashlight and opened the plastic bag. His count was thorough, but Sherman had expected nothing less. The man struck him as a capable NCO and he wondered why the Corps stuck him in the stocks to languish. Sherman wondered if he was a bad apple from the start or had this place broken something in him.

"It's all there."

"Look," said Sherman. "When I do business, I like to know who I am working with. Call it a bridge of trust. I don't want real names, but anything is better than a letter."

The tall one glanced at the wide one and something akin to an answer passed between them.

"Hadz," said the wide, stocky man.

"Deet," replied the tall Marine.

His friend grunted and looked eager to leave, but Deet had a question forming on his lips. It hung like a cloud around his face, never breaking free.

When he spoke again, it was all business. "We expect the last half tomorrow."

"Jones already has fifty," replied Sherman, annoyed with the change in financing.

Deet chuckled and the moonlight danced across his tall

frame as it shook. "Consider it his payment. Same amount tomorrow. Clear?"

Sherman didn't care either way, and he'd anticipated such a turn. Fees were ubiquitous, even in the underbelly of capitalism. Besides, a much bigger issue loomed over the coming sun. With Tripp dead or dying, he'd lost his only source of capital. He knew the Marines were too smart to do the exchange in a single spot, and if he showed up empty-handed, things would not end well. The FBI case would fall apart and he'd be bleeding out on the dirt again, with a few new holes.

"Fine," he replied. "Don't disappoint me."

"Is that a threat?"

"Only if you think it is."

The Marines quietly laughed at some inside joke and Sherman took his cue to leave, disappearing into the folds of night.

***

Landers scarcely spoke a word during the meeting. Her attention focused on capturing everything with a low-light camera. Everything except the captain's face. She planned to keep that end of the agreement. Coming up short was a betrayal of trust and a kernel of guilt was already gnawing through her gut.

By pulling Sherman into their case, she'd simultaneously damaged the only two things she held dear. Her career hung by a thin thread if the captain's methods were ever exposed, and she was endangering the life of a fellow soldier. Both current and former lives had been suddenly mixed up in a single case, and Landers felt an existential dread over the outcome.

From a legal perspective, they had evidence of a payment. Only the exchange remained. Landers had called for reinforcements from the Los Angeles office earlier in the evening. Now, only the waiting remained. A long day awaited them, full of phone calls, paperwork, preparation, and uncertainty.

Both agents were worn-down but they stayed put for fear of being seen. A blaze behind the trailer had illuminated the area, sending up a tendril of acrid smoke into the air. They watched, transfixed by the trailer's rectangular silhouette engulfed in flames.

It reminded Landers of an ambushed convoy outside of Kandahar, long after the screams and gunshots subsided. Some of those Humvees burned for hours until nothing but white ash and the blackened frames remained.

"They're gone," said a voice that raced out of the darkness like a gunshot.

Javier practically levitated off the ground next to her.

"How did you..." she began asking but stopped, her heart rate quadrupling. The captain's abilities were no longer surprising or astonishing. He lived up to all the stories she'd heard about his team and then some.

"We need to talk," he said, still an unseen voice cloaked by the night.

"About what?" she asked.

"I'll need a new motel too," he added without answering her question.

"Why?" asked Javier.

"Call it an abundance of caution."

"Okay," replied Landers. "There is another place across the freeway. We'll make the arrangements, but what do you want to talk about?"

Sherman didn't say anything, and for a moment, she'd thought he disappeared.

"We need a new source of money."

"What happened to Tripp?"

His voice edged to a growl. "It didn't end well."

"I'll see what I can do," she replied. "What time are we meeting?"

She waited for a response, but this time, he was gone, and they were left alone in the dark with their fears and aspirations for the next few days.

Chapter Forty

Two Marines left from the Annex in the early evening, sitting high in a rickety old Ford F-150. Elias recognized them from the photos he'd gotten from the officer on the golf course and followed them into town. The guys were cagey, but not blatantly suspicious. They stayed under the speed limit and used turn signals but doubled back on their route at least twice. Elias had to stop for fear of being spotted. Luckily, Buford was a small, dumpy town with nothing of interest, and he'd spotted them heading west.

They turned on a rutted dirt road under the faded glory of a forgotten housing development.

"Whispering Winds," Elias read aloud and laughed at how many stupid people existed in the world.

Miles of rock and scrub spread out before him like a hot pan of bacon sizzling in the evening heat. He didn't bother following the soldiers. Doing so would only invite attention, and Elias loathed unwanted scrutiny. Unless he paid for it with booze, drugs, or cash.

The cheap burner phone buzzed again. Another emergency, he assumed, and read the text with mild amusement.

Wrap it up, ASAP. Too many questions being asked.

He puzzled over who was asking the questions and typed back with tentative strokes, *Problem?*

They searched his name!

Elias started to ask what name but quickly deleted the characters. Something had the money folk spooked and he enjoyed feeling them squirm with a taste of real-world angst. The detective in him stirred to life thinking about the name.

Of the six pictures, five were standard personnel images. They came from some vast bureaucratic database. Cogs in a government machine. The last photo—the blurry one from a budget security camera—stood out in his mind. He'd known the bearded man was different from the beginning. Seeing him in person at the hotel only solidified Elias' opinion. He had a visceral reaction to the man's presence, sensing they had this deep commonality—a long, violent history.

He left and headed back to the base to wait for them. Everyone heads home eventually.

The short stretch of double-wide pavement leading to the Marine Annex saw little traffic in the early morning hours. Elias noted a shift change for the guards and a couple of locals on the wet end of sobering up.

Among the dead embers of night, he saw a pair of headlights approach from the south. They appeared from nowhere as if built from the sand itself. Elias checked the paper map strewn across the passenger seat. He only found empty space. The faint cream color of blank paper between Buford and the Annex. Yet, the vehicle approached despite the lack of official roads.

He sat up straighter and peered through his binoculars, craning so far forward that the ends touched the windshield. The truck that pulled up to the guard post was a few years newer and steel-blue, not red. Despite the differences, Elias saw two silhouettes wave to the guards, who seemed chatty and lively despite the hour.

Elias looked to the phone for confirmation. The text came quicker than he'd expected—an affirmation of the contract's importance.

Client confirms everyone is in for the night.

Elias made a mental note of the new truck model and color, discarding the outdated information floating like driftwood in his memory.

The phone buzzed again.

All 3 are on leave tomorrow afternoon. Window is closing.

He lobbed a few obscenities towards the faintly glowing screen but replied.

Understood.

More than just a ten-character reply, Elias knew what happened next like a batter sitting on a 3-0 fastball. A meeting was afoot.

He looked at his watch. Ten hours stretched ahead before afternoon. Less time than he wanted, but enough to plan out a sudden ending for all involved.

Elias took an extra burner phone out of the glove box and switched it on. It was an old model but had GPS. The battery showed over eighty percent. Enough for a day on lower power mode.

He tapped out a reply to his contact.

I need a favor from the man on the inside.

Despite the hour, neither man could sleep, so they sipped longnecks on Deet's couch and started into their uncertain futures. Everything was in place. The guns were packaged and ready to move. Months ago, Deet scouted an abandoned borax mine east of town for such an occasion. It felt good, lots of ways in and out, but with long sightlines for most approaches. Sneaking up on them would be nigh impossible.

Yet for all the check marks, Deet couldn't shake the sensation that he'd missed something, like the recurring dream he had in high school. In it, he woke up on graduation day only to realize he'd signed up for a class but never attended. With an F, he wouldn't graduate. He'd never get out of his shithole neighborhood or become a Marine. The few, the proud, the ones not working at Popeye's for minimum wage or getting shot over twenty bucks of weed behind the Sinclair station.

The feeling made him distant, worried, and unsettled.

"That guy has some swagger," said Hadz. An empty beer bottle dangled between two fingers.

"Swagger is all piss and vinegar," Deet replied. "That man walks with intent."

Hadz opened another bottle using the countertop's edge as an opener.

"Kind of like you."

Deet looked over.

"Actually, just like you," Hadz continued.

"What are you driving at?"

"What did the gunny really say, you know, when you asked?"

Deet knew what his friend meant, but that particular truth was better left unsaid.

"Lots of shit. You know the gunny, he's got more words than a dictionary. Why does it matter?"

"Don't fuck with me sarge. I see that two-thousand-yard stare you got glued to those eyes. Ain't nothing bothers you, so if those feathers are all ruffled, well, it pertains to me too."

Deet swirled his bottle and watched as the last sip clung to the sides, unable to escape the centrifugal force. "He's some heavy hitter with JSOC."

Hadz looked relieved. "That's miles better than a cop. Why are you looking so blue in the balls?"

"If he's in that world, why get the hardware from us?"

"Why not?" countered Hadz. "Maybe his normal sources are belly-up. Who cares?"

"Maybe," said Deet, but he didn't believe it.

"See, stop worrying about that shit or you'll end up like my Uncle Charles and die at thirty-five."

Deet saw his friend's point but couldn't agree with the optimistic outlook. "Didn't he snort fentanyl?"

"Yeah, Charlie had the white line fever, but only because he looked under all the wrong rocks. The man had a fine woman and a running truck. What more do you need?"

What Deet took to be a rhetorical question hung in the stale air of his trailer.

"Best call it a night," he said and stood up.

Hadz nodded and took his half-finished beer with him on the way out.

Chapter Forty-One

The hotel room looked no different from Sherman's last, save for one less bed and a broken waffle maker at the continental breakfast. The carpet had similar interlocking triangles with brightly colored circles. It registered in passing like a crack in the sidewalk. The bed was a bed and the shower worked. Everything else was added layers of sheen to justify the price.

He called Landers early, when the sun merely threatened the coming heat.

"It's early, Captain," she answered. Her voice sounded alert but not chipper.

"Yet, you're awake."

"Who said I slept?"

"Fair enough," answered Sherman. She struck him as a lifer, burning the wick from both ends, hoping that retirement never came. They weren't so different in that regard.

"What about the money?" she said.

"What, indeed."

"How short are we?" She didn't sound annoyed but resigned to the facts.

"One hundred and fifty."

Silence crept into the call.

"Is there any way around it?" she asked.

"I don't think showing up empty-handed will end well for me. These guys aren't idiots, and they have no compunction against violence. Elmore is proof of that. You've got taxpayer cash. Use some of that."

Another long pause smothered the conversation.

"I can't," said Landers.

"Why not?"

"Does it matter? The answer is still the same. No cash for the buy and only two bodies for the bust."

It was Sherman's turn for surprise. "They're only sending two agents for backup?"

"All tactical teams are currently deployed elsewhere," she said.

"They're hanging you and the case out to dry."

Landers sighed, deep and long. "They called it a temporary resource constraint."

Sherman laughed at the petty bureaucratic language. Every branch of the government had their own idiosyncrasies, but it all meant the same.

"It's still five on three," he said.

"And the money?" asked Landers.

"I already gave you the answer to that question written on a piece of paper. A combination to a safe full of ill-gotten gains."

"Not a chance," she said. Her tone was sharp.

"The money is just sitting there."

A third wave of silence wedged into the call. Sherman

knew such an ask went well beyond her legal flexibility. He only wondered how far her morals would bend.

"Fine," she whispered. "Meet me at that diner by the Sunset Motel in twenty minutes. We can discuss the details."

"Deal."

A thrum of urgency propelled Agent Landers out of the hotel room. Her partner still snored in his bed. The phone had done nothing to wake him, but Landers didn't want that to change. She'd made her choice and had no intention of dragging Javier into the muck with her.

By the time she entered the diner, shuffling through the early morning crowd and the smell of freshly cooked bacon, Landers knew she was late. Sherman sat in the back, facing the front door. The same seat she normally took because anything else made her feel exposed and small.

His thick hands gripped a cup of coffee, and three empty containers of cream littered the table. He looked tired, in a resigned but not exhausted way. She felt the same but with the exhaustion and significant rings under her eyes.

"You're early," she said and slipped into the booth.

"Coffee is on its way."

And before she could say anything, a waitress appeared with a mug and carafe.

"You need another minute with the menu?" asked the woman.

Landers needed a month somewhere cold, with trees that changed color and misty mornings. A minute with the menu wouldn't change that.

"Scrambled eggs and bacon," she replied.

"Toast?"

"No, thanks."

The waitress turned to Sherman.

"Same, but with sourdough."

The woman nodded and left the carafe of coffee with extra containers of cream.

"I take it this is now a two-person operation," said Sherman.

"Javier is…" she began but trailed off. "He's a good cop. I don't want him involved with this."

"Why are you involved?" he asked.

"I imagine for not so different reasons that dragged you out of bed this morning."

"You can't help yourself," he said with an understanding smile.

"No, not really. I've spent too many years trying to do right. I can't stop now."

"Have you considered a new career choice?" he asked.

"What would you have me do?"

"Go to law school, make furniture… I don't know what makes you tick."

Bullshit, thought Landers, he knew exactly what kept her going. They weren't all that different, and by the end of the day, they'd both be criminals.

"I hear retirement's a bitch," she added.

Sherman laughed and flashed another knowing smile.

"Well, spit it out, Captain. What's your plan?"

"Wouldn't I be admitting to a crime?"

Landers didn't reply. She felt too tired for the extra breath.

"Fine," he continued. "We were there before. It shouldn't be too hard to repeat the process."

She lowered her voice. "We questioned you in the inter-rogation room, not the chief's office."

Sherman looked unconcerned by the difference.

"How do you expect us to get in and him out?"

A wide grin spread across Sherman's face, and Landers knew she was not going to like the answer.

The gas station's buckled pavement shimmered in the morning sun. It reminded Landers of the town itself. All cracked and gouged while facing the earthly extremes. She'd parked the sedan in the side lot, looking up towards Oil Valley. An opening salvo in Sherman's grand plan, the repercussions of which made her stomach spin like a washing machine.

Career over? Likely.

Jail time? Perhaps.

Bullet in the back? Maybe.

An SUV pulled up next to her from the opposite direc-tion and rolled down the driver's window. She recognized the Chief of Police and he did not look happy.

"Special Agent Landers," he said.

"Chief, thanks for meeting me."

He spat a thick wad of yellow snot on the ground and looked her straight in the eyes. "Your message made it sound like I didn't have much of a choice in the matter."

Landers tried her best with an apologetic smile. "I'm sorry my message came across like that. I assure you, that was not my intent."

"No offense to Uncle Sam, but why the fuck am I here?"

"We received some information about the recent trou-bles in Buford."

The chief stiffened and his eyes narrowed.

"What trouble?" he asked.

Landers dodged the question. "The bureau obtained several communications between Tripp Donovan and, well, your son. Now, this Tripp character is a bit player from Hemet, but he has connections running down to Tijuana and it's come to our attention that he owns that bar." She pointed for dramatic effect, but the chief was already looking up the hill.

"So what?" he asked. "That's outside of city limits. I can't do a damn thing about those boys."

Landers nodded ruefully as if such a detail had slipped her mind. "Right, of course. What about Ash? Our evidence suggests a connection between the two men and another establishment called Trotters. You might want to consider checking into their arrangements."

If anger could kill, the chief would have dropped dead on the spot. Landers could see the blood pulsing through his enraged temples.

"With all due respect, Agent Landers, and believe me, I don't have much for your kind, stop talking like your jaw is broke. You ain't making any sense."

"What do you mean?" she asked and steeled herself for the verbal storm.

"It ain't my goddamn problem, lady, that's what I mean. Those places ain't in the city, which means it is a county matter. So, why don't you go and bother that worthless, elected asshole and get him to do something about nothing… because that is what I am hearing right about now—a big fat nothing. Some hearsay on what? A wire? Probably a couple of junkies babbling their crack-addled minds off. And for what? So you can drag me away from breakfast and blow smoke up my ass? No fucking thanks!"

With that, the chief rolled up his window and sped away, leaving Landers inhaling a cloud of sand. She checked her watch. The conversation had lasted five minutes, plus another fifteen minutes worth of travel time. She hoped Sherman used it wisely.

Chapter Forty-Two

Walking into the police station filled Sherman with the same dread as a high school reunion, although he never planned on attending one. A fear of being recognized as who you once were danced in his mind. To camouflage that feat and his frame, Landers loaned him a blue raid jacket and hat from her trunk. Both items had 'FBI' written in large white block letters and he felt both conspicuous and annoying heading into the sea of blue uniforms.

The duty officer behind the desk treated Sherman like he had the plague, staying well away from the badge and paper he produced. If anyone cared to scratch the surface of his disguise, they would have found Landers' face and a year-old warrant.

Luckily for Sherman, the local police wanted nothing to do with a federal investigation or the agents involved. The woman behind the counter was no exception.

Sherman held out the badge with his finger over the picture, and asked, "Can I use your copier?"

The officer looked relieved at the request's banality. "Sure, it's just down the hall. Help yourself."

He nodded and kept the hat pulled down low over his face. The front entryway had cameras, but he guessed the hallways did not. He considered being seen entering the building an acceptable risk, as long as they didn't get a good image.

Sherman remembered the layout from their previous visit. Things like that just stayed in his mind. He passed the front desk and followed a narrow linoleum-lined hallway with blue squares on the floor and smudges on the walls. It led past a few sparsely decorated offices and a row of gray cubicles the same color as the drop ceiling above. Places like that made him claustrophobic. It was as if the thin tiles might fall down on him at any moment. No wonder his father had died after taking a desk job.

Sherman walked with the unhurried, deliberate steps of someone used to giving orders and getting what they demanded. He summoned an old Lt. Colonel as an example of bombastic pomp. An image from the early days of his war, long before he joined JSOC or hunted the Taliban in the deep folds of night. The Lt. Colonel didn't just walk, he stalked around the base like it was a gift from the almighty for him and him alone.

Mimicking that entitled asshole worked. Those in uniform stepped aside, but Sherman could feel the hard stares once he passed, which was fine. It kept their gaze on the big block letters, not his face.

The copy room, like most unwanted things, sat on the fringes of the buildings near the utility closet. Sherman poked his head inside ever so briefly to confirm such a machine existed and that using it would surely baffle him.

At the back of the station, he found a wide, well-lit hallway. Brass name plates adorned the doors and he saw titles such as Lieutenant, Captain, and Deputy Chief. Just beyond was the chief's office, with a much larger font befitting someone who needed to flaunt their power.

He tried the handle and, unsurprisingly, found it locked. A guy in a cheap suit cast a long look in his direction, but Sherman chased him off with a beckoning wave. The suit, like the duty officer, wanted nothing to do with him.

As soon as the cop turned the corner, Sherman landed a well-placed boot below the handle, sending the cheap hollow-core door careening inward. With a lunge, he caught the handle and pulled it back, but not quite shut, and pretended to read the warrant without a care in the world.

A thickly-set bald guy poked his head out of an office down the hall with a startled look on his face. He glanced at Sherman uneasily like someone who found a stray dog in their backyard.

"Did you hear something?" he asked.

"No," replied Sherman. His tone was flat.

"Oh," replied the man, a bit dejectedly.

"Which way is the copier?"

The bald guy pointed around the corner before slinking back into his office.

Sherman waited a beat to see if the police officer would peek again, but the jacket dismayed any interaction. In the space of a breath, he slipped into the chief's sanctuary.

For a small city cop on a bureaucratic salary, the room glowed with the fine grain of mahogany. Opulence dripped from the liquor cabinet and coffee table. Even the highball glasses sitting next to a bottle of fine scotch were crystal. *Taxpayer or drug money?* Sherman wondered as he considered who paid for the chief's extravagances.

The safe was located behind a false drawer in the desk, exactly where Ash had described. Sherman had not intended to uncover such information when he visited Vanessa's ex, but bargaining chips often tumble out when extreme acts of violence hover in the future. Ash started talking, then babbling as Sherman explained the situation to him in bleak terms.

Leave town and never speak to, or of, Vanessa landed at the very top as an unconditional request. Failure to do so would result in a necklacing. Ash appeared confused at this reference, so Sherman went into the details and history of the execution, which involved filling a rubber car tire with gasoline, hanging it around the victim's neck, and setting it on fire. By the time he got to the fifth outcome of failure, Ash was begging for his life with snot streaming down his face and writing out a combination to a safe Sherman hadn't known existed.

With a slow turn right then left, just like his locker in high school, Sherman opened the safe. The soft metallic clink disappeared into the sounds of shuffling feet. From beneath the door, shadows passed in hurried motion. He looked at his watch. Fifteen minutes had passed since Landers became the distraction. Time was in short supply.

Sherman grabbed a reusable canvas grocery bag from the jacket pocket. The contents of secret stashes can surprise, like the newspaper clippings in his father's storage unit, but the chief's safe offered no such shock. It held cash, lots of cash, and a pistol with no serial number. A ghost gun. A throwaway piece, if Sherman's intuition was correct, kept for creating or hiding guilt.

He found the weapon loaded and slipped the imitation Glock into his waistband, well hidden by the raid jacket. The cash slid into the grocery bag with satisfying thumps.

He didn't take the time to count but quick mental math totaled it at over four hundred thousand.

Taking care to cover his tracks, Sherman closed the safe and replaced the false drawer. An angrier Chief of Police further complicated his stay in Buford, and he wanted to prolong the discovery of his misdeeds.

Stopping behind the door, Sherman waited and listened for any activity, be it footsteps or whispered conversation. He heard nothing but the hum of air conditioning and the ring of desk phones. With one final breath, he slipped quickly into the hall and retraced his steps.

Not more than ten feet later, the bald head popped out of its office like a shiny turtle.

"Did you find the copier?" asked the man.

Sherman pointed in the room's direction and kept on walking. "Heading that way now."

"Wait!" said the man a bit too loudly.

Sherman paused and shifted his weight, glad to know the gun was loaded.

"The code is 911. You'll need that to make the damn thing work."

"Thanks," Sherman replied. "I appreciate the help."

The bald cop waved him on like he'd already done his one good deed for the day and needed no further recognition.

Sherman could now count the steps out the front door, but when he rounded the corner, everything changed. Coming down the hall like a bull charging down the streets of Pamplona was the Chief of Police. His red face looked a shade darker, and his nostrils flared with contempt. A subordinate trailed behind, warily bouncing from side to side as if preparing to dodge a flying object.

The chief turned to hurl another insult at the man

behind him, and Sherman took the opportunity to duck into the copy room. A startled patrol officer looked at him with wide eyes upon his sudden entry. He was standing over the copier, relentlessly jabbing buttons. Sherman closed the door ever so slightly, just enough to stay out of view from the hallway.

"The code is 911," he said.

The officer looked down at the keypad and then up at him.

"You have to enter it first," Sherman continued as the voice of the chief boomed in the hall.

"Can you believe the balls on that woman?" he bellowed. "She dragged me away from a perfectly good chicken fried steak, and for what? Fucking nonsense. Second-hand, inadmissible shit about my boy. Get me the agent in charge for Los Angeles. I want to have a word with him."

Sherman stood behind the door, pretending not to listen as the men passed.

"I believe it's a woman," said a smaller voice.

"What?" yelled the chief.

"The agent in charge for L.A., sir... I believe it's a woman."

"For fuck's sake," came the reply, but fainter and drifting around the corner. "Remember the good old days?"

The subordinate said something that Sherman couldn't hear, and he took that as a sign to leave. He wanted to sprint out the front door and be done with the subterfuge, but merely smiled at the officer and gave a polite shrug of indifference.

No one batted an eye, waved, or said anything when he left. *Just like the plague,* he thought.

Chapter Forty-Three

A wave of musty, super-heated air hit Deet square in the face as he opened the door, like an oven full of dirty socks and oil rags. They'd rented the shed from a retired school-teacher who only walked to and from the bathroom or to get another Pepsi from the fridge. She needed the money and Deet needed the space, so there were no questions about what they kept in there and no complaints about the shed's dilapidated state.

Under two large blue tarps lay the sum of Deet's hopes for a future. Crate upon crate lay stacked up to the ceiling rafters, and Deet could barely squeeze inside. It took months to amass it all, but the last twenty-four hours had been especially arduous. The stranger's list contained a few specialty requests and Deet took risks in the process, but none of that mattered. A beach retirement in Mexico floated in front of him.

"You okay, sarge?" asked Hadz.

Deet smiled as sand and cervezas slipped from focus.

"Yeah. Start unpacking the gear. I want everything organized and ready for transfer."

The other two Marines nodded and began the laborious process of unpacking crates and organizing the truck. Great heaping piles of destructive power filled the space.

Deet paused to take in the full scope of morbid potential. He'd never been one to care about others, but the Marines changed that. He found brotherhood, camaraderie, and even purpose. The uniform, the insignia, the motto… it had meant everything to Deet.

Until it didn't. Two wars and a lifetime of loss later, Deet didn't see things the same as through his eighteen-year-old eyes. Those sure-footed steps that carried him into the recruiter's office had faded with each passing year.

At first, Deet chalked it up to a bad lieutenant or captain. Even the Marines let in a bad apple or two. Yet, that kernel of dissatisfaction stayed, growing larger and hotter with each passing year. By his third tour, things came to a head. Specifically, the bulbous head of Major Tucker and all the cowardly, hollow words he spewed at regular intervals.

Deet understood the purpose of a motivational speech. Inspiration was two parts bullshit, even on the best of occasions, so that didn't bother him. It was the major's gleeful ignorance that drove Deet mad. It amounted to treason in his mind, and one day, he stopped listening and took action.

He caught the major exiting the piss-poor excuse for a bathroom. The officer didn't see Deet coming because all he looked at were screens, paper, and mandates. He never looked up to notice they were losing the war and too myopic to see that undeniable fact. In order to rectify that short-sightedness, Deet threw the major into a nearby burn pit, filled to the brim with all the shit—both literal and figurative.

Deet deserved a court martial but received something almost worse—a posting in the armpit of California doing menial work for a commanding officer measures worse than Major Tucker. Hadz stood up for Deet and followed him there as a result. And Boot... well, Boot had always been on the wrong side of the tracks and couldn't have found the right side of the law even if it fell on him.

"What are you gonna do with your slice?" asked Hadz.

"Mexico," answered Deet.

The younger man's eyes danced with iniquity. "Tequila and cheap whores. My favorite."

Deet said nothing.

Hadz watched him intensely for several seconds. "You're not coming back."

"No," replied Deet. "I'm staying."

"To do what? We ain't robbing a bank. I mean, it's a good sum but not that good."

"It'll do," said Deet. "I'll buy a bar in some little town and sleep in a hammock listening to the waves."

"Now I know you're dreaming. Ain't no such thing left in Baja."

Deet nodded, knowing everywhere cost a fortune, and even with all the money they'd earned selling surplus guns, it was barely enough to buy a house in Buford, let alone coastal Mexico.

"I'm still not coming back."

Hadz glanced across the miles of spindly bushes. "Yeah, I hear that."

"They'll have your ass in a vice," said Boot, interjecting himself into the conversation.

"Maybe," replied Deet. "But I'm tired of seeing these

assholes get rich while we get bent. You know that Colonel Spit-and-Polish is making a killing with his little side deals."

The men nodded in agreement. As the War on Terror closed its final chapters, everyone wanted their slice of American largesse. The colonel was no exception.

"We could still take it up another notch and make some stacks in the process," added Hadz.

"No. I'm not selling to the cartel. They'd murder a whole village and not bat an eye."

"And do you think Frank Sherman is any different? For all we know, he's planning an African coup. You know those boys play by different rules."

"What boys?" asked Boot.

Deet silently cursed his friend for bringing that fact into the open.

"The buyer is some wet-work Willie in JSOC," said Hadz.

Boot's eyes darted around. "Are we pissing in our backyard?"

"It's fine," said Deet. "This ain't coming back on us."

The reassurance did not calm the younger man. "That's a lot of hardware back there. Why the hell would he need that?"

"He ain't a cop," said Hadz. "And that's what matters."

"Maybe he doesn't want to start a coup in Africa. Maybe he's starting a coup here."

Deet put a hand on his cousin's shoulder. "You need to stay off 4chan for a while. That shit will rot your mind."

"I knew that dude was spooky. The way he looked right at me through the darkness," said Boot.

"It was spooky," added Hadz.

Deet rolled his eyes in frustration. He needed both men

for the plan to work, and Hadz was getting Boot all riled up before the biggest payday of their lives.

"Cut your shit," said Deet. "He's human like anyone else, and this is probably Iran-Contra part deux."

"If that was true, redneck Elmore was working for the CIA," said Hadz with amusement in his eyes.

Deet unconsciously looked out towards the mountains and the shallow grave they dug. Unease crept back into his stomach, twisting it around.

"Elmore didn't smell right. We agreed on that."

Hadz nodded.

"He had to go," Deet continued. "This Sherman character is different... he knows his shit, so I want everyone to focus on the fuck-up. No skating. Eyes up, head on a swivel. It's payday, boys."

"Yut."

"Now, throw that camper shell on top and let's get going."

As the men closed the storage shed, Deet typed out a quick text to Jones. It contained the instructions for the final payment. He hit send and, despite the ever-present knot in his stomach, a wide grin spread across his face. Retirement, he felt, was just around the corner.

Silence rooted into the room, burrowing in the geometric patterned carpet and veneer-covered table. It held as all six eyes gazed uneasily at the canvas grocery bag and its upturned contents. Javier spoke first, breaking what Landers wanted to endure.

"Did the price go up and no one told me?" he asked.

"No," replied Sherman.

"Then why do you have an extra quarter-million dollars in a Vons bag?"

Landers knew the captain didn't care about the details or decimal places, not like her partner. The good man, the good cop, the type to ask questions that she wished he wouldn't.

"Call it insurance against inflation," replied Sherman.

Javier raised an eyebrow, and Landers knew asking him to stop was pointless. The man didn't know how to let it go, just like a kid with their bag of candy on Halloween night.

"Where did it come from?"

Sherman said nothing.

"Don't toy with me, Captain. You put Tripp in an ICU with a broken mandible, so I know it didn't come from him."

Again, Sherman didn't flinch or bat an eye.

Landers guessed the captain was imagining all the ways he could break Javier's jaw—an empty chalkboard had more detail than his expression.

"I knew it!" yelled Javier. "This has gone too far." He pointed towards Landers. "Did he rob a bank? Did you know?"

"Look, Javier…" Landers began.

"It's Agent Martinez, right now. Remember that and the badge you're carrying."

"They denied my request for funds. We've only got two agents coming for backup. They're trying to bury the case."

Javier glanced between them and the money. "You helped him."

Landers rubbed her eyes. Exhaustion did not begin to cover her current state and her partner's short-sightedness only made things worse. Javier never grasped the greater good or understood her drive, her compulsion to see things through.

"Captain Sherman, acting on his own accord, removed the ill-gotten gains from a rather corrupt civil servant. Nothing more, nothing less, and for his help with that, we are going to look the other way because this case is more than some dipshit meth dealer's missing cash. We have a chance to do some real goddamn good today, and I'm not letting the provenance of his payment get in the way of that. Are we clear?"

Javier nodded and leaned in towards Sherman.

"Where did you get it from?" he asked.

"Do you really want to know?"

Her partner hesitated for a moment. "No, never mind. I don't."

"Can we drop this particular line of questioning and plan for what comes next?" asked Landers, shaking her head at the bickering.

"A text," said Sherman.

Javier did not look amused at the brevity, so Sherman continued.

"For the meeting location. Jones will send over the info via text."

"Easy enough," replied Javier. "We grab them after the exchange."

Sherman's head shook slowly from side to side, and Landers suddenly noticed how quickly his beard had grown back.

"It's not so simple. I show up with the money and then we go somewhere else for the exchange."

Javier rubbed his bald head. "And we won't know where the exchange will happen?"

"Exactly."

"Fine. We follow by helicopter or drone."

"No air support," replied Landers.

"What then?" asked Javier.

A tiny flickering smile crossed Sherman's face and Landers knew her flexibility would be tested again. She had seen that expression before… like the devil dancing a jig and taunting her to step through the door.

"We need a panel van and some extra-large cardboard boxes—the kind refrigerators come in," Sherman explained.

Javier frowned but Landers understood. She played in them as a kid, making forts and castles and princess caves from the discarded boxes. Anything her imagination created got built in cardboard until nothing but crayon-encrusted pieces remained.

"You want us to hide in the boxes?" she said.

Sherman nodded.

"Not a chance," said Javier.

"It's worked before," added Sherman with a flat matter-of-fact delivery.

"When did such an asinine plan ever work?" asked Javier.

"Somalia," Sherman answered.

Javier threw up his hands. "What?"

"I can't tell you the details of the operation, but it involved a high-ranking Al-Shabaab member, a truck, and weapon crates."

"And you were in the weapons crate?" asked Javier.

"No, I was in the truck, but my guys were in there."

"And that worked?"

"That's classified."

"I think the key point here is that the captain is still alive and well," said Landers.

"He wasn't in the box," said Javier.

"They're still breathing too," added Sherman.

Javier folded his arms over his chest. "Why can't we just follow you in?"

"You saw the place they picked last time. That was secluded but hard to access. The entry was long and easy to control. They'll pick something similar, with long sightlines to ensure no one else shows up."

"How do you know?"

"Because that's what I would do," said Landers, interrupting the back and forth.

Sherman nodded in assent.

Javier looked about to throw a fit and express disdain over the plan, but a knock on the door interrupted his displeasure. Their backup stood on the other side and Landers suddenly felt less sure about the plan.

Chapter Forty-Four

The sky-blue truck rumbled across the dirt road like a small drop of water rolling down an endless hill. Deet hadn't seen a soul since they turned off the closest paved highway fifteen minutes earlier. Only the occasional tumbleweed chased after the bloom of dust left in their wake. Deet enjoyed the surrounding silence, he felt free to think, and his eyes roamed across the barren landscape.

The gentle slope upwards revealed nearly everything behind them. There were a few hidden ways into the mine, and it made him feel safer, just like the ballistic ceramic plates in his tactical vest.

Boot fidgeted in the passenger seat and tried to turn on the radio. Deet slapped his cousin's hand away.

"But, Sarge," the younger man replied in protest.

"You need to learn how to be still. Didn't your mama teach you that?"

Boot laughed and the magazines in his vest jangled quietly. "She's your auntie. I'd say the problem is on your side of the family."

"Just keep the radio off," Deet said, but a sudden familial obligation swelled in his chest.

Fear mingled with hope and spite. The complex brew of emotions reminded Deet of his first deployment in Iraq when the surge still lingered as a bitter memory. The city-wide battles were over, but the danger never left. It lurked in the shadows as an ever-present threat. Those were scary days, but good ones too, when his sense of purpose still burned bright.

Deet tried to shake away the thought and the sour taste of regret he felt for leaving it behind. If only he hadn't thrown the major into the burn pit, maybe things would have turned out differently... or maybe not. By then, his war had turned into a burned bag of popcorn where even the good pieces were tainted by the bad.

"Is that it?" asked Boot, pointing towards a hulking wreckage of twisting steel and rust.

"It is," replied Deet.

The mine once flourished in that slim Golden Age after World War Two but before Vietnam when possibility glittered in the future. Deet marveled at the hubris of such brittle ambitions. Cities, wars, and deserts did not mix. Lessons, he realized, the United States always failed to learn.

A thirty-foot-tall rectangular tower stood in the center of the site and Deet parked the truck in its shadow. All around them sat rusted machinery, half-buried by the wandering desert. Shacks of corrugated tin stood peeled open like used sardine cans. A steady wind whistled through, and the mine creaked with unseen life.

"This place is creepier than that abandoned tannery by Uncle Tito's house," said Boot as he spun in slow circles.

"I know," said Deet. "It's perfect."

"Where do you want me?"

Deet pointed toward the top of the tower. "Up there."

"Seriously?"

"There's a ladder around the back."

Boot muttered something under his breath that Deet chose to ignore. He handed his cousin a scope for the rifle and a bottle of water.

"Holler if you see anything. We should hear from Hadz soon."

"How soon?" asked Boot. "It'll be hotter than *abuelita's* cooking up there."

"Soon enough."

Boot shook his head with self-evident disdain and walked off towards the rusted ladder.

Deet glanced at his watch. Somewhere in the valley below, Jones would be making the call. Plans were in motion. He grabbed his backpack from the truck and unzipped it once more. All one hundred and fifty thousand dollars fluttered in a sudden gust of wind. Satisfied, he swung the bag onto his shoulder and set to work as clouds gathered over the distant mountains.

———

The agents looked on with dismay glinting in their eyes when Sherman arrived at the deserted parking lot. He'd told Landers to meet him there and not the hotel for reasons so obvious, he had not bothered to explain them to her. However, the man they encountered at the continental breakfast stuck in his mind like day-old oatmeal, and he debated over disclosing that fact to the agent but decided against it.

Sherman wanted a cargo van, but timing dictated

choice. He bought the only thing left on the lot, which was a fifteen-foot U-Haul truck in its former life. The faded orange words clung to the sides like scabs about to peel off. It was old and clunky but ran well enough. Sherman reckoned he only needed it for a hundred miles or less, so he paid with the chief's cash—not that it mattered to the salesman.

When he unlatched the rear door and it rolled back up inside, Javier's eyes went from wide-open to aghast.

"It reeks in there," he said, taking a step back.

The other agents followed suit, except for Landers.

Fair enough, thought Sherman, but it didn't smell much worse than a lot of places he'd been.

The cargo hold might have been used for transporting roadkill because it smelled of rotting flesh that never got cleaned out. Heat made things worse, baking the rancid scent into the metal.

"You can't be serious," said one of the agents who looked two months short of retirement. Landers had called him Smit or Smith—the accuracy of which did not bother Sherman.

Neither agent exuded competence, reinforcing his belief that the FBI wanted to bury the case. Smit had one foot in a Florida retirement village and the other agent, Hardcastle, looked like she still got carded for cigarettes. Sherman guessed that she and Quantico had parted ways within the last few weeks. Her gear was too shiny for anything older.

Unlike the moving truck, the boxes in the back were genuine. Sherman picked them up from a U-Haul store. He bought nine in total. Four big and five small. The big ones were wardrobe boxes, if the label meant anything. Big enough for a grown adult. The extra ones were decorations. A distraction for any prying eyes wanting to look inside.

"This is not a best-practice," said Hardcastle. Her hands shook ever so slightly.

"It's the best of our bad options," said Landers, turning to face the group. "We believe subterfuge is necessary and Captain Sherman has graciously agreed to drive."

Javier, who had aired his misgivings in private, stepped forward. "Agent Landers is right. We've got one chance here. This landscape is a sieve, and we risk losing them after the exchange."

Sherman couldn't help noticing that Landers looked reassured by her partner's affirmation.

"Look," continued Landers, "I know this isn't what you expected or what they teach at Quantico, but we've been through the plan already. Captain Sherman will let us know when to get out. Once out, we hit them fast and loud. Don't hesitate because these guys won't. Is everyone clear on that?"

Despite the smell, the heat, and the unknown, everyone nodded. Sherman admired the succinctness of the speech. No flowery crap needed.

Landers turned toward Sherman. "Do we have a location?"

He held up the burner phone with a text from Jones. "It's an exit off the highway, ten minutes out of town."

"Anything of interest nearby?"

"Nothing open, but there's an old strip mine a few miles north. Pretty open terrain with good lines of sight. That's where I'd do it."

"Alright, you heard the captain. Exchange is taking place at an abandoned mine. Keep your eyes open and watch your angles."

Everyone nodded again, but Hardcastle's hands continued to shake.

Landers leaned in towards Sherman and whispered, "I'm trusting you."

Sherman understood her meaning. Their relationship differed little from the men under his command. For the next hour or so, everyone depended on his judgment and actions.

———

The moving truck rattled down the highway, swaying with each dip in the asphalt. Such stiff motion felt jarring in the cab, and Sherman knew the effects were multiplied in the back. He'd helped enough friends move to know even the smallest bump brought a crunching response from the cargo area. Personally, he didn't own enough stuff to fill the mom's attic jutting out over the cab, let alone a fifteen-foot moving truck.

In consideration for his passengers, Sherman had cut some ventilation holes through the roof, but he knew it did little to ease the heat. Still, he felt no compunction to suffer with them, and turned up the air conditioning to max. The engine shuddered a touch but did not overheat.

Buford and its highway signage disappeared behind, leaving only the great swath of sunbaked dirt between them and Las Vegas. Sherman's mental map said they were close, and he started looking at the mile markers. The text mentioned it specifically. Small white signs whizzed by innocuously until they didn't, and Sherman slowed down.

He exited left onto a road with no sign or evident purpose. It existed for reasons unknown or forgotten. Without weight, the truck bounced around like a diving board.

On the back side of the first dune, Sherman slowed to a

crawl. Tucked away and hidden from the road was a newer model Ram pickup. The man standing next to the truck had ox-broad shoulders and a crew cut. Sherman recognized Hadz from their late-night meeting.

The man waved him forward until Sherman came to a stop ten yards from the pickup. He slid the shifter into park and waited. The stalemate continued for another minute as Hadz made sure no one else exited the highway, and Sherman made sure he stayed still, for fear of sudden movements and the Marine's M4 rifle.

The young soldier motioned for him to get out of the truck, and Sherman stepped into the heat with his father's pistol holstered on his hip.

"That ain't gonna fly," said Hadz, his hand reflexively grabbing the rifle.

"I'm not delivering all this money without it," replied Sherman.

A prolonged pause followed, and Sherman could feel the guy weighing the costs of the offending weapon.

"It better stay in the leather."

"The feeling's mutual," said Sherman.

"Let me see the cash."

Sherman nodded toward the moving truck. Hadz followed and looked longingly at the canvas grocery bag filled with money.

"You can count it later," said Sherman, unwilling to let his leverage slip away.

"What if I want to count it now?"

Sherman took a step closer. They weren't but ten feet apart and the man still hadn't raised his rifle.

"Like I said," Sherman repeated. "You can count it later."

Backing a Marine down from a fight was next to impossible, but Sherman stood tall because he knew the younger man still respected rank, even if he didn't have the two silver bars on his shoulder.

"You don't want to be the second guy who comes up short with us."

"What happened to the first?" asked Sherman.

The soldier smiled, thin and flaring, then glanced at the ground.

Elmore, thought Sherman. *They buried Elmore somewhere out here to rot with tumbleweeds for company.* Indignation and anger flared inside. Not for the corpse locked away under the sand, but for Vanessa and a lifetime of not knowing.

"Where'd you get the truck?" asked the Marine.

"Somewhere cheap," replied Sherman.

"I'm gonna need to check inside."

Hadz looked at the moving truck like a wary dog, and Sherman bet the guy had seen a few friends vaporized at vehicle checkpoints.

Not that Landers needed the warning, but Sherman rapped his knuckles along the outside, tapping out a rhythm over the faded image of Wapakoneta still visible on the side.

"Can you believe the places they put on these things?" he asked, hoping to disguise his action.

Hadz shrugged, not appearing perturbed. "I used to have family in Ohio."

"And?"

"They dead."

Sherman flipped the latch and the door rolled up, concealing the holes in the roof he'd cut. The stench wafted out, but the Marine wasn't fazed.

"Jesus, are you moving apartments too? What's with the boxes?"

Sherman could almost hear the collective breath as everyone inside waited for his response.

"I don't want the highway patrol opening this up and seeing what's best not seen. I'll load it in the boxes and look like every other asshole moving out of California."

Hadz said nothing for a moment as his eyes processed the interior. Then he turned back to Sherman. "I hope you got enough."

"Me too."

"Come on and follow me. We're going for a drive."

"Where to?" asked Sherman.

"It ain't for you to know until we're there."

Chapter Forty-Five

Sweat poured down his body and Elias felt like a waterslide, slick with effort in the evening sun. To his surprise, the phone trick had worked. He'd watched the little blue dot float out of town and into the vast brown nothingness that engulfed the area. Once it left the highway, he knew where it was going. The satellite image showed only one thing of interest—an abandoned industrial site. *A mine*, he reasoned. Extraction was the only game in an area bereft of creation.

He'd taken a parallel road north not long after the blue dot stopped, knowing the Marines would spot him any other way. From there, he hiked in with a backpack full of water and a rifle slung over his shoulder.

Elias was not a great shooter. Not like some in his profession that could hit a quarter from a mile away and never be seen. He preferred to be close and liked the smell of fear and piss and blood. Success, he'd found, was better savored within an arm's reach.

It came as a disappointment when he realized his current assignment would not allow such proximity. He could have done the job in chunks, taking care of the agents at the hotel and the Marines off-base, but he understood the larger picture. A sting operation was in progress with the bearded man as the key. He bridged the gap between the FBI and Marines, between the money and the guns. Criminality, he'd come to realize, followed a very logical path.

As for the money behind the hits... he didn't ask and they never told. Reason said that the officer from the golf course had something to do with it. Judging by his fancy friend, Elias guessed the guy had his own fingers in the honey jar and didn't want to share. War was money, after all, and people didn't like sharing money.

As Elias reached a small knoll, no more than a blip on a topo map, he slowed and crouched down in a scattering of rocks. Three hundred yards away sat the abandoned mine, a twisting graveyard of industrial dreams. Elias wouldn't have found the spot without the aid of technology, but he didn't bemoan his lack of wilderness skills. On the streets of Baltimore, he could disappear into a crowd in the blink of an eye.

Checking for snakes and scorpions in his newfound hideout, Elias made a mental note to never take another job outside of a major metropolitan area. He laid out a small tarp, a few water bottles, and the rifle. It wasn't the best weapon for the job at hand, but it was the best one he could procure in the time available. It was some version of an AR-15, but Elias did not know which. All he cared about was that it had a decent-sized magazine and 6x scope.

In circular immediacy of the optic, Elias made out two of the three Marines. One was on top of a boxy tower in the middle of the mine with a rifle that looked like his own. The tall one that could have been carved from stone stood by a pickup with a camper shell. He was fussing over items in the back. Guns, Elias assumed, as men like that wouldn't have the gall to steal anything else.

He hadn't waited long when a thin plume of dust danced across the horizon. What began as a single line turned to two distinct shapes as they grew closer. Elias chugged a water and thanked God he didn't have to wait too much longer in the boiling heat.

Two vehicles hardened into focus. One pickup and one moving truck. Elias chuckled when he saw the faded town name on the side of the U-Haul.

"Neil fucking Armstrong," he said to himself.

The pickup parked by the other truck, but the U-Haul pulled up short between two rundown shacks that looked like burst soda cans. Before the Marines could argue with the driver, the back rolled up and four armed FBI agents slipped out. They escaped unseen behind the tangle of rusted buildings and forgotten machinery.

"Clever bastards," Elias mused.

Even he hadn't thought of it and assumed the feds would arrive in a flurry of lights and sirens. Although, he had to admit, it was better like that. Everyone together in one tight spot like fish waiting for the dynamite. He settled in for the show.

The Marines were waving Sherman forward and yelling some obscenities about the army and generally deriding his driving. He started counting to thirty. If his men could exit a Blackhawk in three seconds flat, it stood to reason four FBI agents could make their way out of a U-Haul in thirty.

Ten. More waving and some confused looks.

Twenty. Anger had set in. He raised his hands in good faith.

Thirty. Their guns were raised with menace, but he saw a flash in the side mirror and felt the rear door slide close.

Sherman made a show of trying to shift from neutral to drive, lurching the moving truck forward in staccato bursts.

The big Marine, the one calling himself Deet, stepped forward and pointed forcefully to an open spot in front of an old office building. He looked mad but also relieved... like he was happy no one was shooting.

"What the hell was that?" he yelled through the open window.

"Sorry," said Sherman with a sheepish grin he hoped would pass as genuine. "I got the only thing on the lot, and it's got more miles than Route 66."

Deet looked at the peeling paint and faded flecks of adventure that once adorned the sides. "Next time, spend a little. You don't want to break down with this shit in the back."

"Thanks, but I'll be fine. Just working out the kinks."

The Marine scowled but then his face softened enough for the momentary danger to pass. "You got the money?"

"You know I do."

"I need to count it."

"And I need to see what it's buying."

Deet took his pumpkin pie-sized hand and waved it over his shoulder. "The hardware is in the pickup, but I see you've brought your own."

"You know what they say about plans?"

"They always go to shit."

Sherman nodded. "Besides, I feel naked without it."

The Marine smiled like he agreed with the sentiment. "Is that your deployment piece?"

An even playing field, thought Sherman. With everyone knowing about the other. He appreciated the momentary transparency and equality, however fleeting. The small talk continued as they walked together towards the pickup.

"From my father's collection," answered Sherman.

"Vietnam?"

"More tours than I got fingers," said Sherman.

The irreverence landed close to the truth, and although his father only served three tours, it might have been a lifetime. According to Sophia, he never truly came home.

"A family affair," said Deet.

"Like most addictions, it's been passed down through the generations. And you?"

"My apple rolled pretty far from the tree."

Sherman wished that had been his lot in life, but he knew otherwise. He and his father shared a tenacity for seeing things through, and although he felt a growing camaraderie towards the Marine, he would see things through.

"It's all there," said Deet, pointing towards the tailgate.

"You mind doing the honors?"

Deet glanced between Sherman and the truck. "I don't like to open car doors these days either."

The tailgate swung down, the camper went up, and Sherman saw several million worth of taxpayer dollars sitting on plastic tarps. The Marines had delivered on their end of the bargain, but Sherman felt competing twinges of disappointment. Somewhere inside, he'd hoped it was all a con, but he saw a look of pride and even relief on the man's face and felt disappointment he'd taken it so far.

"Can you help load it up?" asked Sherman.

"Money first."

"Right, money is always first."

They walked back towards the U-Haul, carefully

retracing their steps over the brittle dirt and bits of industrial detritus. In a smudge of movement, Sherman spotted the third Marine on top of a rectangular tower. He suppressed a sudden wave of panic that they'd seen Landers, and he was about to catch a bullet in the back.

Nothing came.

Sherman reached into the moving truck, grabbed the grocery bag, and handed it over to Deet.

"It's all there," he said.

Hadz handed Deet a backpack and the Marine bent down to count his payday, slowly adding new stacks of cash on top of old.

Any time, thought Sherman, trying not to look around.

Finished and smiling with satisfaction, Deet stood up. He swung the pack over his shoulder and dusted himself off.

"Good doing business with you, Mr. Sherman."

He stuck out his pie-sized hand in a gesture of goodwill when the veritable dam broke and the feds moved in fast and loud.

Four voices yelled, "FBI! Don't move!"

Followed by, "Hands up! Drop your weapons!"

Sherman complied, hoping to set a good example, and took a step away from Deet, who still had his arm outstretched like a lowered railroad crossing gate.

"Get your fucking hands up," shouted Javier.

Hadz had not yet fully complied. He had one hand up and the other in his rifle, unable to let go of his training.

"Stand down, Marine," came Landers' voice from out of view to Sherman's right.

Looking dejected and tone raging mad, Deet raised his muscular limbs toward the sky.

Hadz finally did the same.

Only the third Marine remained, and Sherman hoped Landers had seen him too.

As if sensing his gaze, Landers stepped forward with her rifle pointing up towards the tower. "Drop your weapons, soldier!"

"Do it, Boot," shouted Deet, holding his arms up.

Sherman took another step back, already knowing which way he'd jump if the shooting started.

"Drop it," yelled the other agents.

Inch by inch, Boot stood up on top of the tower, his arms and palms facing the sky above.

The agents moved forward, barking more orders. The place reverberated with their voices as an agent edged closer to Sherman, who exhaled a breath he hadn't realized he was holding.

It was over.

Then it wasn't.

A gunshot rolled across the barren ground, pinging around the tin shacks. Even amid all the chaos and yelling, the sound arrived like an out-of-control freight train.

Something warm and viscous splashed across Sherman's face and he struggled to see out of his left eye. Blinded by blood, he knew, from toenails to crown, that it had all gone wrong.

Chapter Forty-Six

With the match struck, chaos followed. Gunshots roared through the abandoned mine, taking on a metallic quality before fading into the surrounding wasteland. Sherman dove towards a rusted-out engine block and the edges of a conveyor belt. Where most people concerned themselves with restrooms or coffee shops, Sherman already knew the automotive remnant was the safest refuge, even though his vision remained blurry.

Sherman wiped furiously, trying to get the blood out of his eyes. A tiny splinter snagged on his shirt and he yanked out a thin fragment of bone from his forehead. Someone else's bone.

That's when he understood.

In a thin sliver of space between rusted metal parts, Sherman saw Hardcastle lying face-down, the hardened dirt wet with gore. A small circular splotch of crimson in her blond hair served as proof of the forgone conclusion.

She was gone.

Their plan had taken a terrible turn.

The FBI agents were shooting it out, but Sherman doubted any of them knew the real threat. From the first distorted, whistling snap, he'd known that they'd missed something.

He'd missed something.

Another Marine made sense, but he felt confident about the number leading up to the exchange. The way Deet ordered Boot to put down the rifle, Sherman thought it was genuine, but it could have been a trap.

A trap he'd missed.

Gunfire erupted from his right, and Sherman circled towards the sound, hoping to flank around the battle. He stayed low, stumbling around an outbuilding. His left eye still stinging and blurry.

A burst from the tower shredded through a piece of tin roofing overhead, rocketing shards of degraded metal in the ground.

Around the corner of the shack, he found Smit on the ground with minutes left to live. Three bullets had hit center mass on the agent's vest, one of which slipped through. Dark, sticky patches were forming along his side and Sherman could hear his punctured lung slowly filling with blood.

A mental act of triage tumbled through his mind—one in a long line of terrible choices he'd been forced to make. They never got any easier, just quicker. It only took a glance, and he knew.

Sherman reached out and squeezed Smit's hand in a final act of kindness for a man he'd only known for a few hours. They locked eyes for a moment, and Sherman felt the same anguish he'd experienced all those times before when he'd seen comrades die.

He took the agent's Colt M4 carbine and two magazines

from his tactical vest. Then Sherman repeated a routine done thousands of times before, like tracing a well-worn memory across time. First, he press-checked the rifle to confirm it was ready to fire, then he removed the magazine. The latter was half-empty, and Sherman swapped it out for a fresh one.

Better armed, he moved further right, circling away from the tower, making sure he kept his back behind cover.

Boot was still fighting from up high, sending bursts down on the remaining agents. The rippling thump of his M16 mingled with the dry pops of Landers' MP5 and Javier's service pistol.

As Sherman crossed from one shack to another, hoping to get an angle, a single bullet punctured a neat hole not six inches from his head. The round arrived with a hiss and snap, just like the one responsible for starting the mess. In that moment, as he dug into the hard dirt, Sherman knew the true magnitude of his own misunderstanding. All of them were smack in the middle of an ambush. A Marine would not have missed by that much.

The bland, pudgy man from the hotel breakfast drifted into focus like a sour gust of bad breath. Sherman silently cursed himself for not saying anything.

For another minute, he crawled between dusty and dilapidated buildings until he found a view of the tower. The burst had slowed and only the occasional pistol answered in response.

Sherman shouldered the M4 and waited, keeping the red dot just above the tower's metal roof. In the briefest of flashes, Boot's head popped up looking for a target.

Then another peak.

On the third time, Sherman fired.

It was an educated guess. A gut reaction.

An M16 tumbled down and thudded onto the ground, sending up chunks of dirt. Then Boot followed, landing with a wet splat.

A primal yell went up from across the site, all visceral and triumphant. It was answered by two quick shots from the mystery shooter.

Silence followed.

Smit, Hardcastle, and Boot were dead, that much Sherman knew as fact, and he guessed at least one more FBI agent was down. That left two Marines and a fed still standing.

Crawling past an old Cadillac hood the size of a California king bed, Sherman caught a glimpse of Hadz—or what remained of him. His limp body leaned against the blue truck... head slumped forward with a thin rivulet of blood falling from his lips.

Two dead Marines, four gone in total. The mental math of carnage ticked by in Sherman's mind. He needed to find the shooter, but if Deet still lived, he was the bigger threat.

Sherman kept circling to his right, knowing that Deet could not have moved in any other direction without risking exposure to the mystery shooter or the FBI. It didn't take him long to hear something.

A faint scuffing of boots caught his attention, even as his ear still vibrated from the conflict.

He crept forward.

The hulking figure of Deet dashed behind a group of metal drums, and Sherman followed, feeling the man's presence lurking nearby.

At the edge of the mine, Sherman found him and it took his breath away. Deet charged out from the shadows and knocked Sherman backward over the edge of a small berm of sand. It felt like a tree trunk hitting his chest.

Several bullets followed their path, upending small plumes of earth.

The men tumbled down into a ravine in a flailing pile of limbs and guns, arriving dazed in the rocks and lacy shrubs. Sherman staggered to a crouch, wincing from the impact of Deet's broad shoulders across his chest. The M4 lay several feet out of reach, and he drew his father's pistol.

Deet whipped around, ready to charge again, but stopped. His heavy breaths filled the sudden silence.

"You fucking traitor," he said, the veins on his forehead throbbing. "You're one of us."

Sherman eased a few steps back. "It won't do any good hanging the blame on me."

"That was my cousin you shot."

"I didn't fire first," Sherman replied, taking another step away from the human ball of rage.

"You shot a fellow soldier," said Deet. His ragged voice rang with sadness and betrayal.

"And your cousin killed a cop two months from retirement."

"Your guy shot first!"

Sherman shook his head and pointed behind them. "Whoever is out there shot first."

Deet's expression softened a touch as confusion took hold. "It's your shooter out there."

"No," replied Sherman. "It's not. It's someone who wants us dead. Do you know anyone like that?"

"You."

"I don't want to kill you," said Sherman.

"Funny sentence from the man holding a gun."

"You damn well know that if I wanted you dead, I would have done it on the first night we met. I wasn't twenty feet from your boys, and you would have never heard me coming. So, don't give me that shit."

"Then why the fuck are you here?"

"Because you killed my friend's brother, and you're disrespecting the uniform, and because I don't tolerate stupid shit like selling military weapons to hillbillies."

"You mean Elmore?" asked Deet.

Sherman nodded.

"I knew that guy was trouble."

"He was, but it doesn't give you the right."

"Hollow words," replied Deet.

"Maybe," said Sherman. "My past is certainly checkered, but I don't go about burying people in shallow graves."

"This is all a diversion, isn't it? You're stalling for your guy to circle around."

"It ain't my guy."

Deet clutched at the backpack over his shoulder. "It ain't fair. This lot we've got."

"No one ever said it was."

"You know my base commander is selling top-secret parts to the Israelis? No one cares about that. No one cares about him because he went to West Point just like his father and his grandfather."

"For what it's worth, I believe you. I've seen worse over the years. Why not testify against him? Get some payback."

Deet's shoulders sagged. "The system doesn't work that way, you know that."

"It never will unless you try."

"Are you gonna shoot me?" Deet asked.

"Not unless you make me."

Deet nodded, and Sherman could see the Marine had

come to a momentous decision—one that could go terribly wrong. He looked down one barrel and picked the other.

"Don't do it," said Sherman.

"I'll take my chances, I always have."

Deet took off running north towards the desert beyond like a man possessed. A man with nothing to lose but a future he'd already sold away. He ran with purpose, zigzagging and ducking. A massive but unpredictable target.

The shooting started as soon as Deet hit open space. A steady rhythm of snaps whistled over the ravine. Five, then ten, then twenty rounds zipped above Sherman's head. His mind absorbed the angle and distance, storing it for later.

Thirty yards out, the first of many bullets found its mark.

Deet sagged from the impact but kept on going, struggling to keep his footing. Sherman silently urged him on, knowing it was too late.

The vest he wore couldn't stop everything. More and more bullets hit until there wasn't any fight left in the man and nothing remained but broken dreams and congealed clumps of sand.

Sherman watched through to the end while his brain cataloged the incoming rounds. He owed the Marine that much. Animosity aside, the man didn't deserve an ending like that anymore than Elmore deserved a shallow pit in the desert or Vanessa the indignities of a shattered life. About the only person Sherman didn't bat an eye over was Colt and he didn't even pull the trigger. A happy accident as far as Sherman was concerned.

Not one to overstay his welcome, Sherman kneeled and debated his options. The ravine petered out after a few dozen yards in either direction, narrowing to thin cracks in the ground no bigger than a fist. He couldn't move up or down it, and he knew what running north ended in.

Grabbing the M4 from the ground and sliding uphill, Sherman did his best to put the shack between himself and the shooter. Going back into the mine was the only choice. From his experience, staying put only ended with a bullet to the side.

He slid over the berm on his belly, staying low enough to lick the dirt. Sherman didn't need a map to tell him the shooter's location. His brain had figured that out. There was only one spot it could be—a small rise around three hundred yards away. And there was only one way to get there.

Slipping between the wreckage of industrial dreams and past spent shell casings, Sherman edged towards the westernmost point of the mine, only pausing long enough to look at Hardcastle one last time. The wind had picked up, whistling through the rickety metal and sending the end of her ponytail flapping in the breeze.

Yet another soul that deserved better, and he added her to the growing tally in his lifetime.

Beyond the blue truck and Hadz's corpse, Sherman discovered Javier. He had his back against a giant sprocket with teeth the size of baseballs. There was a swollen brown stain under his leg. The end had come slowly and painfully.

If praying had been in Sherman's repertoire, he would have done so, but instead, he stripped off Javier's body armor and slipped it on, wordlessly thanking the agent for his generosity.

"You shouldn't do that," said a weak voice.

Sherman turned to find Agent Landers dragging herself around the corner with one arm.

"He doesn't need it anymore."

"Oh," she replied in a distant voice.

Sherman slid across to her. A tourniquet circled her leg just below the crotch and her jeans were dark and sticky. "Where else are you hit?"

"My shoulder."

He grabbed her bag and fished out the med pack. The leg was gnarly, but she'd already done the work to save herself. The bullet missed the bone but must have nicked an artery. He wrapped the wound and injected her with an antibiotic.

Landers' shoulder wound did not look any better and he couldn't find an exit wound.

"This is gonna hurt. Bite down on something," said Sherman. Telling her not to scream was repeating something she already knew.

She nodded and her eyes listed about in the sockets.

Sherman grabbed some gauze, and using his thumb, jammed the material into the wound. Landers tensed and moaned but did not scream or blackout.

"Did you call it in?" he asked.

She shook her head and held up a busted phone.

He grabbed Javier's and handed it over. "Call it in. I'll stay with you."

"Don't," she whispered.

"It's fine. I'll keep the pressure on your shoulder."

"Don't," she repeated.

"Why?" asked Sherman.

"Is anyone else left?"

"Just you and me."

"Then go. I wouldn't stay for you. Get the fucker who did this."

She started dialing and Sherman gladly picked up the rifle once more, hell-bent on putting the shooter in the ground and leaving what remained for the vultures.

Chapter Forty-Seven

Elias had honed his patience over decades as a detective and years more in the law's shadow. He knew how to wait in a parked car or hotel room, but not under the desert sun. The heat was all consuming like it existed in its own dimension. Every article of clothing he wore had drenched through with sweat. His pale skin was a shade of pink he'd only seen in the urinal after eating too many beets.

All but one water bottle remained. He'd pissed so much from the adrenaline and hydration that his little knoll reeked from all manner of bodily fluid.

Elias wanted to head back but a nagging sensation of failure kept him in place. At least three FBI agents were dead, but he couldn't help feeling disappointment over the first shot. He'd been aiming for the bearded man when the first round left the chamber, but the young agent stepped in front as he fired. She took the impact, and despite the spectacular shower of bodily fluids, he missed the intended target.

The Dominican or Puerto Rican agent's demise had given his morale a boost like a shot of whiskey or line of white. When the Marine on the tower caught one to his face, the agent let out some primal whoop of joy, momentarily forgetting all about the threat Elias posed. The fed foolishly stepped out into the open. Pulling the trigger had never come so easily to Elias. He'd missed low but still found flesh and had the added benefit of making the agent bleed out slowly.

Then there'd been the statue-esque Marine who belonged on a recruiting poster espousing virility and strength. Elias saw him tumble out of view, only to run away minutes later. The clever bastard was a hard target to hit with all the serpentine movement, but Elias got him in the end. He put a few extra bullets in the body out of spite.

Counting the carnage and subtracting out his targets left Elias with an awkward sum. It should have equaled zero, but two remained.

He couldn't account for the lead agent, but he'd seen her take several bullets in the gunfight. With everything whizzing around the mine, the odds of her surviving were slim. That left the bearded man unaccounted for.

He might be dead, Elias thought. *Killed in the crossfire.* Yet no matter how much hope he piled onto the side of the scale, it still balanced awkwardly to the other end.

So, he waited and waited, hoping for proof. He stayed until he physically couldn't stand the heat any longer.

The breaking point came as he finished the last of his water.

"To hell with this," Elias muttered.

He could look for the bearded man at the hotel, assuming he lived. Another opportunity would arise—he was sure of it.

Elias eased onto his knees, but everything hurt. His eyes were bloodshot, belly sore from laying on rocks, and his skin felt like someone held a lighter to it.

He stumbled a bit before regaining his balance. Two hours of hiding stung like an eternity.

Besides the bearded man, his only regret lay in the dirt on the far side of the mine. He saw what the tall Marine stuffed into the backpack, and it pained him to leave it out there for anyone to find. Elias made a pact with himself to come back out at night to look for the bag, assuming the local police didn't find it first.

He hobbled back towards his car, slowly gaining pace as the blood returned to his legs. Despite his sunburned exterior, Elias felt quite delighted with how things had turned out. The *mamacitas* could run lotion on him instead of sunscreen, and tequila always tasted good.

Life isn't too bad, he thought.

A thin trickle of blood ran down Sherman's forearm, gifted from a sharp rock, and a few cacti needles had embedded themselves in his legs, but he'd made it out of the mine. The gulley he'd crawled through spat out into a field of tailings left behind by the extractive process—little molehills of waste battered and smoothed by the wind.

Sherman waded through the ejected material as it filled his boots with hot grains of sand. Nothing made a sound except the wind crackling through the dry shrubs and a distant creak from the rusted tin roofs.

Across the valley to the west, rare summer clouds gathered over the mountains like wet wool draped over a saw blade. He loved the starkness of life in the desert, but the view did nothing for him. Only one finite task subsumed the entirety of his concentration. Enjoying the view didn't even break the surface in comparison.

He would kill the person responsible.

No doubts or maybes. Sherman willed the desire into fact like his father and grandfather before him.

A desire for answers swirled in his mind, and he wanted to know why or who had set such a calamity into motion, but answers rarely found receptive ears. Knowing was nice but it wasn't essential. He could live with an incomplete puzzle if no one else was alive to finish it.

A dry streambed headed west, and Sherman followed it for a mile before turning south. A lumpy ridge no higher than a goat separated his gulley from the shooter's escape route.

He knew this fact down to the bone because it was the only way onto the knoll from which the shooting happened. One way in and one way out. That was a certainty because he would have done the same.

Sherman slithered towards the top of the ridge like a snake hungry for a meal. His eyes flitted across the vast cracked land searching for movement. A gust of wind swept up from the valley, and he felt the grit of sand on his teeth.

He saw nothing but wind-worn rocks.

Then a twitch caught his gaze. The swinging arm of a brown smudge a quarter-mile west. The figure wore a safari shirt and peanut butter-colored khakis with a rifle across its back.

Sherman set off in a crouching run, bounding across the rocky terrain without taking his eyes off his prey. The evening was hot, the sun still bright, but he moved with absolute ease. This was more home than anywhere else, with a rifle in hand, eyes on a target, and violence on the mind.

His great loping strides propelled him downhill like the true countryman he was. He closed the gap within a few minutes, stopping only once when the figure slowed to check behind them.

A quarter-mile became a hundred yards, well within his ability to hit the target, but Sherman pressed on. Seventy, then sixty… finally, he pulled up at fifty yards from the figure and steadied the rifle.

The target was male, bald, and pudgy. His arms were the color of Flamin' Hot Cheetos, and he wobbled like a top about to run out of spin.

Sherman waited until the man waddled into a patch of sand bereft of any natural cover and squeezed the trigger. Such an easy, natural movement. Breathe out, squeeze, repeat. Except, he only needed the first shot.

The bullet hit where he'd intended, shattering the man's pelvis on the left side and sending him sprawling onto the ground in a great sandy pirouette. Guttural screams of pain filled the air and faded in the distance with the gunshot.

In predictable human fashion, the wounded man tried to get the rifle off his back, but he had landed on top of it. His arms flailed feebly in the air between choking sobs like an overturned turtle fighting off the buzzards circling above.

The man threw up his hands in front of his face and pleaded. "Please, don't do this. I have a wife and kids."

"What's your name?" asked Sherman.

"Elias," he said. "My name is Elias, and my kids' names are—"

Sherman cut him off. "Look, Elias. This isn't one of

those conversations. You can't change the outcome. The only thing in your control is how much you suffer."

Elias did not immediately reply. His eyes narrowed and hardened. Sherman watched all seven stages of grief play out on his face.

The denial faded quickly. Pain had a way of brushing that aside.

Anger came next. "Fuck you. I'm not doing shit to help you," he wailed.

Sherman said nothing. He stood there and watched the sand absorb more and more blood, waiting for the next turn of the page.

Bargaining arrived with a gritted smile.

"Look," he began. "I have money. Help me out and you can have all of it."

"I don't want your money," Sherman said.

"Drugs? Girls? I can get whatever you want."

"I want to know who paid you."

Elias squirmed and shrieked from the effort. "Ask for something else. Anything else."

"Give me a name."

"And then what?"

"I already told you. The ending doesn't change."

Depression arrived as the realization burrowed deep inside his sunburned skull, and Elias lay still on the clotted sand.

"Please," he whispered.

"The name."

"There is no name! I don't deal with names."

Shadows, thought Sherman. The whole mess was filled with people lurking on the edges, meting out destruction, but when it came down to it, there was someone sitting at a desk ordering the hits and paying the checks.

"You're gonna bleed out. With a wound like that, I give you four or five hours. If you don't name names, I'll put one in your gut. You'll die quicker, but in agony. Give me something, anything worth pursuing, and I'll make it quick."

Elias swallowed hard as snot ran down to his chin. Then, he began bobbing his head up and down to some internal dialogue Sherman could only guess at.

"Fuck 'em," he said.

Sherman kept silent. The words were not meant for him.

"Yeah, fuck 'em," Elias repeated.

"Name?" Sherman asked.

"Never got one, but he was an officer over at the base. Handed me the Marine's pictures in person at some fancy golf course out of town."

"Description?"

"White. Dark hair. Tall. Straight as a fiddle. A general prick."

Sherman nodded, filing away all the details for later.

"Do me one favor. Call my wife…"

Elias never finished the sentence.

Sherman pulled the trigger and fulfilled his end of the bargain. It was an eleventh-hour agreement and he didn't care how Elias felt at the end. The man did not deserve compassion, and Sherman did not give any, but in that instinctual corner of his brain, he wanted to shoot him in the gut anyway.

The sharp crack drifted out and away until only the ringing in his ears remained. He was alone with the wind, the sand, and the stench.

He reached down, found the dead man's car keys, and took a mental note of the direction Elias was headed. Sherman turned back to retrace his steps to the mine.

Landers was waiting alone and in pain, and she deserved his compassion, not some neon pink hitman.

A few steps later, he changed his mind... not about helping Landers, but about what Elias had said. He turned back and relieved the man of his rifle, considering the opportunity it presented before trotting up the rising hill.

Chapter Forty-Eight

Sirens wailed across the unfettered ground like the ocean lapping up onto the beach, pushing further inland until it had no energy left and faded into the sand. The lights caught the dusk air and floating particles of dirt in a strobing glow of red and blue. Across the valley came the clap of thunder as the clouds writhed over the mountains.

Sherman slung the heavy bag of money over his shoulder, trotted down towards Landers, and they watched the storm crash against the jagged peaks and fall onto the town below. She didn't say anything. Not about the extra rifle in his hands or the backpack slung over his shoulder.

"Where's Elmore's sister?" she asked.

"Vanessa? I convinced her to leave town for a few days."

"Why?"

"I didn't want anything worse to happen to her. The house was bad enough."

"Because you didn't think she could handle it?" asked Landers.

"No, I asked her to leave because no one should have to

see the things we have. There was no need to add to the darkness in this world."

"Chivalrous," she said.

"Would you have done differently?" he asked.

Landers paused, her eyes darting around in consideration. "No, I suppose not."

Sherman said nothing.

"Tell her I'm sorry about Elmore. There was decency in him, and I'm sure she knows that, but tell her just the same."

As for his own involvement, Sherman did not expect an apology from Landers. He would have used the same leverage and tactics in the situation if he'd been in charge.

"I will, and try not to be too hard on yourself," he said.

Landers struggled to laugh and winced from the pain. "I'll never let this go any more than it will let go of me, but you of all people know what that is like."

A faint hum from all the memories of loss thrummed in Sherman's mind, and he slowly nodded in agreement.

"If you ever need a fed, look me up," said Landers.

The shrill sirens grew louder, and Sherman stood to leave. "I don't believe they'll ever break you."

Sherman headed towards the dead man's car as emergency responders drew closer. He guessed someone in that kind of dismal shape and in such oppressive heat would not walk for more than two miles.

Surprisingly, it was closer to four in the end, not that Sherman minded the hike or the misting rain that spun off from the clouds in wispy gray arms.

Elias had parked the sedan half-off a lesser-used dirt

road that stretched out of view like endless strands of spaghetti. The car was an Impala and probably black, but Sherman couldn't tell for certain with the cloak of dust covering it.

An innocuous car for an innocuous man. *The interior tracked too,* he thought. Neither spotless nor messy. The right amount of disorganization. The kind of vehicle no one would look twice at or second-guess if they saw it drive by.

Sherman checked the trunk, half-expecting to find a body, but found it empty. He placed the rifle inside and covered some of it with a floor mat. Then he stood in the rain to make a phone call. One of many.

The front desk of the Desert Rose Retirement Village answered.

"Hey, Stan, this is Frank Sherman. I'm wondering if you can do me a favor?"

"I aim to please," Stan replied.

There is that sunny optimism again, thought Sherman.

"Can you pack up my mom's stuff? Keep whatever valuables you can fit in that big trunk of hers and trash the rest."

Stan paused on the other end.

"Frank, are you sure that's a good idea? She's on a lot of medication and change is jarring for those with... uh, memory issues."

"She wants to die by the ocean, Stan. I don't want to deny her that request."

"She may have years left. It ain't cheap on that side of the pass."

Sherman gripped the backpack a little tighter. "I'll manage."

"You're paid up through the end of the month. Should I get the paperwork for departure?"

"I think that's a good idea."

"We'll be sorry to see her go. Your mother is a real fire-cracker on her good days."

"And her bad ones?"

"Well," said Stan. "She's still pretty explosive then too."

Optimistic and polite. If only more people were like Stan, thought Sherman.

"Thanks for the help. I'll be there tomorrow afternoon to pick her up."

After Sherman hung up, he drove straight to the highway in the gathering dusk with the rain slashing down and muddy splotches covering the windshield. He drove without lights for fear of being spotted by the swarm of law enforcement scouring the desert. He didn't stop when the tires found pavement and kept going until the glow of corporate lodging drew his attention to an exit. He skipped the first two hotels and settled on a Motel-8 down the cul-de-sac behind Denny's.

The clerk looked apathetic at best and didn't bat an eye when he paid cash and offered no form of identification. She just pointed at the small stack of twenties on the desk and Sherman doubled down on the cost. He considered it a necessary expense and happily paid the price for anonymity. The woman entered a name not his own and he found satisfaction in knowing the FBI would not discover a Frank Sherman listed anywhere.

The room was on the first floor and Sherman cracked the bathroom window open enough to squeeze out in a hurry but hoped he wouldn't have to use it. Stripping off the blankets, he settled on the clean sheets and made the difficult call—the one he dreaded for its necessity.

"Frank," answered Vanessa with a raggedness that suggested he'd been missing for decades.

"Are you okay?" he asked.

"Not really. Not yet. But enough about me. Are you okay?"

"I'm whole," he answered, unable to process any more of the preceding day.

"That's not surprising. You have a knack for survival, but what about the other guy?"

"Not over the phone. Where are you staying?"

"San Clemente. I'm watching the waves crash and trying not to think too hard."

Sherman recognized his own coping mechanism in action. "Good. I'll find you tomorrow."

"Is it over?" she asked. Her voice rose with the last word, and it hung there as a question and an accusation.

"Almost," he answered. Sherman knew there was one more call to make and one more wrong to right, but that would wait. He listened to her heavy breathing, wondering what she was thinking.

"Frank," Vanessa said, but then paused for an almost uncomfortable silence. "Be careful out there."

"I'll see you tomorrow."

"Where?" she asked, only to discover he had already hung up.

Sherman would find her the same way he found other people in other parts of the world, albeit under very different circumstances. It was all the same process, only the outcomes varied.

He stepped outside onto the walkway.

Stars poked through the final rays of dusk and the storm swirled in the distance, only dirty streaks on the glass remained as evidence of its arrival. He wanted to put away the phone and sleep, drifting beyond all the muck and grime, but one card remained face-down. The odds were slim but worth pursuing.

It didn't take long for Sherman to find the name. It was public record. The final phone call took some searching as the number didn't exist in the usual places. It was a technical struggle to find it, but someone answered. To his surprise, they didn't balk or hang up at his question. Money, it seemed, bought excellent customer service.

Chapter Forty-Nine

The morning was cool on account of the storm blowing through the night before, and Colonel Brandon Wakefield felt lighter than he had in twenty years. Everything was coming together in perfectly joined pieces. All his hard work over the years, all the suffering he'd endured at the Logistical Annex... it was almost over. He rolled down the windows of his Mazda and imagined what the road would feel like behind the wheel of a Porsche or an Audi. All those niceties he'd dreamed of over the years, the watches, cars, and women... they were within reach now. It was payday.

To celebrate his upcoming success and the end to all his financial woes, he'd booked a morning round of golf. It was the least he could do. Golf was his escape. It allowed him to dream bigger. To be fully embodied as the person he envisioned. The type of man people opened doors for and not just saluted because he outranked them. A man with means who commanded respect by the size of his bank account, not the silver eagle on his uniformed shoulder. A man of the world.

He pulled into the parking lot of the private club and relished the view. Something about a sea of green in the desert evoked a sense of power, like anything was possible with enough determination and capital. It felt so very American.

Technically, the course belonged to the corporation across the street, but that didn't bother Wakefield. He didn't care where the money came from, so long as it flowed to him and he enjoyed its privileges.

The concierge opened the large glass front door as he approached and beckoned him inside.

"Good morning, Mr. Wakefield. So glad you could join us this morning," said the man in his soothing British accent.

Everything sounded better to Wakefield when spoken in a posh London intonation. It exuded sophistication.

"Thank you, Landon."

"Mr. Briggs phoned to say he'll be here shortly and to have a drink on the house while you wait."

Colonel Wakefield was not normally a morning cocktail kind of man, but things were changing. He relished the thought that he might now be a morning cocktail kind of man. A man of leisure and golf and mimosas. A man who started and ended his day with extravagance.

He sat down at the gleaming mahogany bar and wondered what to order, not knowing what one drank in the morning at a place so exclusive.

The bartender appeared and smiled. She was young and blonde and dressed in a white shirt one size too small for her frame. Wakefield had never looked too closely at her because women like that were unattainable, or so he thought. This morning was different, and his eyes lingered for longer than a gentleman's should.

"Good morning, Mr. Wakefield. Can I start you off with a cocktail?"

Her voice was soft and layered, and he lapped it up.

"I'm feeling adventurous this morning. Why don't you pick something out for me?"

"Gin or whiskey?"

Wakefield considered the request and went with the opposite of his usual choice.

"Gin," he answered.

"One Gin Fizz coming up."

Wakefield leaned back and enjoyed the view as the woman made the cocktail, and then he enjoyed the drink itself. It was something he could see himself doing more often.

Mr. Briggs walked in minutes later. If he had a first name, it was not given, and the colonel was none the wiser.

"Ah, Brandon, so good of you to invite me for a round. I will never pass up the opportunity."

Wakefield nodded, although he bristled at the use of his first name for business arrangements. The name, however his own it may have been, sounded demeaning. He preferred Mr. Wakefield or Colonel Wakefield or Sir when the circumstances demanded brevity.

"Gin Fizz I see, good choice. They were all the rage at Yale."

The colonel was a state school man and stood a little taller. At least he had that over Briggs.

"Shall we get this round started?" he asked.

"Gladly."

They played through seven holes with the usual small talk of stock market recaps and business news and a few golf scores thrown in. Nothing of real importance, but it filled the time, and Wakefield enjoyed the company. Not because he liked Briggs, but because he wanted to be him or at least someone with his clout and bank account.

Wakefield spent the better part of the eighth hole working up the gumption to ask about the previous night's results. A direct question bordered on uncouth or potentially incriminating, so he went in with a compliment, hoping to appeal to Briggs' ever-so-evident vanity.

"I saw the news this morning. Your man did a fine job out there."

Briggs gave him a stony look of disapproval as if he'd broken some unspoken code of conduct like politics or religion around the dinner table.

He continued, "Those three troublemakers never reported back to base. I'll list them as AWOL this afternoon, just to be sure."

Briggs swung mechanically and landed his drive in the middle of the green. *An unflappable machine,* thought Wakefield.

The corporate man softened a little with the perfect swing. "Our sources said six bodies and one survivor."

Wakefield stepped back from the ball. Mention of a survivor had his full attention.

"Do we know who?" he asked, trying to hide his nerves.

"The lead agent."

Wakefield felt a bundle of nerves tighten in his stomach. "What happened? I thought it was all taken care of."

Briggs smiled but Wakefield wasn't sure what emotion the man felt. He had one of those faces that read like an empty journal.

"Don't worry, she's in the ICU and the investigation will wind down soon enough. We'll see to that."

Wakefield nodded. Briggs had only informed him of the FBI agents and their investigation into missing government property after the company paid for the hit, and well after Wakefield's first suspicion regarding the sergeant nicknamed Deet. He wanted to point out that glaring fact but thought better of lashing out at the hand that feeds.

"Lucky," Wakefield replied, but silently wondered what the slip-up would cost him.

"You've done well by us, Brandon. The Israelis are very happy with the first shipment. Your early retirement is all but assured once we complete the order."

Mention of anything other than one shipment threw Wakefield off. "I thought the transaction was done."

Briggs pulled out a nine iron and landed a near-perfect chip.

"Ah, Brandon. That was just the beginning. We are optimistic for your continued success. In fact, I've got a little sign of our appreciation back at the clubhouse."

Wakefield perked up at the mention of a gift. Nice Rolexes and Patek Philippes drifted through his imagination. Something to cement his rise to prominence.

"I appreciate the opportunity, Mr. Briggs. It's been a pleasure doing business with you."

"Please, we consider you a valuable partner."

Briggs slapped him on the back as they approached the ninth hole. Both men were within putting distance and Wakefield moved forward to grab the flag and set it aside, but he stopped. Something on the flagpole caught his attention.

"Are you gonna stand there all day? I've got a birdie putt here."

Wakefield pointed to the flag and the small piece of paper taped to it. Briggs cocked his head and moved closer to investigate. Neither man made a move to grab it off the pole. Not at first.

They could see clearly enough from where they stood. The piece of paper was a business card. It had a blue seal on the left and a name in the middle.

Special Agent Megan Landers

"Is this some sort of joke?" asked Wakefield.

"She's half-dead in the hospital," said Briggs.

Wakefield ripped the card off the pole. He felt his chest tightening with fear and distrust.

"What's on the back?" Briggs asked, pointing at the card.

The colonel flipped it over and stared down at the two words written in black marker.

Semper Fidelis

Wakefield's heart began to pound and then pick up pace like a marching band.

"Isn't that your motto?" asked Briggs. "What the fuck is going on? This is not funny."

"Always faithful," said Wakefield.

Frank Sherman was two coffees deep and stirring what remained of his eggs and hashbrowns together when the news broke. He looked up at the small television mounted on the diner wall.

The nearest CBS station cut into the broadcast. A well-quaffed woman sat behind a desk, looking serious.

"Breaking news, folks. Another outburst of violence in

Buford leaves two dead this morning. We go to Anderson Steele on the ground."

A blonde man in a polo shirt stood sweatless and blinking in the direct sun like he had just got out of the van. "Good afternoon, Janet. I'm here at an unnamed corporate golf course on the outskirts of Buford."

"What can you tell us about this awful event?"

"Security is tight but my sources at the coroner's office informed me that they recovered two bodies this morning."

"Anderson, that is just terrible. Do we know what happened?"

"Again, details are scant, but they believe both men were shot to death while playing an early morning round of golf."

The camera cut back to the anchorwoman.

"Terrible, Anderson, just terrible. I can't imagine why someone would do something like that on a golf course of all places. Do the authorities have any leads?"

"It's too early in the investigation to say, but my source suggested they may never know where the fatal bullets came from. No weapons or evidence that we know of were recovered from the scene."

"Awful times indeed," said the woman. "That was Anderson Steele at the scene of a golf course double homicide. Now, back to Samantha Teal for the weather. Samantha, I hear it's another scorcher."

Sherman shook his head at the abrupt pivot between death and degrees. He drank his coffee and considered the possible repercussions of his actions.

The police wouldn't find a shell casing or a rifle. He'd taken those with him when he left the scene. Only if they were lucky would they find a mangled bullet driven into the ground by ballistics, and even then, it would tie back to Elias' rifle.

He doubted they'd ever match the writing on the back of Landers' business card. Sherman couldn't help but leave a little message he knew the colonel would understand. A verbal kick in the crotch for Deet, who despite his own unforgivable actions, did not deserve what he got.

Sherman had waited for the Colonel to read the note and look around with wide eyes the size of the gumballs he used to get for a quarter from the gas station down the street. Massive white orbs of shock and fear. Only when reality had sunken deep into the man's face had Sherman pulled the trigger.

It was all done and dusted in three seconds. The length of a long exhale or the time it takes for a Formula One race car to reach the highway speed limit. The men were breathing, and then they weren't.

Shooting them had brought him no pleasure, not the act itself, but deep down, he knew it was the right thing to do. Not by the law or any standard of morality, but his own compass. That guiding principle that everyone navigates their lives with.

He finished the last few bites of his lunch and paid with cash before heading out for one final thing.

Chapter Fifty

By 10:00 AM, the sun had wiped away any trace of the cool morning air. By 3:00 PM, it was in the triple digits and blasting like a convection oven. Sherman had burned the Impala he took from Elias in a sandy field and was driving his mom's gold station wagon, wishing he'd rented a new car.

Sophia was in a foul mood when Stan wheeled her outside of the Desert Rose Retirement Village, but Sherman didn't blame her. Summer weather aside, she looked confused and scared.

"Frank, what the hell is going on? It's hot enough to scald a loon, and this doof packed all my pearls away."

Not a lucid day, Sherman realized.

"I'm moving you to a new facility."

"Why?" she demanded.

"Because you asked."

Sophia paused, and in her distant gaze, he knew she didn't remember.

"Oh."

"It's okay, Mom. Let's get you in the car."

"Couldn't you have got something nicer?" she asked, pointing to the station wagon.

"That's your car, Mom."

"What! I would never buy something so ugly."

"That's what I said when you brought it home."

"Oh. Well, where are we going in that horrible excuse for a paint job?"

"The ocean."

"Christ alive, Frank. Why didn't you just say so?"

Sherman closed the door behind her and shook hands with Stan.

"Thanks for your help with her."

"My pleasure. Say, is Vanessa alright? She kind of ghosted the place."

"It's not my story to tell, but I wouldn't expect her back any time soon."

Stan nodded like he knew some insider information, and Sherman waved as they drove away. The dour star-shaped building disappeared into the distance and Sherman felt a great release of tension in his chest as the latent fears of being a terrible son eased.

"Are we picking up your father?" asked Sophia, glancing around the road.

"No, Mom."

"Then why are you stopping? Do we need a realtor?"

"It's not for me, but it will only take a minute."

"Leave the car running or my tits might melt."

By the time Sherman got Sophia settled, signed the paperwork, and paid up in advance, the early hours of true darkness had settled over the ocean. He left her tucked into bed with the nightly news blaring on the television.

All roads lead somewhere in small towns, and Sherman guessed this one would not disappoint. The cold salty air stung as it soaked into his desert-scorched skin. A few street-lamps illuminated the sidewalk and made yellow glowing circus tents in the mist. Each one a small refuge from the surrounding darkness.

Sherman passed fancy seafood places with white linen tablecloths and valet parking. He skirted the cocktail bar overflowing with designer clothes and a cover charge. He kept going towards the edge of town, where the road petered out into clumps of salal and pine.

He continued until a faint glow drew him in.

Under the warming light on an old Pabst sign, he found the End of the Road. An old bar—a working man's drinking establishment. Something those fancy folks down the street would call a hole or a dive.

The parking lot had gravel in past years, but more dirt than rock remained. Most of the vehicles showed salt-inflicted scars and rusty battle wounds of long coastal lives.

The cedar shake siding was new, but the door was not. The circular window in the center resembled the helm of a ship and it brought back the vague edges of a childhood memory. Fainter than the night, it swirled with whiffs of grease and fried fish and Cal breaking a man's nose.

Sherman walked inside.

The jukebox played a Hank song.

He found Vanessa at the bar humming to the neon and nursing a bottle of beer. Her expression exuded amusement and disbelief.

"You really did find me."

"It seemed like your kind of place."

"You could have called or texted. It would have saved you the trouble."

Sherman ordered a beer and smiled.

"But where would the fun be in that?"

The bartender dropped off the bottle with a clink and Sherman pointed to a small table in the back where they took a seat. Vanessa didn't try to take the seat facing the front door, and he appreciated the consideration for his natural inclinations.

"It's good to see you, Frank. I'd like to say I never doubted you, but that'd be a lie."

"Nothing is ever certain."

"Way to cheer a girl up."

"What can I say, I'm a bundle of optimism."

Vanessa laughed but it had a tinge of sadness that seemed to run down to her toes. Her whole body flinched in grief and she reached for the bottle. Sherman understood the reflex, the hope of numbing what cannot be controlled. He also knew no one survived at the bottom.

"Are you ready to hear it?" he asked.

"No," Vanessa answered. "But I can't live like this."

"The bad news hasn't changed. Elmore's gone."

She sniffed and nodded.

"The slightly better news is, I know where to find him."

"How?" she asked, but then the dots connected. "You know what happened."

Sherman nodded.

"Tell me!"

"It's not easy to hear."

"I'm ready."

"Elmore worked for the FBI as an informant, trying to buy guns on the black market."

"I knew that," she said impatiently.

"So did the sellers... or they suspected as much. When he met them that night, they got spooked and killed him, then buried his body in the mountain's shadow."

Despite her placid exterior, Sherman saw the waves of grief crashing down. He only hoped she found some relief in knowing.

"I suppose that's as good a place as any. He loved it out there in the sand and the wind."

Sherman knew the feeling.

"Did Agent Landers at least catch them? Was there justice for Elmore?" she asked.

Sherman fumbled with her question, trying to answer for himself and failing.

"Frank?" she said.

"I won't call it justice, but ends were met."

"Sometimes you make less sense than your mother."

Being enigmatic was a family tradition, and Sherman struggled for clarity. "I sourced the money and got the feds to the exchange."

"Did Tripp front it all?"

"No, Ash and his father did, albeit unwittingly."

Vanessa leaned so far back, she almost fell out of her chair.

"He told you about the safe?"

"And the combination."

"But how?"

"I explained the consequences of his behavior towards you, and he volunteered the combination. Probably out of some vain hope I wouldn't shoot him."

"Wait," said Vanessa with an incredulous laugh. "You

just threatened Ash and he caved? I don't believe that story for a second. If that was true, I would have been rid of him years ago."

Sherman took a sip from his bottle and looked her in the eyes. "The truth?"

She nodded.

"I told him I would put a tire filled with gasoline around his neck, light it on fire, and watch him slowly burn to death if he ever laid eyes on you again. That may have been after his friend, Colt, accidentally shot off his own manhood, but Ash didn't know that. All he saw was three people on the ground and me. Not to diminish my storytelling, but context probably made him offer up the combination."

"I'm almost speechless. That might be one of the nicest, most fucked up things anyone ever did for me."

Sherman kept quiet.

"What about your deal with the FBI? Did they hold up their end?"

Mention of the dead agents made Sherman's beard itch. He couldn't shake the image of Hardcastle oozing out onto the ground.

"Yeah, but only Landers made it out alive."

"What?"

"You asked about justice, and I don't think that existed out there. What I can say is that most of them are dead. Landers' partner and two other agents, along with the three Marines that did Elmore in."

Sherman almost regretted telling her because Vanessa had a look of pure horror on her face as if all the shit she'd survived paled next to his story.

"I'm so sorry," she began.

"It's fine."

"No, it's nothing of the sort. I should have stopped you from getting involved. How could I have been so selfish?"

"You pushed and Landers pulled, but in the end, it was my choice. My mom is right... I'm not destined for white picket fences and a quiet cul-de-sac."

Mention of Sophia made Vanessa's eyes light up and she changed the subject.

"How is your mom?"

"About that," answered Sherman. "Any chance you're looking for a new job? I just moved her down the street. She wants to die by the ocean, or so she said."

"Good for her, but my life is in Buford."

"Is it?" he asked.

She didn't say anything for a few minutes and Sherman waited with her silence, hoping they would come to the same conclusion.

"I guess not," she finally replied. "But I don't have any money or a place to live or a job."

Sherman picked up Deet's backpack and placed it on the table between them. "They gave me a prepaid cash discount, so there's still some left. Not enough to buy anything outright, not with these prices, but maybe with your equity you can swing a nice down payment."

Vanessa unzipped the bag and gasped. After paying for Sophia's place, over one hundred thousand dollars remained inside.

"I can't," she whispered.

"You can. I even stopped by your realtor's office on the way here. Jones is only too happy to buy your place for cash, assuming you're interested."

"That's too kind."

"It's not. It's selfish. You take great care of Sophia, and I want that to continue. You can handle her on the bad days, and I expect they're going to outnumber the good."

Vanessa smiled. "Does she like the new place?"

"Before I left, she was eating a bowl of fresh peaches. She looked at me and said, 'Sure beats that syrupy shit Jorge served.' So, I think that's a yes."

"I'll take it," she said, pulling the backpack across the table. "But only if I can buy the next round."

Next in the Frank Sherman Thrillers Series

vinci-books.com/last-out

A hero's quest for justice in a world where debts are paid in blood.

In the aftermath of Afghanistan's fall, Captain Frank Sherman faces a year of aimless existence until a friend's disappearance plunges him into the dark world of human trafficking. Haunted by the war on terror's ghosts, Sherman navigates a treacherous path from Afghanistan's peaks to the Rockies, unraveling a sinister web that spans borders.

Turn the page for a free preview…

The Last One Out: Chapter One

Rotor wash from a loitering Blackhawk helicopter rocketed debris through the open trailer door. Captain Frank Sherman watched amusedly as a West Point lieutenant tried to close the flimsy hatch. The young man was late to the war through no fault of his own, but that didn't stop Sherman from smiling at the officer's misfortune.

By the time Sherman sat down that morning, Afghanistan was two-thirds kindling and one-third matches. At any moment, the whole place would go up in smoke along with decades worth of blood and treasure. The question wasn't of when, but what would survive the inferno.

Circumstances aside, Afghanistan was in Sherman's blood as much as any other place. The country could almost claim the title of home for how many years he'd spent there. All his twenties and most of his thirties passed in places no tourist would dare tread. Hot beds like Iraq, Syria, Somalia, and Mali. The places where soldiers like Sherman deployed often.

"Get that damn door shut," shouted Major Sanders.

The major was Sherman's commanding officer. He was short and wide, with hands that could probably bend rebar. As the lieutenant was discovering, Major Sanders was a no-bullshit, get-it-done, kind of man.

The soldiers sat around what remained of their ragtag command center. Troop drawdowns and the impending American exodus left much of the JSOC base in disarray.

"At least we still have a door," remarked Sherman.

"I could run a war from a damnable cave, if need be," replied Sanders, who still eyed the lieutenant like he might fall over from the wind.

Sherman wanted to make a joke about Sanders being old enough to plan the caveman's first war but thought better of it.

"Alright, enough dawdling." Sanders dropped a folder on the table and said, "We have less than twenty hours to finish this."

The officers grabbed copies and examined the contents.

"More asset extraction, sir?" asked the young lieutenant. He was either on loan from some other department or had connections—Sherman couldn't remember which.

Sanders paused and looked in the young man's direction. "Think of it as repaying a debt. Everyone on that list risked their lives to help their country. Getting them out before the Taliban strings them up from telephone poles is the least we can do."

Chastened, the lieutenant returned to his copy and said no more.

"If you recognize a name, call it out," added Sanders. "Otherwise, it's luck of the draw."

Sherman scanned through the dozens of names, looking for one he knew would eventually make its way through American bureaucracy. It hadn't been on the first iteration, nor the five subsequent lists, but he found the name near the end of this one. Lowest of the low priority.

"We'll take Colonel Khada and family," he said.

Sanders looked up for a moment with a question in his eyes but nodded. "Anyone else?"

No one spoke up and he assigned out names and locations to his men. Each glanced down and memorized the details before leaving to assemble their teams. No questions remained and a quiet concentration filled the room.

"Captain, a word," said Sanders.

Sherman stepped aside.

"Your choice comes with logistical difficulties. Colonel Khada went into hiding last night."

Sherman held up the paper listing an address in Kabul, just down the road from where they sat. "How far out did they go?"

"Near Baghlan."

"I see." Sherman didn't need a map to find Baghlan or know that it sat squarely in front of the Taliban advances in the north. "Did they say why?"

"Credible threat," replied Sanders.

"It must have been bad to hide up there. The Taliban will raise their flag there next week."

"Someone threw a grenade through their kitchen window."

"Shit."

"Apparently, there is an old family connection in town. I didn't get the details, but it will complicate the extraction?"

"How?"

"Political sensitivities," replied Sanders with a shrug. "A jackass in a suit decided we shouldn't interfere, remember?"

"Some things never change," said Sherman as he turned to leave.

"One more thing, Captain," Sanders began, and Sherman knew he wasn't going to like what came next. "We've had a request…"

"I'd rather not," replied Sherman.

"You don't have to take the lieutenant, if that's what you're thinking."

Sherman sighed in relief.

"It's a reporter," said Sanders.

"Can I refuse?"

The major smiled sympathetically, and Sherman knew he didn't have a choice. The reporter was coming along, and he had no say in the matter.

"For what it's worth, they say he's very good at his job," added Sanders.

"I'm good at my job. He's a hindrance."

Stepping outside, July swirled around oppressively. The heat had its own weight that pulled you to the ground. Despite all his deployments in the area, Sherman always found the intensity astonishing.

"Captain Sherman," said a man standing in the building's shade. He was thin and wiry with a streak of gray stubble across his face. Short dark hair rested atop a deeply tanned face and inquisitive brown eyes. He was roughly the same age. "I'm Danny Bashir with Reuters."

Sherman stepped into the shade and shook the man's hand. Common decency, his mother always told him.

"Tell me, Danny, what brings you to Afghanistan?"

"It's the graveyard of empires."

"Ours included?" asked Sherman.

"No, I imagine not, but it's the story of our generation. Hard not to cover it."

"Couldn't you do that from the trailer or Kabul?"

Danny smiled and nodded. "I could, but that's not how I work. Have you read any of my pieces?"

Sherman read the news religiously, especially the international section. Knowledge was power and a headline one morning might translate into a mission the next.

"Jog my memory," he said.

"I wrote a bit for the Times on the Ethiopian war in Tigray. Then one regarding the recent Taliban advances in the southwest."

The African article ran a bell in Sherman's memory. The reporter snuck into rebel territory to get the story.

"I read the Tigray one. How'd you get over the border?"

"In a cardboard box full of donated clothes."

Sherman smiled and laughed at the effort. "Alright."

"What about the Taliban article?"

"I'm gonna lay down a ground rule here, Danny. You can ask about the past but not current missions. Is that clear?"

"Crystal."

"Good, I'll introduce you to the team."

Two men stood nearby, chatting casually like any other office job. They stopped when Sherman approached, trailed by the reporter, who wore light brown body armor and a scuffed-up helmet.

"Sergeant Gournsey and Corporal Lopez, meet Danny Bashir from Reuters," said Sherman as a brief introduction.

"Pleasure to meet you both," said Danny.

Sergeant Gournsey gave a half-hearted smile. The affable Kentuckian stood a good six inches taller than the reporter and could have tossed him in the air like a sack of potatoes. The sergeant had served with Sherman longer than anyone else on the team—anyone alive, at least.

"Who are we picking up today?" asked Lopez, who ignored Danny altogether.

The corporal carried a general disdain for anything unrelated to the mission at hand, which didn't bother Sherman. Lopez could have worn a tinfoil hat and babbled about an alien invasion for all he cared because Lopez had a gift. The Central Valley native could shoot a head of cauliflower from two miles away.

"Colonel Khada and family," answered Sherman.

Both men gave a satisfied smile.

"About time," said Gournsey.

Sherman nodded in agreement. It had taken far too long.

"What are we waiting for?" asked Lopez. "I'll drive."

"He's not in Kabul," answered Sherman.

"Credible threat?" asked Gournsey.

"Why is he running?" asked the reporter, who stood at a polite distance.

"I imagine because he doesn't want to see his daughters raped and his wife beheaded," answered Lopez with a remarkably even tone.

Danny nodded politely. "I understand the likely outcomes. My question is, why now? Did the Taliban find them?"

"Danny," said Sherman, "you're already forgetting my ground rule. No questions about the mission."

"Professional curiosity," replied the reporter.

"Killed the cat," added Lopez.

"Where did they go?" asked Gournsey.

"Baghlan."

"Not ideal," replied the sergeant.

"Wheels up in twenty. Grab your gear," said Sherman.

His men nodded but said nothing. This was their twelfth mission in the last week, and the war's unraveling left little time for rest. Endings required as much energy as beginnings.

Sherman walked off to get his own gear as the reporter followed like a bloodhound sniffing out a story.

"Captain, who is Colonel Khada? Why did he make the list?"

"A patriot," replied Sherman tersely.

"I get that, but he must have done something significant to get a ticket stateside."

Sherman swiveled to face the man. "Bring extra water, a few snacks, and ditch any big-ass camera you plan on bringing. We're traveling light and quick."

Danny held up a pen and notepad. "This is all I need."

By the time Sherman reached the helipad, Gournsey and Lopez were already aboard the Blackhawk. The mercury topped triple digits and Sherman handed his men ice-cold bottles of water he'd pilfered from the officer's quarters.

"Thanks, Cap," said Lopez. "What's the plan?"

Sherman retrieved a map from his pocket and spread it out for his men. He pointed to Baghlan.

"You remember it?" he asked.

Gournsey and Lopez nodded.

"We kicked down some doors there last year," added the sergeant.

"Two years ago, but who's counting," said Sherman. "We can't land near the town without making waves and alerting the Taliban."

"I thought we had a fancy agreement," said Lopez. "We both look the other way while this place falls apart."

"Whatever got signed over mint tea in Doha doesn't mean shit up there. Remember, it's their country. We're just passing through."

"Some fucking country," added Gournsey.

"Do you think the Taliban will take over after we leave?" asked Lopez.

"You've seen the Afghan Army in action. Without American air support, they're ruined," said Sherman.

"They have superior numbers, years of training, and a billion-dollar arsenal," interjected Danny, who had just climbed aboard. "Or so we say. Although, it doesn't feel like it."

Sherman sighed. No amount of money ever won a war without the will to fight. It didn't matter how the generals or politicians spun the facts—he knew time was not on their side. American troops would leave in two months or less and the ending would not be pretty.

"I'm checking with the pilots," he said and walked off.

Danny stowed his gear and took a seat next to Gournsey.

"Tell me, sergeant, who is this colonel you're trying to save?"

"He flew helicopters, but I imagine you found that out."

The reporter gave a brief smile. "And that's worth all this?"

"We have a saying in my holler… Blood over Bourbon."

The reporter looked baffled.

"He owes the colonel his life," continued the sergeant.

"Who does?"

"The Cap," answered Gournsey and motioned towards Sherman, who was deep in conversation with the crew.

"What happened?"

"It ain't my story to tell."

"Are any of the stories true? I asked around. Captain Sherman has quite the reputation in certain circles, off the record, of course."

"Like what?"

"I heard he took out a Hind helicopter with a grenade launcher in Syria, killed an ex-Iraqi general with a letter opener, and single-handedly cleared an ISIS cave complex."

Gournsey's grin split wider than the San Andreas fault. "No, none of that shit is true."

The reporter's face fell a little with disappointment as he watched Sherman return to the helicopter.

"Nope," repeated Gournsey and slapped Danny on the back. "It was a spoon, not a letter opener."

Danny's eyes widened as Sherman took his seat.

"I hope the sergeant isn't filling your head with tall tales," said Sherman after noticing the look on the reporter's face.

"Did you really kill a man with a spoon?"

Sherman joined Gournsey and Lopez in a short fit of laughter. "Last time I heard this story, it was a pen."

"I heard fire poker," added Lopez.

"So, it's not true?"

"Just a bunch of smoke," said Sherman, then he motioned for the pilots to take off.

"But I've seen some of your declassified after-action reports. They're not nothing."

Sherman nodded. He had killed a man with a utensil, but it was a butter knife, and the man was a terrorist who blew up schools. He doubted those facts ever made it into a printed report. People just wanted to have their heroes, even if they had to invent them.

"Once we're wheels down, I want you to stick close to Sergeant Gournsey. Do whatever he says. Clear?"

Danny nodded. "Got it."

"Good. Welcome back to Afghanistan. Don't worry, you didn't miss a goddamn thing."

The Last One Out: Chapter Two

Heat swirled so thickly in the tiny apartment that Asal Khada felt like she was inside her grandmother's stone oven —the one she used to make naan bread every morning. The thought of calmer times brought out a tear that evaporated while rolling down her cheek.

Esin, her youngest daughter, lay in Asal's lap, lazily swatting away the flies that buzzed around her face. Asal gently stroked her hair, trying not to think about the dangers lurking everywhere. Only the day before, someone had thrown a grenade through their kitchen window. God granted them mercy that day because no one got hurt, but they'd gotten the Taliban's message loud and clear. Death awaited them as traitors of the state and thus God.

Across the room, Asal's husband peered anxiously through the curtains, straining at every flitter of movement and loud sound. She hadn't seen him so nervous since the night before he joined the Afghan Air Force to help the Americans. That night, Zarak Khada paced across their living room so many times, he left a trail across the rugs.

Asal felt a surge of pride then for her husband and the stand he took against the Taliban. It had been difficult and she often stayed up late waiting for him to return or for bad news.

In time, life normalized—if life in a war ever sits on an even keel. They moved into a nice flat in Kabul. Zarak rose through the ranks and soon earned a colonel's salary. They had two beautiful daughters, born into the dawn of a post-Taliban Afghanistan. The girls went to school. They learned and grew and explored. It wasn't a perfect life and Asal longed for more, but it was a good life, and knowing her daughters might find a wider world gave her hope and comfort. The horizon was wide and colorful.

Those colors faded, and the view constricted to nothingness as the Americans began winding down their war. As if the country was a small child that you could simply put down and leave alone. Asal knew better, and so did her husband. Zarak started the asylum application the first day it opened, but hope dwindled with each passing week. News of the Taliban advances made Asal's chest burn, and even her daughters carried a sallow, forlorn look reserved for adults who know the end is near. Seeing them absorb such fear and hate hurt her soul.

Then came the grenade and a hasty drive away from Kabul. Her great aunt offered them the apartment and she would have refused if there was any other option. Zarak called the Americans to tell them what happened, and someone noted their location. Everything, Asal mused, rode on a note that may or may not exist.

"I hear trucks," said Zarak.

Asal gently placed her youngest daughter's head on a pillow and joined her husband at the window.

"Did they stop?" she asked.

"I think so," he replied.

"No one knows we're here. Maybe they'll pass through," she said, but the words had the taste of lies as they left her mouth.

"God willing," he added.

Asal nodded and went back to waiting, which felt more like melting than sitting.

"Wait... I see something," Zarak said.

The constant fear and heat had numbed Asal's nerves, and she didn't move. "What do you see?"

"Taliban," he replied.

Asal rocked her daughters awake and spoke to them in a frayed voice. "Grab your bags, my loves."

"But, Mommy," protested Esin, the youngest.

"Now, my darling. Do it now."

The girls heard the fear in their mother's voice, and quickly gathered their belongings in their backpacks and held close.

Asal sent up another silent prayer, one of a thousand in the last twenty-four hours, and pulled her daughters closer.

"They're asking people on the street," announced Zarak.

"Should we leave?"

Zarak shook his head. "They would see us go."

Their apartment was on the top floor of a two-story building. An exposed walkway ran in front of the doors leading to stairs at either end. Most of the widows had bars preventing robberies and escapes.

Fear sucked the air from Asal's lungs as she prayed for their lives.

Voices echoed down the walkway. Loud commands to open doors. Commotion filled the building as a few residents gathered in the dirt courtyard.

Zarak shut the curtains and they all ducked behind a wooden table, praying the Taliban would think the apartment was vacant.

Loud knocking followed. Fists pounded on doors. Asal wept with her children while her husband's jaw clamped tighter.

Then came the crash of the first door and a fleeting hope of survival slipped through Asal's fingers like water.

The Last One Out: Chapter Three

The pilot's voice erupted into Sherman's headset, overpowering the dull roar of the helicopter. His daydream of a tropical beach dissipated like shifting sands and the present moment jittered into focus.

"Captain, command just reported significant Taliban activity in the area. They're concerned about a potential issue if we fly much closer and ordering us to RTB."

Returning to base and the colonel's survival were incompatible ideas. Sherman understood that outcome perfectly.

"How far out are we?" he asked.

The co-pilot glanced down at the map to confirm what Sherman already guessed.

"Ten minutes out."

"Did you confirm that order?" asked Sherman.

The pilots smiled at each other. They'd flown Sherman's team before and both men knew Colonel Khada and what he'd done.

"I'll buy you five minutes and have command reconfirm

Taliban activity, but you'll still be hiking in," answered the pilot.

"I never pass up a good hike."

"No guarantee when we'll be back," added the co-pilot. "You'll be on your own."

"Understood," said Sherman before he switched channels so his team could hear. "We've got a situation."

"Did they beat us here?" asked Gournsey.

"The pilot is confirming an RTB order, which means our infil is longer than expected."

"Wait… does that mean we're still going?" asked Danny.

"We are," said Sherman. "You can head back with the Blackhawk."

The reporter glanced around at the seriousness etched into the three faces surrounding him. "This guy must be worth it."

Sherman said nothing.

"If I go back, I'll miss the story."

"Make some shit up."

"It doesn't work that way."

Sherman shrugged.

The co-pilot waved a finger in the air and the helicopter descended.

"Your choice, but time is running out," said Sherman.

"You're not leaving them much choice," said Danny.

Gournsey flashed a maniacal smile and flung open the door. Wind and dust rushed through the opening as the pilots touched down between two poppy fields.

"Damnit," groaned the reporter as Lopez and Gournsey slipped out, moving towards an old stone wall for cover.

"Story of a generation," said Sherman. "There'll be lots of coverage. Doesn't have to be your war."

When Sherman reached the wall, it did not surprise him to see Danny moving towards them. Fear of missing out was a powerful motivator, and the reporter seemed keen on writing the end to this chapter of American history.

"Zulu One, Echo Nine. We are proceeding on foot to the target location. Over," radioed Sherman.

"Echo Nine, the area is hostile. Repeat, the area is hostile. Over."

"The country's hostile," muttered Gournsey.

"Zulu One, understood. Over."

A moment passed, then Major Sanders cut in, "Echo Nine, confirmed. Good hunting. Out."

Sherman winked at Danny. "Let's find your story."

The dust and emptiness of Bagram Air Base with its Hesco barriers, razor wire, and fast-food restaurants was but a memory. Baghlan sounded similar but sat west of the Hindu Kush Mountains in the terraced green wonderland of ancient homes and even older farms. In the valley, where the water flowed, people grew wheat, rice, barley, and poppies. Even in July, the greens boldly splashed across the otherwise brown landscape.

Sherman loved and hated this part of the country. He loved the stark beauty of the mountains, the orchards of fruit, and the hospitality of the locals. He hated that so many friends had died in ambushes, killed to hold territory in an unwinnable war.

"This is an amazing place," said Danny as they crossed under rows of thorny acacia trees. "Reminds me a bit of Libya."

"Reminds me of Lodi," added Lopez.

"You reported from Libya?" asked Gournsey.

"Yeah, during the Civil War, before things totally went to hell."

"What was your take on the place?"

Danny gave a brief chuckle. "I wrote nearly twenty thousand words on the country, and I still don't understand it."

"And Afghanistan?"

"This was my first assignment. Straight out of college. Thought it would be a few months, maybe a year. Yet here I am."

"Here we all are," said Sherman.

"Our generation's Vietnam."

Sherman shrugged. "Different war altogether."

"It's gonna end the same," added Danny. "They hold together this place with glue and paperclips."

"You're not wrong."

"Can I quote you on that?"

"Not a chance," Sherman answered.

The four soldiers hurried towards the outskirts of Baghlan and the colonel's last known location. The city stretched out below them in a cluttered checkerboard of square brown buildings and brightly colored billboards.

Sherman didn't need a map to know where they were going. They could see the apartment building in the distance, next to a vacant dirt field on one side and a gas station on the other. Even without the clear line of sight, he would have found it. Navigation was one of those inherent skills some people possess, like always knowing the time or sleeping on command. Sherman couldn't do either of those, but he could navigate anywhere in the dead of night and end up exactly where he planned.

Angling down the hill, he aimed to approach the building through the empty field, which contained some old mud walls. Had the Taliban not sped up their advance and had the government put up a proper fight, they could have landed the Blackhawk there and gotten everyone out in a matter of minutes. He would have preferred that but let those what-ifs drop to the wayside and focused on the options in front of them.

"Captain, do you think the American withdrawal is fool-hardy?" asked Danny.

"Above my pay grade," he answered, annoyed by the question, which pulled his attention away from the next hundred yards.

"He ain't gonna answer you anymore," whispered Gournsey.

"Why not?"

"He's on point. All he cares about is the next few minutes and us living through it."

"Oh, I didn't mean to…"

"Just keep your voice down and your eyes up," said Gournsey. "They call it the graveyard of empires for a reason."

Minutes slid by in concentrated silence as Sherman maneuvered the team. They passed through a young grove of slender trees and past a toothless farmer who offered them tea. Sherman politely declined but spoke to the man in Pashto for a few minutes. Local intelligence was the best kind.

"What are they saying?" asked Danny.

Gournsey glanced over his shoulder. "The weather, his crops… uh, favorite World Cup team, and if the old man's seen any Taliban."

"And?" asked Danny, his voice edging towards fear.

"The old man is an Italy fan but doesn't think they have a chance."

Sherman returned to the group. "He also said the Taliban are looking for collaborators."

"You speak Pashto?"

Sherman ignored the question. "Sergeant, any thoughts on our approach?"

Gournsey pointed to a battered Toyota that had recently parked by the apartment. "Looks like we're late to the party. Probably not a great idea to roll up in force."

Peering over a mud-brick wall, Sherman saw at least three mujahideen fighters talking with some locals. If four Americans suddenly appeared, it would be a shoot first kind of ending.

Sherman motioned to Lopez, who didn't need any further instruction. The lanky young sniper headed back up the hill towards a spot with better sight lines.

"Post up here and cover our retreat," ordered Sherman. "I'll secure the family. Once I have everyone, we'll move back over the hill to the LZ."

"Where do you want me, Captain?" asked Danny.

"Never over three steps from the sergeant."

The reporter nodded. "Gotcha."

Time slowed for Sherman as he dashed across the open field toward the apartment building. Filled with adrenaline, his mind perceived all the terrible possibilities. All the angles he might catch a bullet. All the places for a cruelly hidden mine. Yet he didn't slow or let up. Those thoughts and threats had not left his reality for years, even when he wasn't downrange.

Grab your copy...
vinci-books.com/last-out